SHOWDOWN IN SALT CREEK

LEE EVERETT

CHAPTER 1

THE STREETS OF SALT CREEK WERE ALIVE WITH
activity as the townspeople milled about, taking care
of both business and pleasures. With the air crisp
and still from the aftereffects of a long, brutal and
lingering winter and then a short summer, the hint
of cooler weather fast approaching was now threatening to cascade over the town again at any time.
The promise of those colder temperatures had
brought a renewed life in the locals as they took
advantage of the last opportunities they would have
to comfortably venture outside and about before the
next unforgiving winter had set in.

Sheriff Vince Redding, or Redding as he was
commonly referred to, walked out of his office,
stretching out the effects of a short nap he had
stolen, and casually leaned against the boardwalk

post outside his door, rotating his arm off to his side as he had grown accustomed to doing in an attempt to stretch the stiffness and persistent soreness from his left side. It was the only movement that he had found that seemed to offer him any sort of relief.

The wound he had sustained almost a year earlier from his then-deputy, Hal Bremerton, had never really healed properly, a fact that had unfortunately been reaffirmed to Redding by Doc Hastings after many weeks of healing. "It will never be quite the same again," Hastings had informed him, much to his dismay, a reality that he had tried numerous times to accept, but was still finding difficulty in doing so. The level of pain was nothing more than a nuisance and nothing he could not handle. In fact, he had grown to ignore it, for the most part. The thought of having such a condition for the remainder of his life was unappealing to Redding, to say the least, but it was one that he was slowly having to come to grips with and it certainly beat the alternative of having died from his wound.

As he stood on the boardwalk, he remembered how he had trusted Deputy Bremerton all the way up until he had discovered that Bremerton was one of the masked men who had attacked him one night in an attempt to run him out of town shortly after he had become sheriff. Redding had been bushwhacked by four men and severely beaten, but not before he got off a nasty shot to Bremerton's face with his boot. When he later saw Bremerton's injury, it was the only thing he could use to verify the man's involvement in the assault.

He had liked Bremerton and since Bremerton had been his deputy; he had foolishly trusted him, something that his father had always warned him not to do so easily. "People are inherently untrustworthy until they can prove to you otherwise," he had heard the elder Redding say to him more times than he could remember. Growing up, he had resigned to the fact that the saying was nothing more than the ramblings of an old, foolish man, but once Hal Bremerton, someone he believed he could trust, had taken part in assaulting him and then trying to kill him, he thought the man's words to be much-needed wisdom, albeit accepted a little too late to do him any good.

Adding salt to the wound of Bremerton's betrayal was when Bremerton had tried to kill him the day he shot him on the road a few miles outside of town. It was Bremerton's attempt to appease the man he was secretly answering to, Slade McMahon, and ultimately, the man who had given the order to kill, McMahon's boss, Roland Bartlett. McMahon had wanted Redding out of the way and had assigned Bremerton to do the dirty work for him, choosing not to be directly involved. But Bremerton made a mistake and had failed to kill Redding, managing instead only to wound him. When he had walked up to check on Redding's condition, Redding had been forced to shoot the man dead. To this day, the pain of Bremerton's betrayal lingered within Redding as much as the bullet hole that he had in his side.

He was still amazed that Bremerton had gotten mixed up with Roland Bartlett in the first place. Roland Bartlett's deception was not of particular surprise to Redding, but he had always thought of Bremerton to be of good character and trustworthy, so his betrayal of Redding was a shock and a disappointment. The fact that Bremerton had been convinced to kill his friend and boss and had been so willing to do so was something he felt he would never get over.

Sheriff Redding took a quick glance up at the morning sun to monitor the weather, causing him to squint from its intensity as he tried to predict how the day's weather would play out. He found himself doing that more since the shooting as a way of his body telling him what to expect. An unexpected side effect of being shot in such a tender location was how it helped him predict the upcoming weather. He could now tell with considerable accuracy, he would boast, of upcoming inclement weather just by the level of tenderness his side experienced. He had heard of such a phenomenon from others but had always dismissed it as folklore and nothing else. It was not a foolproof method for predicting, by any means, but it was still reliable enough to give him a convenient heads-up, which was the only positive attribute he could think of from being shot.

He decided to postpone doing his morning rounds until after he had his coffee at the restaurant. These days, he usually made it himself, but today was different since he had an underlying reason for wanting to visit the restaurant.

Sheriff Redding was due to make rounds but decided to put it off and left his spot outside of the sheriff's office and headed the short distance over to the restaurant, the steam of his breath mildly visible as he walked. He enjoyed the snowfall every winter, but he was also looking forward to the spring when things started settling down more. It had been a harsh winter, and those who did not abide by the law would be coming out in full force to make up for their winter absence.

He entered and was greeted with the usual pleasantries from the usual customers as he wandered over to a back table facing the door. The restaurant owner, Millie Williamson, a middle-aged portly woman, was over with a pot of fresh coffee and his cup almost as soon as he had sat down.

"Morning, sheriff," she said with a gracious smile as she poured his cup.

"Morning, Millie," he responded with a nod and a smile.

"You eatin' today, sheriff?"

"No, ma'am. Just coffee, please."

"Today's the big day," she started, with suppressed excitement. "I'm guessing you've got a lot to keep you busy, don't 'ya?"

"Yeah. I'm meeting the mayor in an hour. He'll fill me in as to whether any of the details have changed. If not, it's still due to hit town at noon."

"Isn't it exciting?" she said, smiling with pride. "I can't believe it's actually happening and that it's already here."

"Yeah, it's really something," he added dismissively, trying to fane enthusiasm.

She left him to his coffee and headed back to the kitchen while he pondered the day's events that were ahead of him. The thought of it all was overwhelming. He already wanted the day to be over, even though it had barely started. Today was the day the whole town had been anxiously waiting for. It was the day the first steam locomotive came through Salt Creek on its new route.

He had not looked forward to this day since he had first heard the news. There was no denying that the railroad being routed through Salt Creek was a major accomplishment, for the town and the territory, but Redding had his reservations as to just how beneficial it would be for the town and how much more difficult it was going to make his job. He had not openly opposed its construction, but he had disagreed with the manner in which it had been accomplished. Had it been a clean, legal and honest acquisition, he could have been more enthused, but its arrival had been marred with controversy.

Hundreds of Chinese laborers had been sanctioned by the railroad to lay the tracks through Salt Creek and beyond because of their accessibility, their abundance and their strong work ethic, but mostly because they could be hired for very little money. The railroad was all about progress and that progress came at the high cost of the men who built it, of which some paid with their lives. These workers were housed in shoddy makeshift shacks and lived under deplorable conditions. They were forced to work from sunup to sundown, six days a week with their safety and health never being taken into consideration. The railroad had been more concerned about timelines and schedules with their prime attention being focused on keeping costs to a minimum with their potential profits firmly in their sights and they were willing to sacrifice those who they considered in their eyes to be expendable. That kind of selfish greed did not sit well with Redding and, thus, had soured his opinion of the railroad before it had even made it to town.

But there was another reason why Sheriff Redding was concerned about having the railroad come there. It was no secret that the railroad brought riffraff with it, be it those running from the law looking for a quicker way to place as many miles between them and those that they had wronged, or those of questionable character who might, as of yet, not been caught in their unlawful ways. The railroad was a way for lawbreakers to move around quickly and almost without detection. As long as someone had the money for a ticket, their reason for leaving one town and traveling to the next was not questioned and they could get lost in the crowds that would be arriving at the same time. This type of obscurity came in handy for those dodging the law and made his job considerably more difficult.

It was true that the railroad would bring businesses and newcomers to Salt Creek, but Redding preferred the town to prosper on its own merits and at a conformable pace. That would almost guarantee that those who decided to take up roots and plant them there would likely do so out of a sense of business and not as a questionable opportunity. Redding had heard of other towns who rallied for the railroad to pass through them, and once it had, the rate of crime had skyrocketed. It was simply too easy for some unscrupulous individual to flow into town, try their hand at dishonest business and, once their deception was discovered, leave on the next train out. Instead of riding into town alone and drawing everyone's attention, they could easily blend in with the visitors and virtually escape detection.

Sheriff Redding also had a foul taste in his mouth about the railroad running through Salt Creek because of how it had come to be. His previous employer, Roland Bartlett, the owner of the biggest spread anywhere around, had cheated and swindled those in authority with the railroad to make the rail line running through town a reality. Those who could not be bought were bullied. People had been hurt, and some even killed, such as his friend, Dave Fancher. He himself had received the bullet wound to his side because he had refused to back down and let Bartlett run him out of town for not going along with his corruption. There were reminders of Bartlett's deception all around him, reminding him of it on a daily basis. Bartlett had threatened the lives of both him and his new wife, Grace, and had almost made good on those threats. His good friend, Dave Fancher, had also taken a stand against Bartlett's tyranny and ultimately, it had cost him his life.

"I said 'hello, sheriff,'" a voice repeated as a man's head bobbed down in front of him, interrupting his line of sight, stirring Redding out of his state of thought and bringing his attention back to the restaurant. He looked up to see Mayor Bradbury standing in front of him, earlier than expected and already looking flustered and worn, despite it still being early in the day.

"Oh, hello, mayor," Redding said with a soft, awkward chuckle. "Sorry, my mind was just wandering."

"Now I know you've got a lot on your plate, sheriff, but don't you go sideways on me, at least not now," the man said fervently. "I need you at your best today with the railroad coming through town. Then, when that's over, you can fall apart."

"Don't worry, mayor," Redding convinced him with a smile. "I'm all here."

"Good," Mayor Bradbury responded with an aggressive nodding of his head. "Lots going on today. Lots of important people coming into Salt Creek for the first time. We want to make sure they get a formal greeting and that they don't regret bringing their train through here."

"Don't worry, mayor," Sheriff Redding repeated. "We'll make 'em feel special."

"Good, good. That's what I want to hear. Now, don't forget to be on the platform at…"

"Eleven o'clock. I've got it, mayor. I won't be late."

"Don't be late," the frazzled mayor spoke, as if he had not heard Redding's response. "I must go. Lots to do before they arrive. See you at eleven," the mayor spoke as he whirled and headed for the door, tossing Redding a farewell wave behind him in the process. Redding dismissed the excitement that permeated from the mayor and returned to his coffee. He wanted the whole thing to be over with and for things to settle back down and get back to normal. He had grown tired of the whole commotion about the railroad. His thoughts went elsewhere as he took a casual sip of his coffee, only to discover that it had already become tepid in the short amount of time that he had been talking to the mayor and letting his thoughts wander. His simple, disappointing frown was not lost on Millie as she suddenly appeared, as if out of nowhere, holding a fresh pot of coffee. He was so engrossed in his thoughts that he had not even noticed her walking over to him.

"Freshen that up for ya', Sheriff?" she asked as she stood, poised, ready to pour. "I think you got the rest of the last batch. Sorry about that. No charge for it."

"No, thanks, Millie," Redding answered with a simple smile. "I need to get going, anyway. Got to be ready for the train."

"We need to get ready, too," she said with a hint of excitement. "We're closing down for the ceremony, but we'll reopen as soon as it's over in the hopes of seeing a bunch of new customers coming here. First time we ever shut our doors during business hours since I started the place. Didn't even close when the sheriff was gunned down. Well, I guess we'll see you there."

"Yeah, I'll be seeing you."

Despite Millie's offer, Redding dropped a coin on the table and put on his hat as he walked to the door and out onto the boardwalk. He glanced up and down the street before starting back towards his office, deciding to put off his rounds a little longer. He wanted to believe that the train coming there was a blessing and that it was only going to mean good things for the town.

He wanted to believe that, but something deep down inside of him knew better.

CHAPTER 2

As expected, the fanfare for the arrival of the train was almost too much to contain. The crowd was immense and spilled over from the depot platforms and onto the sides of the streets, with some standing in wagons conveniently placed nearby and others perched on the rooftops of neighboring buildings. Everyone was talking, a dull murmuring of voices intermixed with contained excitement while everyone stood anxiously lumped together on the train depot platforms, some periodically stealing glimpses down the tracks, hoping to claim the title of being one of the first to see the spectacle that would soon be arriving. For many, it was the first bit of excitement to hit the town in as many years as they could remember. For Sheriff Redding, it could not be over soon enough.

Though it was barely eleven in the morning, there was a constant checking of watches as impatience began to take over. Some overenthusiastic onlookers had to be herded from the tracks by Sheriff Redding and his deputy, Clint McNeil, as their eagerness to see the new train easily took over their senses and put them in danger.

Redding and Deputy McNeil had finally managed to somewhat quell the excitement of the crowd, although just barely, when the sound of a whistle could be faintly heard off in the distance. Someone hushed the crowd just in time for the sound to be repeated before the entire group burst out in celebration and their cheers easily drowned out any chance of ever hearing it again.

Sheriff Redding had to fight his way through the sea of people to make it over to the train tracks where he could place himself between the crowd and the train and keep a better eye on anyone who might get too close to the approaching locomotive engine. Getting caught up in the news frenzy tended to cause people to lose reasoning and put themselves in harm's way and chance falling in front of a moving train.

The train arrived right on schedule to the fanfare of the townspeople and the greetings from the town band playing a jaunty, joyful tune. Its grand arrival excited the group of spectators from the moment they first heard its whistle blasting off in the distance until it eventually came into sight and up until it began to slow down right in front of the newly constructed train depot and telegraph office.

The celebratory music the band generated was overpowered and drowned out by the loud hissing of the locomotive releasing the steam which had built up during its travels and caused the children and even some of the adults to cover their ears from its deafening outbursts. Those parts of the crowd that were the closest to the train engine briefly disappeared in the midst of the plumes of white smoke as they overtook and glided past them and then casually floated off into the distance, quickly forgotten. Everyone was busy waving and attempting to shout over the noise until the engine came to a solid rest, their enthusiasm beaming from them as if they had never seen a train up close before, of which many had not.

There was an added excitement in the air knowing that the appearance of the locomotive would now be a routine thing and knowing what people and commerce it would bring to the growing town of Salt Creek as it charged towards the new century.

Sheriff Vince Redding watched from the sidelines as the passengers filed out from the train and were greeted by the locals who met them with broad smiles and gracious handshakes, their revelry undaunted even by the noise and the commotion. Redding glanced over the passengers to get a better look at those who had been brought to Salt Creek in such a new and grandiose manner. They looked like the average crowd of travelers that one would expect to see departing from a train. Redding saw no one in particular that stood out to him, a welcome relief and a sign that perhaps he had misjudged these people and was possibly looking a little too much for trouble that wasn't necessarily coming. Maybe his instincts were wrong, and he had built up the antici-pation into something more than it should have been all along. Maybe, but even this casual flow of newcomers wasn't enough to entirely convince him that he had nothing to worry about.

After the dedication ceremony and congratula-tory exchanges from the city council to the railroad representatives and back to the townspeople had concluded, the excitement began to fade, and the townspeople began to part ways and disperse as the ceremony came to an official close. Sheriff Redding stayed behind at the mayor's request, to make sure things returned to normal and that the train was sent on its way to the next stop on its route.

Towards the end of the group of travelers disem-barking from the train was a man who caught Redding's attention. He looked to be a businessman in a fresh, well-tailored dark-colored suit and matching Bowler hat, carrying a formal long coat purposely draped over his arm and a pair of leather dress gloves in his hand. Redding had only seen pictures in advertisements of such flair and distinguished taste, but never had he ever seen them in person. It was clear when seeing him that he was obviously a man of wealth, someone who either had a family that came from money or represented a fortune that he had amassed on his own. Redding could tell from the man's demeanor and the way with which he carried himself that he was accustomed to getting what he wanted, no matter what the cost, or how it was derived.

Having seen pictures of the type of clothing the man wore, Redding recognized it as being from back east. The style and the craftsmanship that went into making it suggested that this was a man of higher standards and considerable means. The man carried himself well as he paused on the platform just long enough to take in his surroundings, the sharpness of his movements mirroring that of his confidence before his expensive matching leather bags were brought to him by a porter. He then followed the man across the span of the depot and off into the street towards the nearest hotel without any sort of hesitation from the man.

The man looked to be around Redding's age and

roughly the same height, but with a stockier frame, carrying a good extra twenty-five pounds on Redding. This was no stranger that had just happened to wander from town to town until he had chosen to be let off here. This was a man with purpose.

Satisfied that the ceremony had proved to be uneventful as far as disruptions, Sheriff Redding made his way back to his office, fielding residual complements and enthusiasm from the townspeople along the way. He stopped in at the land office briefly on the way to check on a new filing Abigail Bartlett had made on a parcel of land adjacent to her own ranch, the J.B. Bar, to make sure everything had gone through. Although it was of no concern to him that she obtained it, he still felt an obligation to make sure she had not encountered any legal complications, especially after what she had gone through within the past few months trying to maintain control of her own property.

The J.B. Bar Ranch, which had been started and grown by her late father, Roland Bartlett, had now become the property of his daughter and only child, Abigail Bartlett. Roland Bartlett had started out as a fair and honest businessman, growing his ranch from nothing into one of the largest and most successful in the territory. But when rumors spread of a possible line of the railroad running through

Salt Creek, Roland Bartlett lost all sense of reasoning and, as a result, he had lost his way. He had to do what was necessary to persuade the railroad to abandon running a line through any of the neighboring towns and pick Salt Creek for its route. Obsessed with making sure the railroad picked Salt Creek for its newest route, Bartlett threw away everything he had worked so hard to build over the years. He threw away reason and rationality and turned to any type of unlawful practices that were necessary to ensure the railroad passed within the town limits, putting his ranch and the future of his only child in jeopardy in the process.

But convincing the officials to divert the railroad through Salt Creek was no easy task. It required money. Lots of it. And far more than he had available to him through his assets. He needed outside funding to ensure that he accumulated the necessary equity to sway the decision-makers who were responsible for plotting the course of the railway. He had to act quickly before the railroad lost interest in Salt Creek altogether. As a result, he got desperate. And as is often the case, desperate men do desperate things. Roland Bartlett let the fear of losing everything he had worked for disappear and began to acquire properties and cattle through unscrupulous means. Some were bought out at a fraction of what they were worth, and those who resisted his offers were ultimately forced off of their properties using questionable means and sometimes even brute force. He turned a blind eye to the law and continued to build his empire through the sweat and pain of others, causing many to lose everything they had owned and worked for. In the end, the railroad did come through Salt creek, but not without a significant cost. His plan to control everything failed as his drive to bring the railroad through town came to pass, but it ended up costing him everything from his daughter's love and respect to his own life. Ironically, the very same man who had rallied so hard for so long to bring the railroad to town didn't get to live long enough to see it come to fruition.

Since her father, Roland Bartlett, had acquired land by forcing its owners off of it, and since the Barrett name had been tarnished and its credibility severely compromised, Abigail had her work cut out for her. She wanted to clear the Bartlett name and wanted to make sure that any growth of her ranch, the J.B. Bar, was done legally and ethically from then on without question. Although Redding had no reason to believe that she would involve herself in anything dishonest or illegal, when it came to the acquisition of land in his jurisdiction, Abigail still wanted to make sure that there were no disagreements about the dealings.

Although the child of a successful rancher,

Abigail Bartlett was a strong, confident woman who was not afraid to work hard in order to succeed. She had witnessed her father build his empire from the ground up and knew what it took to continue on doing the same after his death. There were those who had a hard time accepting that Abigail could follow in her father's footsteps and continuing running the ranch, but she had proved them all to be wrong. Whether behind a desk or on the back of a horse, her drive and determination showed that she was genuinely involved and committed to the J.B. Bar's success and would not let anyone, or anything, stand in her way. In that respect, she was just like her father.

Sheriff Redding caught Abigail in the office, finalizing the deal on the new parcel of land. She saw his movement waiting outside the office and passed a simple wave to him. He waited as she finished and walked outside to meet him.

"Hi, Vince," she greeted him with a smile.

"Hello, Abigail. Everything go okay?"

"Yeah," she said with a dismissive wave of her hand. "I just needed to fill out the rest of the paperwork to finalize the land purchase. I hated getting the land this way, but since Mr. Capwell died, his wife couldn't run the place by herself. She had no choice but to sell, and it seemed like the right thing for her to do to get out from under it. Thankfully, it butts up to my land so I can expand my pastures."

"Well, I'm happy for you," Redding smiled. "If anyone deserves to grow, it's you."

"Thanks, Vince. Say, would you and Grace like to come out for supper tonight? You two can help me celebrate the expansion."

"I'd have to check with her, but I'm sure we can pull away long enough to come out there."

"Great," she replied with a satisfying smile. "Say, about six?"

"Sounds good. Can we bring anything?"

"Just your appetites."

"Don't worry. If Consquella is cooking, that won't be a problem."

"Good. I'll look forward to seeing you then."

Redding tipped his hat and continued on to the sheriff's office while Abigail climbed into her buggy parked in front of the land office. As she settled her belongings onto the floor of the buggy and reached for the reins, she saw him– a tall stranger, impeccably dressed in a dark suit and matching Bowler hat with broad shoulders and a confident smile step out of the front entrance of the Imperial Hotel and apse on the boardwalk.

She watched him, mesmerized by his good looks, probably a little too long, she worried, but long enough for him to see that he had caught her attention. He locked eyes with her and politely tipped his hat for a brief second before continuing on towards the center of town. She watched him all the way until he disappeared inside a building as she felt her face flush. She had lost her breath briefly watching this man, this stranger, whom had obviously just come in on the first run of the new train line.

She had to find a way to meet him.

CHAPTER 3

BLAINE WALKER HAD WALKED UP TO THE FRONT DESK of the Imperial Hotel and waited patiently to garnish the clerk's attention. A mousy-looking man with wire glasses working behind the counter picked up on his arrival and turned to him, flashing a practiced smile.

"Good morning, sir. May I help you?"

"Yes, I'd like a room," Blaine Walker said with a vacant but stern expression as he draped his over-coat down onto the counter, "preferably one facing the street."

"Yes, sir," the clerk responded. "And how long will you be staying with us?"

"At least a week, perhaps more."

"Yes, sir." The clerk spun the register around facing Walker as he retrieved a key from the board behind him and placed it on the counter just as Walker finished. The clerk craned his neck to look at the upside-down signature. "You're in room five, Mr. Walker," he said as he handed the key to him. "Upstairs, second door on your right. Facing the street, just like you requested."

"Thank you," Walker replied, reaching for his overcoat, but the clerk was too mesmerized by Walker's dapper appearance that he had to find out what he could about the stranger.

"You come in on the train? It's exciting to see it here, y'know. It was the first train to come through here, ever. Where did you pick it up at?"

Walker sidestepped the question and glared at the clerk, his features not changing. "Thank you," he responded with a weak smile as he motioned to the porter to follow him upstairs. The clerk stood quietly, his enthusiasm diminished.

Blaine Walker keyed his door and pointed to a spot at the foot of the bed for the porter to dispose of his luggage. After tipping the man, he closed the door behind him as he left and walked over to the window, pulling back the side curtain to peer outside. He had a full view of the entire length of main street, from one end to the other. He even had a clear view of the unloading platform of the train station, giving him clear sight of anyone who would be coming into town. It was the perfect location.

He began unpacking his carefully arranged belongings and dispensing them in their appropriate drawers. When he reached the Smith & Wesson Model Three revolver and rolled up gun belt, he placed it under his pillow, smoothing out the wrinkles of the pillow to avoid detection. Although skilled with a handgun, he didn't want to have to resort to using it, but whether or not he had to would depend on the local law and how much resistance he would get from them.

The bite of the late afternoon breeze had kicked up and put an especially cooler chill in the air than was normal for that time of year.

After finishing up his standard barrage of paperwork, Sheriff Vince Redding had finished off his third cup of coffee and decided it was time to go on rounds to check out the town before making his way home to get ready for supper at Abigail Bartlett's house.

After a brief exchange of his intentions with his deputy, Clint McNeil, he cinched up his coat to brave the breeze that would inevitably have to face once he cleared the door of the sheriff's office. Even so, the first contact with the stiff wind was enough to shake awake any weariness that he had from the laborious day he had just endured.

Redding wanted to believe that the railroad coming into Salt Creek had been a good thing. Good for the economy, good for the potential growth of the town and good for the people. It meant big changes for them, changes in technology and changes in the way business was conducted and improved.

But Redding had seen the darker side of progress before. Despite the good it produced, he had seen what type of shady individuals it also attracted. Individuals who saw the increased prospect of taking from those who had worked and sacrificed so much to make it and how simple it was to do so. He had seen the rate of crime spike in these towns and how the townspeople of these towns had to be even more vigilant than before to protect what was theirs. He had seen businesses lose everything, through no fault of their own, and he had seen good people hurt and even killed for no reason other than greed. He vowed such a thing would not happen to the good residents of Salt Creek, railroad or no railroad.

Sheriff Redding had covered most of the west end of town and was circling back up the two side streets and entered the Palladium Saloon for a routine check and to check in with the bartender there, who was a friend of his. As he passed through the closed front doors, he was greeted with the familiar sights and sounds of a frontier saloon that he had grown to appreciate, from the casual visitors loitering about engaging in the customary topics of conversation to the brass spittoons precariously positioned at the ends of the long inviting bar. He had always loved the charm of a saloon and took in a deep breath to take it all in, feeding off of the tranquility that the atmosphere provided.

As he entered the Palladium, he locked eyes with the bartender, Stan Granger, a large burly man who had always reminded him more of a mountain trapper who had shunned civilization and had become accustomed to living in the wilderness than a barkeep stuck in a frontier town.

"Sheriff!" Stan's booming voice echoed throughout the establishment as he greeted his friend with a large, toothy smile. "Come in out of the cold and sit a spell!" the man suggested as he waved him over. Redding nodded and weaved his way through the surprisingly dense crowd until he reached the outstretched hand of his friend.

"How are you, sheriff?!" Stan resounded as his massive fist clamped down on Redding's. As usual, it was almost painful to shake hands with a man of such stature and strength. He had always feared ever having to subdue his friend at any point if the man became violent, realizing it would probably be necessary to shoot the man just to be able to get him under control.

"Fine, Stan," Redding replied as he tried to shake the crushing sensation from his hand as usual, causing an amused chuckle from the bartender.

"I saw you coming in and you look like you could use something to help take the chill off," Stan suggested as he slid a cup of coffee over to him. "Knew you were coming around soon so I just made it."

"I appreciate that," Redding replied as he cupped the cup in his hands and enjoyed the instant warming sensation it generated before he dared try to sample it. The refreshing warmth of it sliding down his throat was well worth the stinging bit it generated. "That's good," he added as he gingerly tried another sip.

"Glad you like it, sheriff," Stan resounded happily as he innocently patted Redding on the arm with such intensity that he almost spilled his coffee. He was enjoying another sip and had turned to take in the customers when a man spoke.

"Who comes into a bar and drinks coffee?"

At first, Redding did not think the man was talking to him, but then as he glanced down the length of the bar, he realized he was the only one not consuming alcohol. He turned to see a man off to his side, facing him. He believed the man had been drinking, but from his demeanor and speech, he did not appear to be impaired. The bartender spoke before Redding could respond.

"Show the man a little respect. This is our sheriff that you're talking to," Stan offered as his boisterous demeanor suddenly went serious.

"I'm not talking to you, fat man," the customer rudely responded while still locking eyes with Redding.

An enraged Stan started to reach under the bar for his hidden shotgun, but Redding held up his hand to stop him. "Don't," he added simply and cautiously, stopping his friend's movements. Redding turned to fully face the man, his eyes level and hard. "I think you need to leave, mister. Right now, or I'll arrest you for disorderly conduct." Redding added as the sound of sliding chairs and the rumble of stampeding boot steps filled the cavernous room as customers began to push back up against the walls and out of the possible line of fire.

"You think I'm scared of that badge?" the man taunted Redding. "That hunk of metal don't mean nothing to me."

"Then forget the badge," Redding uttered in a calm, cool tone. "*I'm* telling you to leave now before things get ugly."

"I heard you was fast, Redding. Why don't we see if it's true?"

Redding tried to talk the man down, but it was

obvious that he was getting nowhere. "Nobody's bothering you. If you're looking for a fight, you don't want to do that. Why don't you go home and sleep it off?"

"I ain't drunk, you ignorant fool!" the man shouted as his body tensed. "I'm stone cold sober!"

"Then you can't blame this on the liquor. All the more reason to back away," Redding suggested.

"I heard about you, sheriff. People say you're not to be pushed. That's mighty high talking for a man who comes into a saloon and drinks coffee. What's wrong? You ain't man enough to drink a grown man's drink?"

"I drink what I want, when I want it."

"They also say you're fast," the man stated, followed by a loud scoff as he glanced up and down Redding with a sarcastic smirk. "You sure don't look fast to me. So, tell me: *are* you fast, sheriff?"

Redding's eyes went hard. "Let's not find out."

"I ain't scared of you, lawman!" the man suddenly snapped belligerently. "I say you're a coward for hiding behind that tin star! And you're a sissy for not drinkin' like a real man!"

"Alright, that's it. You're under arrest for public disturbance," Redding demanded as he started towards the man.

"No, I ain't!" the man exploded as he reached for his gun.

The man was fast, by all standards, but not fast enough. Redding's hand was cool and controlled as his bullet ripped through the man's midsection, buckling him just as he had cleared leather. Even though he was shot, he still tried to pull the trigger of his revolver, but his hand would not cooperate from the stifling pain coursing through his body that had distorted his grip. He glanced up at Redding, his eyes filled with a mixture of anger and hatred as he worked to fight through the pain. His gritted teeth seethed through gasps of labored breath as he toppled over and onto the wooden floor. There was no more movement.

After holstering his revolver, Redding walked over to the man while checking around him for any others who might have been associated with the fallen man, but when no one moved to check on him or seemed interested in his condition, Redding took it to mean that the man had been alone.

He reached down and picked up the dead man's revolver from his holster and tucked it into his waistband as he spoke to the men who had gathered around to get a close-up view of the dead man. "Somebody go get Emmett," Redding said, referring to the town's undertaker as one of the men peeled away from the growing crowd and ran for the door. The bartender, Stan, had walked up behind Redding, who had squatted to check the man for identification.

"Do you know him, sheriff?" Stan asked as he leaned over Redding for a closer look.

"No, never seen him before," Redding answered, while rummaging through the man's pockets. In the dead man's vest pocket was a wad of cash in folded bills. Redding fanned out the money to verify the amount. "He's got almost a thousand dollars on him. Now, why would a man walk around carrying that kind of money?"

"Maybe he's a gambler," Stan suggested.

"If he's that good at gambling, he wouldn't be so eager to go around picking gunfights with strangers." He shot Stan a look. "You're a witness to how much is here. I'll turn it over to Wainwright at the bank, in case he's got kin that could claim it."

"You sure you don't know him, sheriff?"

Redding continued staring down at the man as he softly shook his head. "Nope. Never seen him before."

"Well, he sure knew you," Stan pointed out. "Even called you by name. Wonder where he came from?"

"Must have come in on the train," Redding reasoned. "I haven't seen him around town before today."

"Me neither," Stan added. "I would have remembered him."

"I know him," one man admitted after breaking through the dense collection of men, drawing Redding's attention and causing him to stand and step over to him as the man pointed down at the body. "That's Jack Folsom."

"Folsom," Stan repeated with a nod. "I've heard of him. He's a lower-class gunman. Hires out a lot," Stan added as he glanced over to Redding for a reaction.

"A gunman?" Redding replied. "What would he want with me? I haven't shot anyone."

"Maybe you locked up a friend of his?"

"That wouldn't warrant trying to kill me, just because I locked up someone he knew."

"Maybe you had a run-in with him before and you just don't remember him."

"Believe me, I remember when someone's trying to kill me."

"But if you've never seen or heard of him, then why would he have a beef with you?"

Redding shook his head, confused. "Don't know. Maybe he just didn't like lawmen."

Stan scoffed. "I don't know about all lawmen, but he obviously didn't like you."

CHAPTER 4

WITH SO MANY PATRONS HAVING BEEN INSIDE THE saloon at the time of the shooting, witnesses filed out of the saloon and began spreading word throughout Salt Creek about the shootout between Sheriff Redding and the gunman, Jack Folsom, like a wildfire out of control. There was the usual suspicion that the gunman, Folsom, was hired to take out Redding, even though there was no evidence to back up the theory. Witnesses to the shooting speculated on the reason behind the standoff, with details immediately being embellished to generate more attention to the storyteller. With no apparent grudge or vendetta pushing Folsom's actions, it was looking more like Folsom was nothing more than a madman looking for a fight.

He had found one.

For Sheriff Redding, it was one more case providing further validation that the railroad was not as beneficial to the town as everyone else thought. He was the only one in town to look at the train as a problem. *It had already started. What he knew would happen. Yes, it brought growth and commerce to their town, but at what cost?*

Mayor Bradbury had been aware of his skepticism and chose to overlook it because there was too much riding on Salt Creek being a stop on the rail line. It meant a lot of money for a lot of people, so to them, the possibility of having gunmen using it to come into town was well worth the risk. After all, that was why they had Sheriff Vince Redding in place. It would be his job to keep them at bay.

But Redding knew the odds were against him since it wasn't feasible for him to be there every time a train came through there. Instead, he would have to wait and see what type of individuals it brought to town. Hopefully, word of the shooting would spread and hopefully it would deter others from coming there looking for an opportunity to cause trouble.

Hopefully.

Redding returned to his office while the body of Jack Folsom was being removed from the saloon and taken to the undertaker's office. The shooting had bothered him. Not because he had had to kill a man, something that he never took pleasure in, but the fact that the man had obviously come to Salt Creek on the railroad. It was the first run of the rail line and the safety of the townspeople had already been placed in jeopardy. He thought nothing of having his life threatened. That part did not bother him, but rather the fact that he had already been proven right. He sat back, contemplating his next move.

Redding was no fool. He had seen this type of situation before in other towns and even if no one else believed him, from his experience, he had every reason to be worried that this was only the beginning.

As dark descended over the town of Salt Creek, Blaine Walker stood diligently by his window, watching. Waiting.

The man he was on the lookout for would be coming into town tonight. At least, that was the plan. He would be riding a horse, a chestnut with a white mane, he had been told, in order to properly identify the man. He knew the type, anyway, and knew what to look for. His hope was that the man could slip into town without being noticed so it was impera- tive that the man arrive after dark when there were fewer people out and about and fewer eyes to notice his arrival since they would know what to look for to be suspicious of, as well.

Walker had chosen this man based on a recommendation from someone who had used his expertise to resolve a similar situation to his own. Walker had never met the man, but that wasn't necessary. From what he had heard of him, this was, without a doubt, the right man for the job.

There was always a gunman or an ex-soldier with no real skills who used his experience of killing during the war to try to make a living afterward. The man he had sent for was a professional, and if there was one thing he needed here in Salt Creek, it was a professional. Someone that he could point in a direction and not have to worry about monitoring him, although he did have a contingency plan, just in case. Regardless, this was someone that he had confidence in who would get the job done. He would have enough on his plate without having to worry about watching over someone else to make sure they were doing their part that they were being paid for. The plan did not allow for such interruptions. Once he, Walker, set things into motion, they had to be completed on time and without interference or all of this that he had worked so hard for would be in vain and he would lose everything. And that was not an option. Blaine Walker was not accustomed to losing.

He began to grow impatient as he released the curtain, wondering if something had happened to the man to delay his arrival or even prevent it, but he quickly doubted both notions. Things did not happen *to* this man. Things happened *because* of this man.

Growing more impatient from the delay, Walker was just about to concede and walk over to the restaurant when he saw a man riding into town on a chestnut with a white mane.

It was him.

Ike Harrington was young, but experienced far beyond most others his age, and some even older. He pulled the chestnut to a stop in front of the Emporium Saloon and climbed down, his spurs jingling as his lean, solid frame stepped onto the dusty road. Harrington carefully took in his surroundings as he surveyed the town, his matching pair of Colt Army revolvers low and tight against his thighs, his movements smooth and intentional, never taking his eyes off of those around him and always aware of where they were. Because of his line of work, it was a habit that was necessary and one that he had honed to perfection. He had made it this long by being careful and not taking anything, or anyone, for granted or by taking unnecessary chances. He also made no assumptions about anything and especially about anyone, since such assumptions could get you killed.

Over the years, there had been plenty of men who had wanted Harrington dead, with most of them having died by his hand in the process. A few had escaped, but he didn't worry about those. If a man knew he was going to have to face Harrington and he somehow managed to get away, he could consider himself lucky beyond measure, because no one who had ever faced Ike Harrington had managed to make it out alive.

Blaine Walker watched as Harrington scanned the buildings until he saw Walker standing in the shadows of the window. When he saw Walker nod to him, Harrington started for the hotel, cutting down between buildings and coming up the rear stairs instead of the front to avoid detection as much as possible. A soft rap on the door and it was opened, with Walker motioning him into his room. Walker took a seat at the small table in the room while Harrington removed his leather gloves and stuffed them into his back pocket.

"You must be Walker," Harrington stated coolly as he glanced over to Walker.

"And you must be the infamous Ike Harrington," Walker replied, equally calm. "Your reputation precedes you, sir. I take it by your presence here that you got my telegram."

"I got it," Harrington said. "I would have been here sooner, but I was tracking a man."

"And what happened?"

Harrington glanced at him slowly. "I found him,"

Harrington spoke softly, dismissing the question any further.

"I sent for you, Mr. Harrington, because I'm going to need your expertise," Walker started, as he took the seat across from him. "I'm looking to get into the ranching business and I need your help in order to do that."

"I don't know who you talked to, but I don't do ranching anymore, Walker. Had my fill of it years ago. I watched men work their fingers to the bone from sunup till past sundown and still fail. Too much work and there's no money in it."

"No, I'm afraid you misunderstand, Mr. Harrington. I'm not looking to bring you on as a ranch hand. I need your services to watch over things while *I* become a rancher."

Harrington turned a curious eye to Walker. "How you plan on doing that, mister? All the good land around here is already taken. You're about twenty years too late."

"Which is precisely why I need your gun," Walker stated boldly. "I'm going to be acquiring ranges and combining them together until I have the largest and most successful in the territory."

"No, thanks," Harrington shook his head, removing his gloves from his pocket and starting to put them back on. "'Acquiring ranges' sounds like a slippery slope. I came here because I thought this was a legitimate job, not a suicide mission. I don't go up against those kinds of numbers. It's too complicated and way too messy."

"That's not what I hear," Walker commented, casually leaning forward in his chair. "I heard that you were ruthless. Unconscionable. Not afraid of anything, or anyone. That's what I was looking for. That's why I chose you. You actually disappoint me, Mr. Harrington."

"You watch your mouth, Walker," Harrington sneered, pointing his finger angrily at the man. "I don't take that kind of talk from you, or anybody else."

"Then stop hiding behind your reputation and at least hear me out," Walker snapped as he abruptly stood. "I need someone on this job to field things for me and to keep the law off my back. They need to be dependable and they need to be good with a gun. I thought you were the man for that job, which is precisely why I sent for you before anyone else. So, tell me, Mr. Harrington: did I make a mistake by sending for you?"

Harrington's short fuse had allowed his anger to keep building, pushing him to want to pull his gun and use it on this man– this arrogant, know-it-all city fella, fancy-dressed, newcomer. But he wanted to hear more, whether he took the job or not. He sighed heavily to try to calm himself. "Alright,

Walker. I'll listen to you. Tell me what you had in mind. And make it quick."

"I'm building the largest ranch in the territory and then I'm taking over this town," Walker spoke, his enthusiasm building as he continued. "I've had my eye on this town since I first found out that the railroad was coming through here."

"So?" Harrington snickered. "Railroads go through lots of towns. If you missed your opportunity here, then go somewhere else. Why is this one so important?"

"Because since the announcement of the railroad coming through here, Salt Creek has almost doubled in size in citizens, and in business growth. That's double the activity in less than four months. That's virtually unheard of."

An unamused Harrington was shaking his head. "I still don't see your point. If the land isn't available, then it isn't available. It's that simple."

"My point, Mr. Harrington, is that this explosive growth represents more opportunity. The largest ranch in the territory owns seventy percent of the total amount of land in this territory."

"Exactly. That's what I was saying before. It's already taken."

"But the ownership can still be transferred," Walker suggested. "All I have to do is get in good with the owner and work my way into owning it."

Harrington chuckled softly. "You're crazy. No one in their right mind is going to just let you waltz in here and sign over their land to you, even if you had the money to buy them out, which I highly doubt you do. I don't care how fancy your clothes are or how slick you can talk. It ain't gonna happen."

"You let me worry about that," Walker said confidently. "I just need you around to help clean things up as I go."

"I'd be wasting my time working towards something that's never going to happen. Walker. I don't enjoy wasting my time."

"I wouldn't have brought you out here if I thought it was wasting your time."

"I still think you're biting off more than you can chew, but I'll have to think about going along with your plans, Walker. I'll let you know something in a day or two," Harrington said as he turned to leave.

"That's not good enough," Walker responded, a solid harshness in his tone. "I need an answer *now*, Harrington."

Harrington turned back to face Walker. "It's going to have to be good enough for now because I'm not ready to give you an answer."

Walker was clearly agitated by his indecisiveness. "Then, obviously, I hired the wrong man."

Harrington took offense to the comment. It insinuated that he wasn't up to the task. He could feel his anger building again. "Listen here, Walker. I work by *my* rules, *not* yours. I work *when* I want and I do *what* I want. Understand?"

"Not if you're working for me, you don't," Walker professed as he took a step closer to Harrington. "If *I'm* paying you, you work for *me* and you do *what* I say, *when* I say, and *how* I say it. If I tell you to do nothing, then *that's* what you do. Those are the terms and they are non-negotiable. Now, I'm a busy man, Mr. Harrington, so do you accept my offer, or should I move on and find someone else?"

Harrington could feel his hand instinctively and slowly slipping down to his revolver. He had to catch himself before he acted on his natural impulse to settle things with a gun. Slowly, he calmed himself and began to relax again. "Alright. Say I accept it. What does it pay?"

"Two thousand dollars up front and another thousand when I have what I'm after."

Harrington took in the numbers versus the risk with a simple nod. Finally, he decided. "Alright, Walker. I'll take the job."

"Good," Blain Walker responded with his own satisfying nod. "Your first act is to find out what you can about the J.B. Bar Ranch. That's the biggest ranch that I was talking about. They own seven out of every ten acres in the territory. I haven't been able to gather much information so far. I need you to get a job there so you can get me inside information on their operation."

"Like I said, I don't do ranch work, but I'll go lean on the owner. He'll talk to me."

"*She*," Walker corrected him. "The J.B. Bar is owned by a woman, Abigail Bartlett."

The news caused Harrington to smile coyly. "Even better."

CHAPTER 5

ABIGAIL BARTLETT WAS SEATED ON THE TOP RAILING of the corral, watching some of her men breaking new horses, when the small plume of dust being kicked up by an approaching rider caught her attention. She watched the man draw nearer, realizing she did not recognize him or his horse. Such visitors here were not uncommon for a ranch in the territory, especially one as large and well-known as hers. Drifters often came there looking for work as they passed through the area, searching for temporary employment just long enough to scrape and save enough of their wages to then allow them to move on to the next cattle ranch where they would do it all over again. Abigail had grown accustomed to such visitors, seeing her father experience it her whole life growing up. It was one of the things to be expected as word spread from one drifter and one town to the next and it was part of the price that came with owning a successful ranch.

"Ms. Bartlett?" Luther Gilroy, her main foreman, uttered while he watched the approaching rider.

"Yes. I see him." She climbed down and turned to the other two men who had been seated next to her and Gilroy. "Matt? When you finish with these, I need you to take them out to Charlie and the others."

"Yes, ma'am, Ms. Bartlett," the ranch hand replied with a respectful tip of his hat. Abigail nodded and started towards the front of the Bartlett house with Luther Gilroy right beside her to draw him away from the other men. They met the rider just as he was pulling up to the hitching rail. It was a routine she and Gilroy had been through many times since her father's death. And like other times before, she did not like the looks of this stranger, especially the twin Colt revolvers she saw hanging on his hips.

This man was trouble.

"Can I help you?" she asked.

"I'm looking for the owner," the man replied.

"I'm the owner, Abigail Bartlett. What can I do for you?"

"I was looking for work."

"I'm sorry, but I don't need any more hands right now," Abigail said without hesitation.

"I was told you were looking," the man replied, slightly agitated.

Abigail's expression did not change or falter. "Then I'm afraid you were told wrong."

"Look, lady…"

"Ms. Bartlett," Gilroy quickly corrected the man, his eyes stern and constantly watching for movement of either of his hands towards a gun.

The man partially nodded his error. "My apologies, *Ms.* Bartlett. I only came out here because I heard you were looking for hands."

"Well, I'm sorry you had to ride all the way out here for nothing but, as I said, I'm afraid we're not hiring at this time, but you might want to try to see if one of the neighboring ranches can oblige you."

The man stared down Luther Gilroy and then passed his attention over to Abigail as he forced a half-smile and then tipped his hat. "Then good day to you, ma'am," he said as he gave a final glance over to Luther Gilroy and then turned his horse and walked it away, up the road. Abigail and Gilroy watched him leave, making sure he was not changing his mind about doing so. Once, the man turned and glanced back to see if they were looking.

"Do you know him?" she asked, as they both continued staring.

"No, ma'am. Never seen him before."

"He sure was a sketchy character, wasn't he?"

Abigail offered, as she continued to make sure he had, indeed, left. "I didn't like the looks of him. I wouldn't have hired him, even if I did have an opening."

"I agree," Luther Gilroy added. "Any legitimate ranch hand knows that a cattle ranch doesn't hire *more* hands going into winter. You can't move cattle till spring. It's hard enough keeping the ones you already have employed busy. I also didn't like the fact that he carries two guns. I can't ever remember seeing a true ranch hand that did."

"I wonder who he really was," she pondered out loud.

"Want me to have one of the men follow him and find out for 'ya, Ms. Bartlett?"

"No, Luther," she answered, "That won't be necessary. Where is the majority of the herd being held right now?"

"The north pastures."

"Then go have the lookouts on the far north pastures doubled until I say otherwise. He could be a scout for rustlers."

"Yes, ma'am," Gilroy replied as he turned and walked back towards the corral. Abigail continued to watch Ike Harrington until he had disappeared over the small knoll just beyond the J.B. Bar Ranch sign.

She had a bad feeling about the man. And something told her it wouldn't be the last time she saw him.

Blaine Walker glanced in the mirror, tidying himself one final time before grabbing his bowler hat and leaving his hotel room. His intentions for the day were clear. He had to find a business to buy.

He strolled through the lobby of the Imperial Hotel and out the front door, forced to adjust the brim of his hat to compensate for the morning sun as he stepped out onto the boardwalk. After lightly passing his walking cane into his open hand, he tossed a smile and tipped his hat at a passing woman before he started for the bank, his attention to only her, causing her to blush innocently. Even if he wasn't successful with the bank president, perhaps he could gather information on businesses that were struggling and might be interested in a buyer or, at the very least, maybe a partner. That would still allow him to get his foot in the door somewhere.

Walker confidently walked across the street and down to the bank entrance, politely removing his hat as he entered and flirting with the secretary until she brought him back to the office of the bank president, Mr. Wainwright, to meet him.

Their meeting was long, but produced nothing of substance as far as an opportunity. It appeared, much to Walker's dismay, that no one in Salt Creek suffered from a lack of business. In fact, businesses were thriving and new ones coming in every week. If he were going to have any sort of chance to make his move in this town, it would need to be soon.

As he walked to nowhere in particular, he spotted a saloon that caught his eye. Its appearance was appealing and located in an ideal spot right in the heart of town and at the junction of two major streets. He stood next to a column in the shade and watched the activity coming in and out of it for some time to confirm his theory. The place was unusually busy, even for this early in the day, which was quite surprising. He decided to take a look inside and find out what all the interest was about.

Walker parted the batwing doors and entered, aware that he was grossly overdressed for such an establishment, but not caring. Besides, if he were to make a name for himself in Salt Creek, the towns-people needed to become accustomed to seeing him about.

As expected, his entrance drew everyone's atten-tion, causing the low murmuring in the place to completely shut down as everyone stared at the man in the fancy clothes and a cane, who seemed so adamantly out of place and who had apparently wandered into the wrong place. They watched him in awe as he strolled confidently up to the bar, leaning his cane up against the front of the counter, and dropped his hat off to the side as he awaited the surprised bartender's arrival. A man, who Walker perceived to be the owner, came over to him, his mouth partially hanging open and still too shocked to say anything.

"Whiskey, mister bar owner," Walker spouted, followed with a grin. The bartender retrieved a bottle and slid a glass over to fill, all the while still unable to produce a single comment. Walker took the glass, quietly gestured a toast to the bartender and downed it in one gulp, seething the stinging aftertaste through a sharp exhale. He glanced back at the bartender and smiled broadly. "That's one thing I enjoy about the frontier," Walker commented. "You always have plenty of good whiskey." Walker slid his glass closer to the bartender. "How about another one for the road?"

"You're not from around these parts, are you, mister?" the man asked as he refilled the glass.

"No, my good man, I am originally from Chicago. I just arrived in your fair city only a few days ago and, I must say, it is even more intoxicating than this fine beverage that you are serving."

"Well, let me be the first to tell you that you're a little overdressed for this place," the bartender said under his breath. "You're asking for trouble coming into a place like this, dressed like that."

"My friend, there's nothing wrong with a man wanting to look one's best," Walker announced loud enough for everyone to hear now that his arrival had startled the entire crowd into silence. "And as for generating disturbances, I assure you that I have no intentions of quarreling with any of your patrons," Walker insisted as he reached for his glass, but a hand clamping tightly onto his wrist stopped him. He looked over at the man holding onto him and smiled faintly. "Would you mind removing your grip from me, sir?"

"What do you think you're doing coming in here dressed like that?" the man asked, while refusing to release Walker's wrist. Walker tried briefly to pull away, but the man's grip only tightened that much more. "You trying to rub our noses in the fact that you've got more money than us? Is that what you're saying? You come in here to flash your money around at us and shove it in our faces like we're nothing?"

"No, I would never think to commit such a demeaning act to you or anyone else in this establishment," he tried to reason. "I simply came into your charming abode for a drink," Walker stated calmly, while still trying to pull his arm away, but the man would not relinquish it.

"Well, you decided to come in spouting off a bunch of fancy words in the wrong place," the man said firmly as another man edged his way up behind the first man to back him up, the second man's deadpan expression unchanging, his eyes steadily watching things as they unfolded.

"Yes," Walker replied calmly, as he glanced at the two men in front of him with a confident smile. "I can see that now, you ignorant wretch." The man holding his wrist started to advance.

Without warning, Walker grabbed the neck of the whiskey bottle with his left hand and crashed it into the side of the first man's head just below his hat but slightly above his ear, splitting his scalp and creating a painful grunt from him as he was sent to the floor. The second man took a step closer to Walker, but before he could get to him, Walker kicked him hard in the stomach, doubling the man over. He quickly followed it up with a sharp right that knocked the man backwards onto his back on the bar. Still holding the remnants of the broken bottle, he pinned the man down against the bar, his face only inches from the battered man's, as he pressed the broken edge of the bottle against the man's throat. The saloon was dead silent as a small dribble of blood began to ooze from the cut and run down his neck, but even so, he dared not move. The man stared at Walker, wide-eyed and frightened for his life, his hands shaking as they were held up in surrender. "We didn't mean anything by it, mister!"

the terrified man exclaimed loudly. "We were just
fooling with 'ya!"

Walker did not ease back. "I may be a gentleman,"
he spoke through gritted teeth, his voice suddenly
icy and unyielding, "but I won't hesitate to cut you
from ear to ear if I ever have the misfortune of
running into either one of you two idiots again. Do I
make myself clear?"

The man shook his head adamantly, unable and
unwilling to move for fear that he would be dead
soon thereafter. Walker hesitated briefly to make
sure his words sunk in before releasing the man
before he slowly backed away and dropped the
broken bottle onto the floor. He continued watching
the second man, who had slowly eased himself up
off of the bar as he gently felt the cut on his neck.
Walker adjusted his coat and retrieved a silver dollar
from his vest pocket, dropping it onto the bar, his
demeanor quickly relaxing again.

"I apologize for the disturbance, my good man.
This is for the bottle, and the mess," he exclaimed
calmly as he picked up his hat and cane. He glanced
down at the unconscious man with a steady stream
of blood gushing from the side of his head and then
up at the second man, who had yet to move. "You'd
better get him to a doctor," he stated coolly as he
donned his hat and started for the door. "He's going
to need stitches."

CHAPTER 6

WHILE BLAINE WALKER WAS SEARCHING FOR A NEW investment, Sheriff Vince Redding was kissing his new bride, Grace, goodbye and climbing into his saddle, heading to his office in town as the first splash of sunlight filtered into the streets.

Even at this early time of the day, the town was already bustling with activity, the renewed energy that the railroad had brought with it still lingering fresh in the air. The townspeople were firmly convinced that the new railway station in Salt Creek would bring even more commerce to the already-thriving community. They were deeply embedded in their beliefs and it would take some time for their enthusiasm to wane, if it ever managed to.

The arrival of the railroad had been anxiously

anticipated by some much more than others. Bringing the railroad to Salt Creek had been the vision of rancher and local businessman Roland Bartlett, and it had paid off handsomely, ironically for everyone but Roland Bartlett, himself. Bartlett had died before seeing his vision come to fruition and, in the process, had already made a lot of money for a great many people with future earnings predicted to be more than anyone could possibly imagine. Those people, and the other residents of Salt Creek, owed a tremendous debt to the Bartlett family, which now consisted only of Roland's daughter, Abigail, herself. The town, which had already experienced significant growth even before the leg of the railroad arrived, had seen that growth explode even more now that the railway line had officially been opened.

Sheriff Redding fielded their pleasantries until he had reached his office, wishing the day and the hoopla were over. As he slid from the saddle and was tying off the roan, he saw the same well-dressed newcomer that had arrived on the first run of the railroad the day before step out of the front door of the Imperial Hotel, tipping his hat as he stopped on the boardwalk to graciously greet two women who were passing by him. Redding could hear their girlish giggles and watched them blush as he threw them a coy smile while doing so.

For a brief second, their eyes locked as Redding politely nodded to the man, who gave him a condescending glance and turned away without acknowledging his presence and started down the boardwalk towards the center of town. The gesture irritated Redding, who dismissed the man's rude behavior and walked into his office where his new deputy, Clint McNeil, had already made coffee. McNeil was sitting at the sheriff's desk looking through wanted posters when Redding entered.

"Oh, sorry, sheriff," a flustered McNeil coughed up as he scrambled to collect the stack of papers and quickly remove his cup from the desk.

Redding was amused by McNeil's embarrassment. "You're here awful early."

"I wanted to get a set of rounds in early."

"I told you it's alright if you use my desk," Redding reassured him as he placed his hat and coat on the coatrack and proceeded to pour his own cup. "This is just as much your office as it is mine."

"I know, sheriff," McNeil stammered nervously as he relocated himself at the nearby table, "but I still feel funny sitting behind it when I ain't the sheriff. It's like I'm taking your clothes or something."

"Well, just don't try to take my wife and we'll be fine," Redding replied jokingly.

The young deputy's face went into shock as his mouth partially fell open, and he froze. "Oh, sheriff," the man stuttered, "I think the world of Ms. Redding, but I'd never try to take her from 'ya. Honest, I wouldn't."

"It's okay, Clint," Redding said calmly with a reassuring smile, touching the young man on the arm. "I was just joking."

Deputy McNeil's face suddenly relaxed as he smiled broadly and chuckled from embarrassment. "Boy, sheriff, you really got me that time."

Redding laughed off the reply and then changed the discussion. "Clint, did you see that man getting off the train yesterday? Big fella, dark hair, flashy dark suit, bowler hat, had a porter dragging his luggage behind him?"

"No, sheriff, I didn't see nobody," the young man replied. "Why? Is he wanted for something?"

"I don't know," Redding stated. "I was just wondering if you knew anything about him."

"No, I don't, but give me his name and I can find out. Do you want me to go ask around?"

"No, there's no need. I don't have his name, anyway. Besides, I have no reason to check up on him. I don't want it to look like we're harassing visitors coming to town. If word got out, it'd be bad for business and people would shy away from coming here."

"Is he still in town?"

"Yeah. He checked into the Imperial. I just saw him out on the street."

"Sorry, sheriff. I don't know nothing about him, but I'll keep my ears open in case someone talks about him. You say he's a big fella, dresses fancy?"

"Yeah. Always carries a walking cane. Can't miss him."

"I'll be on the lookout for 'ya."

"Yeah, do that for me," Redding said. After testing his coffee only to find that it was still too hot, he placed his cup on top of the pot-belly stove and grabbed his coat and hat. "I'm gonna make a quick round through town. Just leave my cup there to keep it warm. I'll be back in a half-hour or so."

"Sure thing, sheriff."

Redding stepped for the door, but stopped and turned back to his young deputy. "Oh, and Clint, you can sit at my desk," he said with a smile as he closed the door behind him and walked out into the chill of the early morning, leaving a sheepish grin on the young man's face.

He started down main street, stopping in at Greer's Bakery for a sample of a hot biscuit like he had grown accustomed to doing of lately. After a friendly exchange with Mr. Greer, he left with his spoils as he juggled the bread between his hands until it was cool enough for him to devour it just as he saw a wagon coming into town driven by Abigail Bartlett. He met up with her in front of the mercantile store as she stopped.

"Morning, sheriff," she called out with a smile as he helped her down from her wagon.

"Morning. And thanks again for inviting us over for supper."

"You're welcome," Abigail responded in her usual outgoing demeanor. "You know that you and Grace are always welcome out at the ranch."

"I appreciate that. You come into town for supplies?"

"Yeah. We're getting low on a lot of things, so I thought I'd take advantage of the cool morning and get it out of the way before the day got away from me. I just need...."

Her voice trailed off as he noticed her looking over his shoulder at something behind him. He turned to see that the well-dressed stranger was coming down the boardwalk towards the Imperial Hotel, pausing just long enough to speak to the bank president, Mr. Wainwright, in passing. When he glanced in their direction and caught them looking at him, he proceeded to walk their way.

"You know him?" Redding asked as he turned back to face her.

"No," she said, lowering her voice. "I saw him

when he came into town on the train yesterday. Do you?"

"No. I saw him come in, too. Hard to miss him. A fella that dresses that fancy sure sticks out around here, that's for sure."

"You can't blame a man for wanting to look dapper," Abigail stated, without taking her eyes from him. "He's only drawing attention because no one else in town dresses that nice."

"Well, he certainly got your attention, didn't he?"

"Who do you think he is?" she asked, sneaking a final peek around Redding.

"I guess it doesn't matter because it looks like you're about to meet him," he added as the man made it over to them.

"Good morning," the man said with a beaming smile as he tipped his hat in Abigail's direction, initially ignoring Redding's presence. "Allow me to introduce myself. My name is Blaine Walker from Chicago. As you already know, I just arrived in your lovely town yesterday on the maiden run of the new railway line. And you are?" he asked as he stared at Abigail.

"I'm Abigail Bartlett," she replied, holding her hand out for him as Walker bowed and kissed the back of her hand.

"It's a pleasure to meet you, Ms. Bartlett," he said

in a smooth tone with a broad smile before he reluctantly turned his attention over to Redding and extended his hand. "And I take it from the large tin star pinned upon your vest that you, sir, must be the law and order in this area. Am I right?"

"Sheriff Vince Redding," he replied as they shook.

"Pleasure to meet you, sheriff. So, what can you tell me about your charming little town?"

Redding tried to be dismissive. "It's just your run-of-the-mill frontier town. The only difference is that we just got the railroad, as you said."

"And a spectacular railroad it is, too," Walker beamed, turning his attention back to Abigail. "And what business are you in, Ms. Bartlett?"

"Please," Abigail said, blushing with an awkward smile, "call me Abigail. I own the J.B. Bar Ranch, a few miles outside of town."

Walker's curiosity amplified. "How interesting. Do you manage it yourself, or is it a family endeavor?"

"No, it's just me," she replied with a genuine smile. "I'm not married."

"Forgive my intrusion into your private life, my dear. I meant no disrespect."

"None taken."

"Well, then fortune has truly smiled upon me today for having met such a beautiful, and available, woman."

Redding was not as easily impressed by his charm as was Abigail and knew Walker was laying it on thick. "What brings you to Salt Creek, Mr. Walker?"

"Please, sheriff, call me Blaine. I am a businessman seeking to expand my business network, and Salt Creek seemed like the perfect place to do so."

Redding decided to dig a little further. "What kind of business do you own?"

"My assets are scattered throughout different business ventures, sheriff, but I have never delved into ranching, which is why I am here. The frontier is now experiencing quite explosive growth and there seems to be no end to it in sight, especially with the railroad now coming through town. Cattle are going to be in short supply and great demand. I intend to capitalize on that demand."

"Do you have a ranch in mind to purchase?" Abigail asked.

"No, I do not. But I am open to suggestions, if you happen to have some inside information on individuals who are in dire straits or are looking to sell for whatever the reason. It could be a win-win situation for us both."

Redding shook his head slightly. "I don't know of anyone right offhand, but I'll keep my ears open for you."

"I will, too," Abigail added with a smile.

"That's very nice of you, Abigail." He paused, ignoring Redding's contribution, and then asked. "I know we've just met, but I am quite intrigued by you, Abigail. May I be so bold as to ask you out to dinner?"

Abigail giggled softly as she shyly looked at him, melting from his words. "Why yes, that would be nice."

"Wonderful," Walker said enthusiastically. "Then I shall call upon you around five this evening. I will send a buggy to fetch you and bring you to my hotel so that we may dine together. The food there is absolutely exquisite, for a frontier town. Will that suffice?"

"A buggy isn't necessary. How about I ride in and meet you there?"

"A beautiful woman and a frontiersman all wrapped up in one sensational package. How fortunate I am, indeed. Then I look forward to seeing you then, Abigail," Walker said with a courteous bow before turning to Redding. "Sheriff Redding, good day to you, sir." Walker added as he tipped his hat to him, turned and walked away, smiling broadly. Redding watched Abigail's gaze follow him as he did so.

"Hello? I'm still here," Redding joked, breaking her concentration and forcing her to face him again.

"What?" Abigail smirked. "Oh, now Vince, don't tell me you're jealous?"

"You don't even know this guy," he started. "I'm just saying to be careful."

"I've been careful since Slade died," Abigail pointed out, her mood softening. "It's been a lonely existence for me, Vince. Lonely and quiet. Don't I deserve to have some excitement and enjoy my life, too?"

"Well, you do need time to get over what happened. You lost your father, and you had been in an abusive relationship then. But this is different."

"You're right," she replied, somewhat curtly. "This is a gentleman. Something that's rare in these parts."

"Well, that's a little hurtful," Redding admitted through a slight smile.

Abigail grabbed Redding's arm and pulled him in to hug him. "Oh, Vince. You know you'll always be my favorite."

"I'm not saying this guy isn't decent, Abigail. I just want you to be careful, that's all. You're my friend. I still worry about you, whether you want me to or not."

"I know you worry about me, Vince, and that's sweet and I appreciate that, but I'll be okay. Y'know, I can take care of myself." She leaned in and kissed him lightly on the cheek before she turned and walked away. Redding watched her as he gently rubbed at the spot where she had kissed him, catching the eyes of several of the locals who had witnessed her display of affection.

"Yeah," he said to himself. "I know."

CHAPTER 7

Sheriff Vince Redding spent the rest of the day bothered by the introduction to Blaine Walker. He wanted to like the man and give him the benefit of the doubt, for Abigail's sake, if for nothing else, but he couldn't. Not yet. He couldn't quite put his finger on what it was that dug at him about Walker, but he felt as if there was something there that Walker was hiding that he wouldn't like. It was there. He could feel it.

He tried to go back to his routine, but something kept gnawing at Redding. Maybe he was just worried about Abigail after her tumultuous relationship with Slade McMahon, Roland Bartlett's right-hand man. Redding later found out that McMahon had physically abused Abigail, not to mention the stranglehold he had over her with trying to run her life and, in the end, even threatening to kill her when he realized she was too head-strong for him to tame. Such an incident had caused Abigail to put her guard up, and for good reason. But now, it seemed as if she was letting that guard down, and all because of a smooth-talking, charismatic stranger.

Redding had another theory about what was happening. He hated to admit it, but maybe he, Redding, was just worried that she was traveling down the same path she had gone down before. Was he too close to her? He questioned if Abigail had been right in that it was only deep-rooted jealousy that had worked its way to the surface, but he quickly dismissed such a notion because he knew he was in love with his wife, Grace. He never had to question his relationship with her, not even when Abigail was involved and Grace had never had enough reason to do so.

He knew nothing of this man, Walker, but something didn't add up. Walker said he had come to Salt Creek to buy a ranch, but the word about the train coming through town had been well known for some time. All the surrounding ranchers were aware of it and, therefore, had no reason to sell, seeing the opportunity for continual growth coming their way. What would cause Walker to believe that he could find a ranch that would be for sale, considering the opportunity that they were about to experience with the new railroad coming into town? No rancher in their right mind would even consider doing something so foolish. The only reason Abigail had stumbled upon the ranch that was available was because of the sudden death of Mr. Capwell, Abigail's long-time neighbor. It had been the only property she had acquired since being on her own. So how did Walker think he was going to get his hands on another seller? The question was a legitimate concern, and a worrisome one for Redding.

Redding began to question why he was so worried about Abigail. She was one of the most level-headed women he had ever known, and she had taken over when her father had died and continued running the ranch all by herself, and very successfully at that. She wasn't about to let a stranger come in and undo all of her hard work. It just wasn't going to happen. She was smarter than that, no matter how charming or good looking the man was. Once he thought about it, he was beginning to think that maybe he was overly worried about her for nothing.

Maybe.

But then again, maybe not.

He began to question himself. Was he rushing into something? Had he given Walker a fair chance?

He returned to the sheriff's office and looked through the new wanted posters, looking for anything on Blaine Walker while also hoping that his hunch was wrong, but instead he found nothing. He remembered that Walker had stated he was originally from Chicago, but there was no easy way to check up with the local authorities to see if Walker was wanted there, either. There was something there, somewhere. He just had to find it. But it would have to wait, at least for now. He was sitting quietly, thinking about how else he could check up on Walker, when the door opened and Abigail Bartlett walked in.

"Well, hello again," he said with a smile as she walked over to his desk, removing her shawl as she did.

"Hi, Vince. I know you're busy, but I just wanted to see if you and Grace would like to come over and have dinner with Blaine and I tonight at his hotel?"

Redding was taken back by the offer and wasn't really sure how to react. "I appreciate the offer, Abigail, but I don't think he would approve of us being there. I was under the impression that Walker wanted you all to himself."

"I suppose he does, but I just met him and it seems a little awkward having supper alone with him when I know nothing of him. I would appreciate it if you and Grace would accompany us. I know it might be a little awkward, but it would make me feel better, at least until I have the chance to get to know him more. If not, it's okay, I'll understand."

"No, it's fine with me," Redding agreed, "and I'm sure Grace wouldn't mind. I just didn't want it to be uncomfortable for you."

"I'm fine with it or I wouldn't have suggested it."

"That's true. It's just odd seeing you like this."

"Like what?"

"Uneasy. Almost… vulnerable."

"I'm still the same strong woman you've always known, Vince," she insisted. "It's just that I haven't dated anyone since Slade and I want to take it slow and be careful this time, so I don't get in over my head. I gave up my independence once. I don't plan on ever doing that again."

"I can respect that. It makes total sense."

"So, you'll come?"

"Yeah. We'll come."

Abigail looked at him curiously. "I feel like you don't really care for Blaine."

"I didn't say that. I don't know anything about him."

"Neither do I, Vince, but he seems like a decent man and you may not know this but, besides you, decent men are hard to come by around here."

"I get it. I just don't want it to feel like we're intruding on your relationship with him, if there turns out to be one."

Abigail smiled softly. "Trust me, Vince, you know me better than that. If I think something, I don't have any problem letting you know."

Redding scoffed softly. "Believe me, I know that better than anyone."

When Abigail walked into the dining lobby of the Imperial Hotel, she saw Blaine Walker sitting at a table facing the front door, as if he had been waiting for her. When he saw her, his smile broadened, but then suddenly fell away as she saw his eyes look past her. When she turned to see what had garnished his attention so, she saw that Sheriff Redding and his wife Grace had happened to walk in behind her. The expression on Blaine Walker's face was less than amused as they followed her over to his table. Redding, however, was amused at the uncomfortableness he had imposed on Walker.

"Good evening, Blaine," she said with a smile as he stood and stepped over to pull out her chair for her.

"Good evening, Abigail," Walker said, almost choking on his words. "Sheriff Redding. And I must assume that this is your wife?"

"Yes," Redding replied as he helped Grace into her chair. "This is my wife, Grace. Grace, this is Blaine Walker."

"How do you do?" Walker responded with a forced, unsettling smile.

"Nice to meet you."

Walker was fighting to find a way to relay his displeasure without it being so obvious. "Forgive me if I seemed a bit surprised by your presence. I wasn't expecting company. I was under the assumption that this was only going to be the two of us, Abigail," Walker stated, a slight hint of agitation present in his tone, but never wavering from his practiced smile he was using to cover up his agitation.

"Oh, I didn't know," Abigail replied, trying to avoid the discussion of the subject. "I only invited them along so we could get to know one another better. Vince and Grace are some of my closest and dearest friends."

"I'm sorry if I sounded rude," Blaine spoke as he quickly tried to overcome the discomfort of the matter. "This is quite alright," he replied with an approving smile. "I don't mind sharing a meal with new friends. It will be nice to have mutual friends here in town."

Abigail returned the smile to him and then passed it over to Vince and Grace, who were both trying to settle into the awkwardness and tension in the air by not speaking.

They ordered their food and talked amongst themselves while they waited, dropping from one stale subject of small talk to the next, trying to overcome the obvious uneasiness that being placed so close to one another was creating. Redding could feel the tension building within them. He knew it was because Walker did not want them there, but was too afraid of hurting Abigail to say so.

"This is a nice hotel," Redding commented as he glanced around them. "I've never really paid it much attention before now."

"Yes. I always like to surround myself with luxury. It is a trait that I have grown rather accustomed to over the years, but I'm sure it all seems rather excessive for a lawman."

Redding knew that the jab was intentional and the comment did not sit well with him, as he darted his eyes at Walker, but he still tried to dismiss it as nothing more than an unintentional insult. "I can appreciate finer things, Blaine," Redding smiled and replied. "I just don't think they're necessary in order to be happy."

"I'm afraid I'll have to disagree with you on that, sheriff. You see, I've sought to live this type of lifestyle and I find that it suits me quite well. Wanting to live in the lap of luxury is not an evil thing. In fact, I find that it is responsible for my happiness and when I am happy, I experience continued success."

"Vince has been quite successful as the town's sheriff. Haven't you, Vince?" Abigail interjected, but the comment was lost on Walker, who was giving Redding a silent, disapproving glare. She shared a quiet glance over at Grace, who had decided to stay out of the awkward discussion.

Walker gave Redding a condescending glance as he spoke. "I'm intrigued. And how does one become a 'successful' sheriff, Mr. Redding? It seems as if it would be a rather daunting task to maintain."

Redding took in a calming deep breath as he sidestepped the patronizing use of the title. "Not really, Mr. Walker. You do it by keeping the undesirables and riffraff out of town," he said calmly, "the ones who only come here to prey on those who have worked for their success and are trying to take it from them." It was apparent from Blaine Walker's expression that he did not like the insinuation, since he knew that Redding was referring to him.

Walker gave him another condescending glare as their eyes locked. "And how do you determine which individuals are the undesirables and the riffraff?"

"They usually show themselves for who they really are," Redding stated as he continued staring at Walker. "Sometimes, it's rather obvious and sometimes it isn't. Sometimes, they're able to hide their intentions well, but you can still find them if you know where to look and what to look for."

Walked leaned confidently closer to the table.

"And do you feel *you* are skilled enough to uncover these deceptive individuals, Sheriff Redding?"

Redding returned the stare with a soft, satisfying nod. "Oh, yeah," he said confidently as he glared back at him. "They may fool others, but they don't fool me. I can spot 'em a mile away."

Walker nodded away the comment dismissively with a coy smile as he turned his attention back to Abigail. "I should love to come out and take a look at your enterprise, Abigail, if you don't mind. It will give me a working sense of how a ranch should operate and would aid me in my search for one of my own."

"I'd like that," she answered with a smile. "Say tomorrow morning around nine?"

"That sounds good," Walker said with a returning smile as he searched for a disapproval from Redding.

"Don't worry, Blaine," Redding added dryly with his own jabbing smile before Walker could ask. "Grace and I won't be there. You'll have her all to yourself."

CHAPTER 8

THE VASE BLAINE WALKER HAD THROWN SHATTERED against the wall, sending tiny fragments of it all around his room as he stomped about in utter anger and disgust. Ike Harrington, who was sitting at the small table in the room, witnessing it all, wanted to comment on the childish behavior, but knew it was better to stay out of things, at least for the moment, until Walker calmed down some.

"Sheriff Redding thinks he knows everything," Walker spouted through gritted teeth as he paced back and forth along the length of the room. "He thinks he's got me figured out, but he doesn't know anything. He's just an ignorant country sheriff. He thinks I'm just some lowlife conman who doesn't know what he's doing, but he's going to find out that he's wrong."

"Redding could become a problem for us," Harrington cautiously spoke, hoping his words were somehow reaching Walker, even in his enraged state.

The statement caused Walker to whirl around to face him. "No, he won't. That's what I'm paying *you* for. That's why you need to get rid of him as soon as possible before he ruins everything."

"Not that I'm opposed to killing," Harrington said flatly, "but I didn't know I would be asked to dispose of a town sheriff. I thought I was supposed to focus more on ranchers."

"It shouldn't matter who I need you to go up against. The money is the same, regardless. I never specifically said who you would be up against," Walker snapped. "I simply said that you were being hired to keep the law off of my back. Well, the law of this town is on it now and I want him removed. Immediately and permanently."

"Not that I couldn't take care of the sheriff, because I can, but the town is still being focused on too much because of the railroad. I don't know if I want that kind of heat on me this early in the plan."

"You'll take whatever heat you need to take to get the job done," Walker uttered sharply as he stopped pacing to face him. "I have more important things to do. I don't have the time or the patience to sit around and hold your hand through this. If I did, I'd just do it myself. But it's what you were hired to do. So do it."

"You want the sheriff killed? I'll kill him," Harrington professed calmly. "But if I'm gonna bring that much attention to myself and put my neck out there on the line, it's gonna cost you an extra thousand dollars."

Walker was clearly insulted by the demand. "Why you lowlife snake! You can't change the rules on me now," Walker swore defiantly. "We had a deal. You stick to your end of the deal, and I stick to mine."

"I'm the one with the gun," Harrington admitted as he drew his revolver and cocked it as he pointed it at Walker. "I can change the rules anytime I want."

Walker stared the man down, his anger fueling his reaction. He was furious that Harrington was now demanding more money for something that should have been taken care of with the original payment, but he was in no position to argue the point. Harrington had made sure of that. He realized it was a moot issue now, but he wasn't quite ready to cave in so easily to Harrington's demands. His demeanor softened somewhat as he spoke.

"Y'know Harrington, I'll bet there are others who would be interested in hearing about a professional like you not being able to stick to an agreed-upon plan. Say, other gunmen looking for a way to capitalize and get business from you. Such rumors would make their way through the territory rather quickly, don't you think? Might tarnish your reputation. Might be bad for business. Might even put you *out* of business."

Harrington stepped closer to Walker, leveling his gun at him. "You threatening to try to ruin me, Walker? Because if you are, that would not be a healthy thing for you to do."

"I don't like having the rules being changed after a deal is agreed upon, that's all." Walker professed as he tried to shrug off the comment and stood his ground. "It's not good business, and I'm all about business."

Harrington looked at him with a cold stare. "I'm in business to make money, just like you are, Walker, but sometimes deals change. You either go with the changes or you kill the deal. In this case, you're the deal. You telling me you wanna kill the deal?"

Walker stared at the man. It was obvious that there was a hidden threat in there that if he didn't agree to this new plan, Harrington could gun him down now and walk away with his initial payment, without having to have done anything for it. It was a losing situation for Walker and Harrington knew it. He struggled to find a way out of this, but it appeared as if there was none. As much as he hated the notion, he had no choice but to go along with the demand. "Fine," he finally conceded. "But this is it.

I'm not doling out any more money until I see some results from you, understand?"

"See it from my perspective, Walker. If I'm gonna get rid of a sheriff, I'm putting myself at a bigger risk, so I expect to be paid more for doing it. Nothing personal. It's just business."

"Just make sure the sheriff isn't going to foul up my plans," Walker insisted. "I can't afford to lose this opportunity because I won't get another one like it."

"Don't worry about me," Harrington said confidently as he causally holstered his gun. "I know how to handle people like him. It's what I do best."

"Fine," Walker resolved, retrieving his pocket watch and changing subjects. "It's almost three. I need you to go meet an associate of mine at the train depot," Walker stated. "Name's Spurlock."

"Who is this fella?"

"Someone special that I sent for."

"What does he look like?"

"Big fella, a little over six-feet tall, medium-build, sandy-colored hair, wears a black Stetson. Looks like he can handle himself. Should be carrying saddle-bags and a bedroll. Everything but a saddle."

"What? You mean no horse?"

"He sometimes has one, but he doesn't usually ride long distances on horseback. Prefers the train whenever possible. Picks up a new horse in each town and sells 'em when he's ready to leave."

Harrington scoffed. "Hard to believe you would associate yourself with someone that soft, Walker. He sounds like a real lightweight to me."

Walker stared at the man with warning. "I wouldn't say that to him if I were you."

The afternoon train arrived in Salt Creek as scheduled, right at three o'clock. The newness of the first train arrival had already passed and the fanfare of the townspeople had subsided, but there were those who still enjoyed seeing the novelty of the locomotive slowing into the station at a crawl, pumping out large plumes of white smoke as it screeched its brakes to a final lazy stop. As the engine hissed its final dose, people started disembarking from the individual boxcars onto the platform. The conductor walked the distance of the train to ensure everyone got off safely as he made his way up to the train engineer to ready for the next leg of their journey.

Ike Harrington stood back in the shadow of the depot overhang, leaning against a support post, while he watched all the passengers begin to step off the various cars of the train. When there was a lull in the people, he thought perhaps Walker's man had not made his train, but just as he was about to give up waiting, a man in his mid-thirties with shoulder-length blond hair appeared carrying saddlebags, among other things. Harrington walked over to the man to meet him halfway across the platform, but the man was alerted by Harrington's interest in him before he even started walking towards him. Harrington could see that it was a gesture that the man did not like at all.

"You here to see Blaine Walker?" Harrington asked when they met.

The stranger stopped and eyed him cautiously. "Who are you?"

"I work for him. Sort of as an advisor."

"He sent for me," the man said coolly while he waited for a reply. "That's all I know, so far."

"I'm Harrington," he said, offering his hand.

"Will Spurlock," he responded with a simple, uninterested nod as he ignored the gesture and glanced over at the small crowd. "Where's Walker?"

"Imperial Hotel. It's on…"

"I'll find it," Spurlock cut in sternly. "First, I gotta get a horse. Which way is the livery stable?"

"East end of town. I guess I'll see you back over at the Imperial, then."

Spurlock stepped around him without saying anything and started walking towards the eastern center of town, still lugging his saddlebags, rifle and bedroll while Harrington rode back to the hotel and walked up to Walker's room and knocked to announce his presence. The door opened and Walker cautiously scanned the hallway in both directions before allowing Harrington to enter, closing the door behind him.

"Did you meet up with Spurlock?" he asked before anything else.

"Yeah. I found him. Not a very talkative fella, is he?"

"No, he isn't, but that's fine. I didn't hire him to talk."

Harrington looked confused. "Then what exactly is he here for?"

"He has other talents that I need to put to use."

"You're talking in circles, Walker. Whatever it is, spit it out."

Walker conceded. "He's here to assist with anything you need."

Harrington was taken back by the notion. "That was a waste of money. I can take care of anything that happens. You don't need him, or don't you have faith in me?"

"Faith has nothing to do with it. I wanted to be sure. I can't afford to miss out on this kind of opportunity."

"Yeah. You already told me that."

"Well, it's true now more than ever. Some people are watching me very closely and waiting for me to make a mistake so they can take me down."

Harrington suddenly got a disturbing thought. "What're you saying, Walker? You don't trust me to get the job done by myself? Is that it?"

"Trust has nothing to do with it," Walker insisted. "I just always like to have a backup plan."

"So, what is all this for? What are you planning?"

"I'm going to take over this town, one business at a time, and I'm going to start with the J.B. Bar Ranch."

"How are you gonna do that? That woman that owns it ain't interested in selling. Even *I* know that."

"She won't have to sell," Walker admitted confidently. "I'll automatically become partial owner of it when we marry."

"When you *marry?*" Harrington spouted with shock. "What makes you think she'll marry you?"

"Because I'm going to court her until she does," Walker added.

"She ain't stupid and she didn't get where she is by being blindsided, either. She'll see your intentions a mile away."

"Not if I cover them up correctly. I'll court her until she agrees to marry me and then, when I have what I need, I'll dispose of her so she doesn't get in the way."

"What about her ranch hands? They aren't going to just sit by and let you run over their boss. They'll have something to say about that, for sure."

"I'll worry about them when the time comes. I can always find new ranch hands if I need to."

"Trying to take over her ranch is going to tip off the law, Walker. Besides, nobody said anything about killing no woman."

"Well, I can't very well let her remain behind, now, can I? She'll keep coming back over and over and she'll halt anything I try to do. It's the assets of that ranch that are the key to taking over everything. It's better to take on just one person than an entire town. Without that ranch, I don't have a hold over anyone."

"I don't care about that," Harrington reasoned. "I ain't getting involved in killing no woman. It ain't like killing a man. Men are expected to get shot and most of the time the law looks the other way because you can always claim self-defense. But you start shooting women and there ain't no coming back from that. They'll hunt us down and hang us for sure."

"Then we need to make sure they don't find out about our little plan, won't we?"

Harrington was already shaking his head vehemently. "I don't like this, Walker. I don't like this at all and when I don't like things, I walk."

"No one told you that you had to like it," Walker professed as he walked closer to Harrington and stared him down. "You're worrying too much about something that hasn't even happened. You just need to do your job. Let me handle the details of how it's going to happen and the repercussions."

"Say you do manage to convince this woman to marry you. What's your plan? You think a piece of paper is going to convince her to hand over everything she's worked for?"

"As half owner of the largest ranch in the territory, I'll have access to everything I need to finish off my plan. I'll have the resources available to liquidate and use the money to buy out anyone in town that I choose to. Once I start buying out businesses, there'll be no stopping me. I'll have the momentum and the money to keep going."

"That's a mighty ambitious plan, Walker, but I think you're planning a little too far ahead. And you're assuming the owner of the J.B. Bar is going to trust you enough to hand over half of her property right from the beginning. She ain't gonna roll over so easily. In fact, from what I hear about her, I don't see that happening at all."

"You let me worry about that," Walker insisted firmly. "You and Spurlock just focus on being there to clean up the mess as I go."

CHAPTER 9

WILL SPURLOCK RODE THE GRAY HE HAD JUST purchased out of the livery stable and over to the Imperial Hotel, as instructed, where Blaine Walker was staying. The gray seemed to be a docile horse and was bridle sensitive, according to the stable owner. It was a large horse, the top of his back standing almost even with Spurlock's shoulders, and well-muscled, a trait that might have to be called upon should he have to leave town suddenly.

He took in the sights of the town as he trotted down the main street, catching the attention of a few of the townspeople along the way. Their curious stares met with his cold, hardened gaze. He did not care for people as a whole, but, unfortunately, it was necessary to converse with them in order to find work. The only people he had any use for were the ones who were willing to pay him. Other than that, he preferred to be left alone.

This town was no different than the others, the dozen or so towns he had been called to over the years. The same people. The same problems. The same solution. They all needed his help, and he was glad to offer it to them. For the right price, he would gladly work for anyone and do their bid.

But always for a price.

He was a man without a conscience; he made no apologies for that. It was a necessary part of the life he had created for himself. Having a conscience meant becoming emotionally involved in his work. That he could not risk. He had to stay detached if he wanted to live. Once he gave his enemies a face, they would become real to him. They may have been actual people to others, but to him, they were just a business dealing. That's all. Nothing more than a task. And one that he was paid quite handsomely for, he would profess.

There was always work to be had. There were always people who wanted, often needed, others eliminated, but they didn't have the courage or the nerve to do what needed to be done, so they gladly turned to men like him and paid him to make their problems go away. It was a line of work that only a select few men could carry out. Others had tried their hand at it, but they quickly found out that they didn't have the stomach for it. That's why he was so good at what he did. He was one of the few men who could carry out the task at hand without remorse. Men who were cold. Calculated. Unforgiving.

Ruthless.

He was a man who believed that force was the best and only option. Over the years, Spurlock had built a reputation for himself as being a dangerous man. He had hired his gun out many times before over the years, and each time he had delivered as promised. Because of his lack of trust, he had no interest in partnering with anyone and always preferred to work alone, usually demanding it. He trusted no one, not even those who paid him handsomely for his gun. He didn't want their friendship anyway. Just their money. It was a philosophy that had kept him alive all these years, and it was something he was not willing to compromise on.

He trotted the gray until they stopped in front of the Imperial, taking in its grandeur as he climbed down and tied him off. He thought such a grandiose building out here in the frontier was nothing short of a waste, as was the high society that typically frequented such establishments and who always looked down on him and his kind. He had just as soon put a bullet in anyone who disapproved of him, no matter how much money they had. None of them were better than him and he would be glad to convey those feelings to them if need be.

His approach to the front desk was met by a suspicious clerk who allowed his stare to last a little too long for Spurlock's taste. Spurlock did not like it. "Yes, sir," the clerk sheepishly asked. "May I help you?"

"Blaine Walker's room," Spurlock said abruptly with a deadpan glare as he watched the nervousness of the clerk increase to his annoyance.

"Uh... y... yes, sir. And is... Mr. Walker expecting you?"

"Just give me the number," Spurlock demanded through furrowed brows, his voice hardening. Unfortunately, the harshness of the comment clearly made the clerk even more anxious than he already was.

"I... I'm not... not allowed to do that, s... sir," he stated through fractured speech. "It's our policy..."

Spurlock suddenly reached over the counter and grabbed the clerk by the front of his shirt and yanked him hard against the back of the counter. The move was so quick and unexpected that the clerk lost his glasses as they toppled to the floor. His expression was of pure fear as Spurlock locked eyes with him. "Five!" the clerk struggled to say, his eyes widened from pure fear as he stammered. "He's in room five!"

Spurlock hesitated a brief instance just to give the clerk more to think about before he tossed him backwards away from the counter, almost causing the poor man to fall back against the wall, an expression of shock and fear still covering his face as he watched Spurlock start to ascend the stairs.

Halfway up, Spurlock turned just in time to see the clerk starting to go around the front counter to leave. He knew the man would be heading straight to the sheriff's office to report the incident. As soon as the clerk saw that Spurlock had stopped and was staring at him, the man changed his mind and quickly darted back behind the counter and through the door into the back room, shutting it quickly behind him. Spurlock made it the rest of the way to Walker's door and knocked, satisfied he had changed the frightened clerk's mind about reporting him. When Walker opened the door and saw who it was, he was less than amused.

"What the hell are you doing here?" he uttered as he grabbed Spurlock by the arm and forcibly pulled him into the room, shutting the door behind him without even taking the time to look for other guests, as was customary. Spurlock pulled his arm away as he half-stumbled into the room right as Walker slammed the door shut. "You know I didn't want to be seen in town with you," Walker said in a whisper that was laced with so much anger that it was as loud as if he had not tried to disguise it. "You're supposed to be a drifter. You draw too much attention to yourself."

"You worry too much," Spurlock haphazardly uttered as he causally tossed his hat onto the table and fell onto the bed, relaxed and comfortable, propping up his feet and crossing his legs.

"And *you* don't worry enough," Walker chimed while he reached down without thinking and swiped Spurlock's boots from off of his bed, causing the man to abruptly sit back upright again. Spurlock did not take kindly to the move and made it known in his disapproving glare at Walker. Walker caught himself for what he had done, picking up on his disgruntled tone and realizing it was best to somewhat relax his tone with the man. "I just didn't want people to be able to associate us with one another," he tried to explain in a somewhat softer, calmer voice. "At least, not this early in the plan. Don't you worry about that?"

"I never worry, Walker. That's why I'm still alive. Because I make sure I never have anything to worry about. Now, you sent for me," Spurlock spouted in an impatient manner, "so tell me why I'm here or watch me leave with the down payment you paid to get me here."

"I came here to start some businesses, but things haven't moved forward as quickly as I had hoped they would. No one in this town is willing to let me buy them out. I tried to work out a deal from Chicago for months before the railroad finally came through and I've been trying since I arrived in town, but to no avail."

"Is there an explanation in there somewhere as to why I'm here?" Spurlock asked impatiently.

Walker gathered his thoughts and took in a deep breath before he could continue. "I need you here to help me convince some of these owners to let me buy them out. I don't care how you do it. I don't even want to know how it's done. In fact, the less I know, the better. I just need you to get it done."

"So, you want me to lean on them until they break?" Spurlock reiterated.

"I said I don't want to know *how* you do it. Just do it. And the quicker you do it, the better."

"Fine. I'll get to it right away. Now, who is this Harrington fella you had meet me at the train station?"

"He's an associate of mine. He's here to help, too."

"Let's get one thing straight: whoever you hired is on you, Walker. But I'm here to tell you that they're *your* problem, *not* mine, and I'm not going to make them my problem. I don't babysit anyone. You're responsible for them, and I'm only responsible for me. Just don't let them get in my way," Spurlock warned.

Walker nodded. "Fine. I'll keep them out of your way."

Spurlock picked up his black Stetson and started for the door, pausing with it open. "Oh, and Walker?" he added as he stopped in the doorway.

Walker turned to face him. "Yeah?"

Spurlock looked at him, his eyes chilling and darkened with warning. "Don't ever put your hands on me again."

Sheriff Redding was pouring a cup of fresh coffee when Deputy Clint McNeil came inside, his rifle tucked under his arm as he rubbed his hands together to generate warmth. He proceeded over to the pot-bellied stove and quickly poured himself a cup of coffee, ignoring its temperature and taking a painful drink before ever putting down his rifle. Redding took note of the move.

"Clint, I've always wanted to ask you: why do you carry a rifle?" he asked curiously. "Why not a revolver like everybody else?"

"I tried it, but I never was any good with a handgun, sheriff," McNeil said as he contemplated risking burning his mouth with another sip. "Just didn't feel right."

"And a rifle feels right to you?"

"Yes, sir," McNeil agreed as he proudly patted the

rifle. "This baby's got fifteen rounds and I'm such a lousy shot that even if I miss, I still got plenty more chances to try to hit something."

"Okay. That's your call."

"Hey, sheriff?" Deputy McNeil suddenly called out, startling the silence in the room. "Did you hear about what happened in the Sidewinder yesterday?"

"Nah," Redding answered, drawing his attention away from his paperwork. "What happened?"

"That Walker fella that's dating Ms. Bartlett busted up two cowboys," he said gleefully. "One of 'em had to have stitches. Split the side of his head wide open with a whiskey bottle."

The information got Redding's full attention. "What started that?"

"Mr. Reynolds said that Walker fella came in dressed all fancy and wanted a drink. A couple of the others started picking on him for the way he was dressed and they got into a fight. Well, the other two didn't really do that much fighting. Never laid a hand on that Walker fella. Guess he sure surprised them. I didn't think that city slicker had it in him to fight. He doesn't look like the fighting type. Are you gonna arrest him?"

"No," Redding answered reluctantly. The thought of housing Walker in his jail was appealing, but it would have to wait until he messed up somewhere else. "Dell Reynolds didn't say anything to me about it, so he must not have worried too much about it. And no one has come by here to press charges, so I guess Walker is a free man."

"Man, I wish I could have been there to see that!" McNeil said excitedly. "I'll bet that was something, especially since I didn't think Mr. Walker knew how to fight!"

"Neither did I."

"Are you gonna tell Ms. Bartlett about it?"

"Nope."

The answer surprised McNeil. "You're *not?*"

"Why would I? It's none of my concern."

"On account of you not liking Mr. Walker. I figured you'd be anxious to tell her something bad that he did."

"As long as no one is pressing charges, it's none of my business."

"But doesn't she deserve to know?"

"No. Just let it go."

Redding was getting frustrated. By him not telling Abigail it made it look like he was protecting Walker, something that he had no intention of doing, or presuming to do. Walker needed to be exposed for the conman that he was, but if it were coming from Redding, it would make it look like he had a personal grudge against Walker. Abigail had already warned him about accusing Walker of things he could not prove. Trying to convince her again, while still having no proof, would only shut Abigail down from ever listening to his warnings again. As much as he hated missing the opportunity to prove to Abigail that Walker was no good, he would have to let this one go and do nothing.

The more he thought about it, the more it dug at his gut.

CHAPTER 10

IT WAS JUST BEFORE NINE O'CLOCK WHEN BLAINE Walker rode up to the J.B. Bar Ranch in his rented buggy to tour Abigail Bartlett's home. After he tied off the reins, he looked around and took in the expansiveness of what she and her father had built. Now it was all hers. And soon, it would be his, too. After smoothing down his hair one final time, his hat was respectfully in his hand when Abigail answered the door.

"Good morning, Blaine," she said with a perky smile at the sight of him. "Thank you for coming."

"Thank you for inviting me," Walker replied with a customary nod. "I'm glad to see that it's only the two of us today," he added.

"I thought we could use a little alone time. Would you like to see the ranch now?"

"Yes, I would."

Abigail motioned to one of her ranch hands who was working by the barn and asked him to saddle two horses for them, which he brought to her shortly thereafter while they chatted. "I hope you don't mind," she said, "but the only way to take in everything and get the whole experience is on the back of a horse. The ranch is too large to try to do it all on foot or you wouldn't get the full effect of it."

"That's perfectly fine. I want the grand tour, my dear," Walker said affectionately.

"Good. Then follow me." Abigail smiled and pulled her horse towards the land behind the house and up through the north valley, pointing out certain landmarks along the way and giving him a brief history of how everything had transpired from the time she could remember growing up until her father had died, and then now. They rode casually, taking in the sights, with Walker being as interactive and interested as he could muster. As they rode, his thoughts drowned her out as he contemplated what he could do with such a massive piece of land, and its resources, at his disposal.

She gave him an extensive tour of the ranch, ending up at the south pasture on a small knoll over-looking part of her cattle. Walker was immediately impressed by the sheer number of the herd. "Look at all those cattle," he gasped as he studied them in amazement. "Exactly how many do you own?"

"Well, of course, with a ranch this size it's impossible to know at any given time because they're constantly moving about, which makes it almost impossible to count them, but we estimate that there's roughly thirty thousand head."

The number was almost too much for Walker to comprehend. "*Thirty thousand?*"

"Mind you, that's taking into consideration that a few will become lost or die off for whatever the reason."

"What about rustlers?" Walker asked. "Don't you ever worry about that with having so many cattle?"

"Rustlers have never been much of an issue for me. We keep a tight watch over the herds and we never leave them unattended in the far-off pastures for too long of a period. I think our presence around deters anyone from trying to take them. But make no mistake, Mr. Walker. These are my cattle. I watch over them and I own them and if anyone tries to come on my land and take what is rightfully mine, they will have to suffer the consequences. I will not tolerate a thief."

"A wise conviction, indeed," Walker replied. "Well, Abigail, I am thoroughly impressed with your operation. I can't imagine how one person is able to manage so much, but you seem to do it beautifully.

You are to be congratulated on your continued success."

"Thank you," she responded with a warm, satisfying smile.

The two spent the next several hours walking their horses around the land and talking. Abigail had never met anyone like Blaine Walker before. Unlike her past fiancé, Slade McMahon, Blaine was a gentleman and treated her with respect. He didn't appear to have a jealous bone in his body, or if he did, he had not exposed it as of yet. That, by itself, was enough for her to be interested in the man.

As they sat below a large sycamore tree overlooking the ranch, they talked to find out more about one another. Walker told her of his upbringing in Chicago and his business that he had grown there and decided to leave behind to follow his dream and venture out west, where the prosperity seemed to know no boundaries. He told her of his interest in starting a saloon and possibly another freight office now that the railroad was in Salt Creek and the number of incoming and outgoing shipments would be increasing dramatically. He spoke of how his intention was to get in on the ground floor and see his businesses grow as the town did. Abigail was impressed with his vision and how it seemed as if he had planned out everything very carefully.

"Are you sure Salt Creek needs another saloon?" she asked jokingly.

"My dear, if there's one thing I've learned since coming out west it's that there's no such thing as a town having too many saloons," he responded with a chuckle, "because there will never be a shortage of drinkers." He looked at her longingly. "Abigail, would you accompany me into town to have lunch with me?"

The notion caught her by surprise. "I thought you were only coming out to look over the ranch."

"I was," Walker admitted sheepishly, "but I've had such a good time being with you that I don't want it to end. So, would you join me for lunch? I'll bring you back out here and it'll give us more time to talk alone."

"I'd like that," she nodded her acceptance, followed by a bright smile. "Just let me tell my foreman that I'll be leaving." He watched her hand the two horses over to Luther Gilroy before she walked back to the buggy, where he helped her up into it and headed into town.

Blaine Walker escorted Abigail Bartlett into the lobby of the Imperial Hotel, where they were seated at a table. The atmosphere in the lobby was relatively quiet, with only the low murmuring of the guests breaking the silence. Walker and Abigail were enjoying their food when a familiar face entered the lobby. It was Sheriff Vince Redding. When she saw him, Abigail eagerly waved him over to their table, much to Blaine Walker's dismay.

"Hi, Vince," Abigail said as she motioned to the empty chair next to hers. "Have a seat. Have some lunch. You don't mind do you, Blaine?"

Redding shifted his eyes over to Walker as he tried to dampen the smug expression that was trying to come through. Walker was struggling with his own outburst, but neatly tucked it away, covering it with a forced smile. "Why, of course not, my dear. Sheriff Redding is always welcome to join us. But I'm sure the sheriff has other pressing matters, my dear," Walker interjected with a rough, forced smile, trying to quell his building resentment. "After all, he is the law in this town. Therefore, he must constantly be on the move to keep the peace."

Redding took the insinuation, but chose to ignore it. "I don't have time to eat, but I suppose it won't hurt if I sit for a few minutes," he replied with his own smile as he removed his hat, pulled out the chair and sat. He noticed Walker's mood becoming even more edgy, and he became silent, making the interruption even more satisfying for him. "Well, what have you two been up to today?"

"I gave Blaine a tour around the ranch," she answered proudly.

"Oh, did you?" Redding turned his attention to Walker. "So, what did you think, Blaine? Pretty impressive, isn't it?"

"Yes, it is, sheriff," Walker admitted through his tightened breathing as he fought to maintain his control. He could feel his anger building inside him, but he had to keep it in check. "I was telling Abigail how impressive it is that she's managed to continue running the ranch all by herself."

"That's right," Redding responded while looking Walker in the eye with a deadpan expression. "She's doing just fine alone. She doesn't need *anyone's* help."

Walker picked up on the implication and stared back at Redding, his hatred for the man intensifying with every passing second. Redding could read Walker's thoughts and reveled in the fact that he was getting to him. He decided to see just how far he could push the man.

"So, what are your plans for Salt Creek, Mr. Walker? What keeps you here?"

"Oh, call him 'Blaine,'" Abigail interrupted with a dismissive wave. "He doesn't like to be called Mr. Walker. He prefers for his friends to call him Blaine."

"Like I was saying, Mr. Walker, what plans do you have for our town?"

The insult dug at Walker's gut like he had been

stabbed with a hot branding iron. He could feel himself fighting to maintain his control over not losing his temper. He had to pause long enough to take in a deep, calming breath before he could force another smile as he answered. "I was telling Abigail that I'm looking into opening a saloon or perhaps buying an existing one."

"He also wants to open a freight office that works with the railroad," Abigail added in a contained excitement, unaware of the quiet dispute between the two men. "He's very ambitious, isn't he, Vince?"

"Yes. I'll give you that," Redding agreed with a telling glare. "He is ambitious."

"You speak about it as if it's a fault, sheriff. Do you not approve of industry being brought into a town to improve it and help it to grow? Or have you ever had the pleasure of owning your own business?"

Redding's jaw tightened. "No. I have not."

Walker continued his berating. "Perhaps your resistance towards growth is limited because you've never had the opportunity to venture outside of this town."

The comment angered Redding, though he tried not to show it. "No, Mr. Walker, I have ventured outside of this town. That has nothing to do with it. I have no reluctance to growth as long as it's done legally, and no one gets hurt or cheated in the process."

Walker sighed heavily. "I'm afraid someone always gets hurt from growth," he declared confidently, "whether it's the small business who cannot, or will not, conform to change, or the little man who is ousted by a bigger entity who is more determined, has a well-thought-out plan, and is well-financed. You see, sheriff, there is *always* going to be someone getting hurt in the name of progress."

"Not if I can help it," Redding warned as he slid his chair back and stood, donning his hat in the process. "I need to be getting back to work," he said offhandedly. "Abigail. Mr. Walker," he said before turning and walking out.

"Bye, Vince," Abigail called out as he made his way down the boardwalk and disappeared around the end of the building. Walker watched him until he was out of sight.

"Your friend, sheriff Redding, is a rather suspicious fella, wouldn't you say, Abigail?"

"Who, Vince? Oh, he's harmless," she said, shrugging off the comment. "He's just a little protective of me, that's all."

Walker did not like the claim. "Why would he be protective of you specifically?"

"I used to have a thing for him when he first came to town," she replied as she waved dismissively, "but that was before he met his wife. And he watched over me and protected me after my father died. He's always been there for me."

Walker did not hear the comment concerning her father and focused, instead, on the other. He could feel his anger building again as he fixated on what she had said. "You had a *thing* for him? Did you ever date him?"

"No. I tried to get to him, but he just wasn't interested. I even threw myself at him and he still turned me down."

"How interesting," Walker mumbled under his breath as the waiter brought them their food. He exchanged smiles with Abigail while they started eating as he quietly stewed over what she had told him.

She had a thing for Redding. Interesting. He could have done without knowing that. It was just another reason for him to hate the man.

CHAPTER 11

A TROUBLED SHERIFF REDDING WANDERED AIMLESSLY back to his office, the events of his encounter with Abigail and Blaine Walker still too fresh in his memory to ignore. As he tossed his hat onto his desk and sat down, his mind wandered. He had feared that Walker was up to something and his conversation with him just now had all but confirmed it. Walker was all wrong for her. He knew it, but Abigail was so mesmerized by Walker's charm and his personality that she could not. *How could she not see it?*

He worried about his friend, but the situation had placed him in a bad position. If he said anything to Abigail, she would assume it was based on nothing more than jealousy, even if he denied it. If he did nothing and she ended up getting hurt, and she *would* be hurt, he would never be able to forgive himself for not intervening in time. What was he to do?

Over the next several weeks, Redding watched as the bond between Abigail and Blaine Walker grew even closer. He hoped that Walker would slip up and expose who he really was and what he was after, but it never happened. Walker was too slick for that.

He thought many times of pulling her off to the side and warning her, trying to convince her not to get involved with the man, but at the same time he also knew that it would do no good. Walker had embedded himself so much into Abigail's world that she was not thinking clearly. Besides, he had no proof and no one to collaborate his suspicions. Everything that he was telling her was off of nothing more than speculation and opinion, and he knew well that his thoughts on the matter wouldn't get him anywhere in convincing her. He needed hard evidence. Evidence that he did not have.

Early one morning, just as the sun dusted the streets with its brilliance, Sheriff Redding was already sitting in his office, unable to sleep and deciding to go into work early instead of possibly causing his wife, Grace, to have to stir before it was time. He had been there for some time pondering his agonizing uneasiness in his quiet solitude when the door opened and Deputy Clint McNeil walked in sporting his customary smile.

The man was always smiling. In fact, Redding could never remember a time he had ever seen him when he wasn't. That made McNeil very affable, and it was one of the main reasons why he kept McNeil on, besides the fact that he was a damn good deputy, if for nothing else. Clint was good-natured and everyone liked him. It was impossible not to, but he was also honest and hardworking, too. He never tried to take the easy way out of things– something that had come in handy more than once since Redding had appointed the young man as his second-in-charge.

Once Sheriff Redding had confronted a group of ranch hands who had become a little too boisterous in one of the saloons and Redding had been summoned there by the saloon owner to remove them. The men had been drinking heavily for quite some time and the alcohol had turned them from meager ranch hands into dangerous men with short tempers, loaded guns, and less than questionable judgement.

When Redding arrived, the group was full loaded with liquor and confidence and stood up to Redding, defying his authority to disperse and challenging him as a whole. His intuition told him to wait for Deputy McNeil to arrive to assist him, but Redding was impatient to remove the men from the saloon before they caused any more damage than had already been incurred, and he made a hasty and bad judgement call. Before McNeil could get there, things escalated into a shootout, leaving two of the ranch hands dead and Redding wounded in the arm. Deputy McNeil arrived and held the entire group at bay while he disarmed them and tended to Redding's injuries until some of the other townspeople arrived to back him up and escort the rowdy men off to the jail with McNeil overseeing the entire operation. During the entire exchange, McNeil never once lost his nerve. He could very well have saved Redding's life that day.

After an exchange of greetings, and pouring himself a cup of fresh coffee, McNeil picked up on Sheriff Redding's quiet dilemma and finally decided to question him about what was bothering him.

"Sheriff? You alright?" he asked as he tested the heat of his coffee.

"No," Redding answered casually, without looking over at him. "I'm not."

"Anything I can help you with?"

Redding readjusted in his chair to face McNeil. "Have you heard anything about new about Blaine Walker, the man who's been seeing Abigail Bartlett?"

"No, nothing. I would have heard something if there was something there to hear. Why?"

"He strike you as being suspicious?"

"Not really," McNeil replied, "but I ain't really been around him, either. I just know him from seeing him around town with Ms. Bartlett. Why? Did he do something?"

"That's just it," Redding reluctantly spoke. "He hasn't done anything. At least, nothing that I can pin him to. But I just don't like the guy."

"Just because you don't like a fella doesn't mean he had to have done something wrong."

"I know, but there's something about him that rubs me the wrong way. Either he's done something and we just don't know about it yet, or he's about to do something. Either way, I don't like it."

"Well, he seems to make Ms. Bartlett happy."

"Yeah, but she could be too close to him to see him for what he really is."

"And what's that?" Deputy McNeil asked.

Redding agonized over the question. "That's just it. I don't know."

He was lost in thought when he heard someone running down the boardwalk in his direction until they were right outside his office when the door suddenly burst open and one of the young men from town came inside, fighting to catch his breath before he could speak. "Sheriff! Come quick! Mr. Reynolds has been shot!"

.   .   .

Sheriff Redding bolted for the door, followed closely by Deputy McNeil after he quickly grabbed the rifle he swiped from the gun rack. Redding followed the messenger over to the Sidewinder Saloon that was owned and run by a friend of his, Dell Reynolds. He knew the shooter was either gone or possibly could be waiting for the arrival of the law to face them, which he doubted since either would only increase their chances of being caught. It was possible that they had been overpowered by bystanders and were being detained. Redding hoped for the latter, but didn't have much faith in it.

When Redding arrived, only one of the front doors of the Sidewinder was open. He halted and drew his revolver as he grabbed the messenger by the arm to stop him from entering. "It's alright, sheriff," the young man uttered excitedly. "There's nobody here. Mr. Reynolds is in there alone."

Despite the warning, Redding pulled the young man back enough to allow him to enter the establishment first, with Deputy McNeil hot on his heels. After a quick look around, he verified that the saloon was empty and holstered his gun as the young man managed to scurry past him. "He's over here, sheriff," the young man exclaimed as he went around to the back of the bar and stopped as Redding walked around him. There, lying in a pool of blood, was Dell Reynolds, dead.

"I found him like this when I came in this morning," the young man explained, still in shock at what he had discovered. "I knocked and knocked, but he wouldn't come to the door, which wasn't like him, so I checked it and it was locked. I went around and came in through the back door and this is how I found him."

"So *you* were the only one to come through the one front door that was open?" Redding asked while he knelt down and carefully studied the dead man and the surrounding scene.

"Yes, sir. That was the door I came out of when I came to get you."

"Clint, go next door on both sides and make sure nobody heard anything."

"You got it, sheriff," Deputy McNeil answered on his way out of the saloon. Redding doubted McNeil would find anyone who saw or heard anything. Whoever had shot the man knew he would be alone that early in the day and wasn't concerned about anyone outside hearing the shot.

Redding dipped the end of his finger in the blood, rubbing the sticky consistency between his fingers. It was still wet. There was no need to check to see if the man was alive. He had been shot straight through the heart and had probably been dead before he hit the floor. He looked around him for any type of clue or something that would help him in his investigation, but nothing like that existed. He turned back to the young man.

"You say you worked for him?"

"Yes, sir. I clean up for Mr. Reynolds every day before he opens from the night before. But I've only been working here for a little over a couple of weeks."

"Anyone unusual come in here lately while you were here? Anyone that looked suspicious, or maybe even a drifter?"

"No, sir. I haven't seen anyone, but I'm usually out of here before Mr. Reynolds opens for business. He didn't want me around when his customers came in. Said it might not be safe, so it was always just me and him when I worked."

"Did you hear him arguing with anyone? Even if it was a local?"

"No, sir."

Redding was deep in thought when Deputy McNeil slipped in the door and past the young man, drawing Redding's attention.

"Anything?" Redding inquired.

"No, sir, sheriff. No one heard anything."

Redding nodded, not surprised by the response. "We need to know if there's any sign of a struggle or a forced break-in."

"I'll go check the back door, just in case," he said as Redding quietly nodded his response.

Redding was running the possibilities through his mind when he first settled on robbery. He immediately stood and checked the register and saw that the drawer was partially opened. "Have you been in here today?" he asked the young man while pointing to the register.

"No, sir. I don't ever go in there. Mr. Reynolds wouldn't approve of it. I wasn't ever supposed to handle the money. Just clean."

Redding knew the young man was telling him the truth, so he dismissed that theory. But since the register had been emptied by someone other than the young man of whatever meager amount was in there, he had to assume that the basis of the killing was a robbery gone bad. Someone had surprised Reynolds and obviously gotten enraged when they saw what little money their efforts had reaped them.

Redding stood as Deputy McNeil emerged from the back, his face perplexed and filled with questions. "Back door wasn't forced open, sheriff. Whoever killed him must have slipped in after Mr. Reynolds opened it."

"Or slipped in *as* he was opening it," Redding added. "But that doesn't make any sense, either. Anyone would have known Reynolds wouldn't have that much cash on him this early in the day. They had to have known that, but yet they killed him, anyway."

"Maybe he resisted," Deputy McNeil offered.

Redding shook his head at the response. "Why would he resist? There was no money. He had no reason to resist. So why kill him? Why not just knock him over the head? Why go out of your way to kill the man when it isn't necessary…"

Redding's words trailed off as the answer suddenly came to him. Deputy McNeil caught his reaction and eyed him curiously. "What is it, sheriff?"

"It was made to look like a robbery, but it wasn't a robbery," Redding replied coldly. "It was an execution."

CHAPTER 12

AFTER SENDING FOR THE UNDERTAKER AND FINISHING up his investigation, Sheriff Redding went back to his office, his thoughts and his mood dampened. He had nothing to go on. No suspects. No eyewitnesses. And no evidence to support his theory, though he still thought it to be true. But there was something else that was bothering him. Deep down, he knew that Blaine Walker was somehow behind it. Maybe Walker wasn't the triggerman. He would never chance putting himself in that position, but he definitely paid someone else to have it done. He knew it, he just couldn't prove it.

Since his own efforts into finding out more about Walker had uncovered nothing, he decided to pay a visit to Abigail Bartlett to see if she had found out anything else about her suitor. With Walker and

Abigail spending so much time together, he had not seen much of her in recent weeks, but even when he did, she was always on the arm of Blaine and he made it impossible for Redding to have a chance to talk to her. It was as if Walker was going out of his way to keep him and Abigail apart, and he was doing a good job of it. So good, in fact, that no one could get near her.

After relaying his plans to Deputy McNeil, Redding mounted the roan and started for the J.B. Bar Ranch. He had to talk to Abigail and warn her of what he suspected she was getting involved in before it was too late, if it wasn't already.

Redding was no fool. He had no beliefs that Abigail would even listen to him. He knew she was going to side with Walker because she had not witnessed anything that he had done wrong. At least nothing that could be tied back to him directly. But it was coming. That was for sure. And when it did, he could bet that Abigail would come out on the short end of things. He didn't know just how far Walker would go to get what he wanted, but it worried him that Walker might think Abigail to be expendable, and he wasn't about to stand back and watch that happen. *That* much he did know because it had already happened to Dell Reynolds.

As he rode, he mulled over what he was going to say to her. Whatever it was, it needed to be convincing, for her sake. Abigail Bartlett had always been a rational and level-headed person, but he wondered if that was still the case, or had all of that changed since she had started dating Walker? Had he gotten in her head? Would she be willing to listen to reason, even if it came from him and especially since there were no facts or proof to back up his suspicions? He hoped so, but he still had his doubts.

He rode up to the Bartlett ranch and climbed down just as Abigail spotted him and came out the front door to greet him. She appeared to be happy, as if beaming from excitement. He secretly hoped she would remain in her good mood after their discussion.

"Hi, Vince!" she exclaimed happily. "What brings you out here?" she asked as she hugged him tightly.

"I had some time on my hands, and I just wanted to come out here and see how you were doing," Redding lied through his forced smile. "Haven't seen much of you lately," he added to help ease in the conversation.

"Well, good! Come on in and we can have lunch together."

"Thanks for the invite, but I can't stay. I've got to get back."

"Why? What's the hurry?"

"Well, there's been a murder in town."

Abigail's expression immediately dropped to one

of concern. "Oh, my gosh. Who was it? Was it anyone I know?"

"Dell Reynolds down at the Sidewinder Saloon."

"Oh, my gosh! Not Dell! What happened?"

"Someone followed him inside when he went to open up this morning and they shot him."

Abigail almost teared up from the shock of the news, her expression visibly painful. "That's such a shame. Why would anyone want to kill him?"

"I don't know," Redding admitted. "They didn't have to. There wasn't any money there. It was as if they went there specifically to kill him," he said to note her reaction, but its true meaning was lost on her. Still, Abigail was taken aback by the notion.

"Who would do such a thing?" she asked innocently. "Dell Reynolds never hurt anyone. He was a sweet man. Everyone liked him."

"That's just it. Everyone that knew him liked him. That's why I don't think it was a local that did it," Redding surmised. "I think someone was brought in to eliminate him."

The word caught Abigail's attention. "Eliminate? That's an odd label for it."

"Well, what else would you call it? If it wasn't a robbery and no one had a vendetta against him, why else would they feel the need to shoot him in cold blood? There just isn't one. They had nothing to gain by it."

"Like you said, it had to be someone who stood to gain something from Dell being killed," Abigail said. "It would be the only reason to shoot him down."

The comment led Redding to open the subject that he had feared opening. "I know Blaine was looking for a saloon to purchase. Has Blaine said anything about talking with Dell Reynolds? Y'know, about possibly buying his saloon?"

Abigail sharply cut her glance over to Redding. It was obvious from her expression that she was protective of Walker. "You don't honestly think that Blaine had anything to do with this, do you, Vince?"

Redding hesitated only for a second, but it was long enough for her to see his true feelings on the subject. "I'm not saying that," he resounded.

"But you aren't denying it, either," she pointed out. "How could you think Blaine could do something like that? He isn't the type of person to order someone to be gunned down, especially a kind man like Dell Reynolds. Blaine would never do such a thing. Shame on you, Vince Redding," she scolded him, "for even considering it. What a horrible thing to do."

"I'm not accusing him of anything, Abigail. I just wanted to know if he ever mentioned talking to Dell Reynolds about buying his saloon, that's all."

Her posture stiffened slightly, just enough for

him to pick up on it. "No, he hasn't. As far as I know, he hadn't even met Dell."

"But don't get me wrong, he did mention having a desire to open his own saloon, right? I think he even mentioned it when we ate together that night at his hotel."

"Yes, but that doesn't mean he would kill someone to make that happen. He could always just build one of his own. He is quite well off, y'know."

"So I've heard. But how well do you know about his finances? I mean, where does his money come from?"

"That isn't any of my business, Vince, nor is it yours. It would be rude enough to ask him such an inappropriate question, much less to imply that he had someone killed for financial gain when he doesn't need it."

"So, you've never heard him explain where he got his wealth? How do you know he's even as well off as he claims to be?"

Abigail pulled away from Redding slightly. "You're getting out of line, Vince," she retorted. "I'm getting offended by your line of questions. I don't know where this is coming from, but it's unjustified, that's for sure, and I don't think we need to continue talking about this."

"I'm sorry if I upset you, Abigail," Redding

offered. "I just wanted to know that you're safe and not being taken advantage of."

"Blaine cares too much for me to ever take advantage of me," she professed, "and your suspicions for him are unwarranted. Why do you have such a problem with me seeing him?"

"I don't have a problem with him, I…"

"Yes, you do," she interrupted. "It's quite obvious to me and to everyone else. But I don't know where it comes from. He's never done anything to you, has he? Or has he done something to you that I don't know about?"

"No, he hasn't."

"Then why are you so interested in finding something on him?"

Redding felt an uncomfortable feeling closing over him. "I consider you a close friend, Abigail, and I just don't want to see you get hurt, that's all."

"I'm not getting hurt, Vince," she said, her tone softening a little. "I'm happy for the first time in a long time, even before Slade died. Blaine makes me happy. Why can't *you* be happy for me, too?"

Redding's exterior somewhat melted as he smiled. "I am happy for you, Abigail. I just can't help but to worry about you, too."

"Well, there's no need to," she insisted. "I was taking care of myself before Blaine Walker came along, or you, for that matter, and I'll still be taking care of myself for a long time to come."

"Okay, I get it," Redding caved. "No more accusations about Blaine."

"I appreciate you looking out for me, Vince. I really do. I just want you to know that I won't let anything happen to me or this ranch."

"And I want *you* to know that *I* won't let anything happen to you or this ranch."

She reached over and hugged him again. "Ah, thanks, Vince. That means a lot to me. You sure you can't stay for some lunch?"

"No, thanks. I need to get back to town and see if anything new came up on Dell's killing."

"Let me know if I can do anything to help," she offered as she turned and started for her house.

"Thanks." Redding climbed into his saddle and pulled the roan towards town. The trip out there had been a bust, and he had not learned anything new from Abigail except that she was very protective of Blaine Walker, something he already was aware of. Redding just hoped he could be as protective of her.

When he arrived back at Salt Creek, Redding went straight to the bank to see the bank president, Mr. Wainwright, hoping that he could shed some light on Dell Reynolds and his financial status. If nothing else, maybe he had heard something that could be useful in helping him solve Reynolds' murder.

He tied off the roan and waited patiently just outside of Wainwright's office as he watched through the window as Wainwright finished up with a customer. As the woman passed by Redding, he motioned for him to step inside his office. "Well, sheriff, to what do I owe the pleasure?"

"I'm afraid it's not a pleasant visit, Mr. Wainwright. I'm here to ask you a few questions about Dell Reynolds."

Wainwright's demeanor suddenly turned solemn. "Oh yes. I heard about his death. Such a shame to happen to such a good man, wasn't it? I am truly sorry to hear about it. He was a fine man and an asset to this community."

"Mr. Wainwright, did Dell ever come to you to talk to you about any financial issues he was having? Was he even having any financial troubles, as far as you knew?"

"Not that I'm aware of. As near as I could tell, his saloon was quite profitable. He built that saloon up to be very successful, one of the most successful ones in Salt Creek, in fact."

"So, he wasn't overextended here at the bank?"

"Overextended? On the contrary. He didn't even have a line of credit here. We talked about it a few years ago when I was trying to get more of his business, but he wasn't interested. He always paid cash for everything. Said he didn't want to rack up any debts. Smart business man. Very savvy. Sharp. Did you think he was having money problems, sheriff?"

"I didn't know whether or not he did. I'm just following up on any ideas I could come up with."

"Since there hasn't been any town gossip on the subject, I take it that his killer hasn't been found?"

"No, not as of yet. But I'm still investigating. I wanted to talk to you first because I needed to cover all my options."

"I understand. I hope you're successful in your work and let me know if I can be of further assistance to you, sheriff. I'll let you know if I come up with anything that could be of use to you," Wainwright added as he stood and shook hands. "I'd hate to see Salt Creek gain a reputation as being an unsafe town."

"Thanks for your time, Mr. Wainwright," Redding replied as he donned his hat and stepped outside. The crispness of the oncoming autumn was beginning to bite at his face while a stiff breeze from the north kicked up as one last taste of winter trailed away. As he casually scanned around town, his attention was caught by a man standing next to a horse across the street a short ways down, staring at him. At first, Redding thought it to be nothing more than a coincidence, but as he continued staring back at the man, he realized the man was intentionally looking directly at him. He stepped off of the boardwalk and into the street to get a closer look as the man turned the horse and started him towards the alley between the general store and the barbershop, stopping just short of the end of the boardwalk. Redding initially started walking toward this office, but the sight of the man continuing to stare at him tugged at his curiosity and he altered his path towards the man.

Once the man realized Redding was walking in his direction, he led his horse into the alley and disappeared. Redding made it to the front of the alley and glanced down at it, but saw nothing. He unhooked his trigger guard, just in case, and started down the alley. Redding stopped a few feet short of the back of the buildings and listened, but there was no sound, so he proceeded down the rest of the way and glanced behind both buildings, but saw no one. Apparently, the mysterious man with the horse was already gone.

CHAPTER 13

As Ike Harrington was walking back to his camp from relieving himself, he was shocked to see the shadow of a man casually sitting by his campfire, drinking coffee. The sudden presence of the man startled Harrington, causing him to stop and draw his gun while keeping an eye on him as he slowly approached the camp. Despite being quiet, his approach was detected by the man.

"No use in trying to sneak up on me. I know it's you, Harrington," Will Spurlock noted calmly. "And you can holster that revolver, too. I don't like having guns pointed at me for no reason or I tend to want to shoot back."

Harrington was somewhat relaxed as he holstered the gun and entered the camp, his agitation showing on his face. "Then don't sneak into someone's camp uninvited and you won't have to worry about it. You're lucky you didn't get shot."

"Relax. I could have killed you long before now, if I wanted. I've been watching you for a while. I could have come in here a dozen times before now, if I'd had a mind to."

Harrington resented the accusation that he was easy to sneak up on. "And you would have been shot each and every time you tried," Harrington responded as he took a longer, second look at the cup Spurlock was using. "Is that *my* cup?"

"I didn't think you'd mind," Spurlock answered nonchalantly as he took a sip. "Didn't feel like digging mine out of my saddlebags."

"You're a strange man, Spurlock," Harrington uttered. "Walker told me you don't ride horses between towns. Why is that?"

"Personal choice. I don't like being alone out in the open, sitting in front of a fire like some kind of target. Too easy to get picked off."

"No more than anyone else."

Spurlock cut him a glare. "In my line of work, it is. I've made a lot of enemies over the years. There's a lot of people out there who'd love to see me dead."

"That's true with any hired gunman. Comes with the job."

"Yeah, but they've tried several times. The last

one damn near succeeded. Lucky for me, he was a bad shot."

Harrington was getting more and more agitated by the second. "What do you want, Spurlock? Why are you here?"

Spurlock stared down Harrington to make sure he had his attention as he casually sipped Harrington's coffee. "How well do you know Walker?"

"Enough to know that he pays well," Harrington snipped. "That's all I need to know. Why?"

"I think he's reckless. He doesn't plan well. He acts first and then thinks about the consequences after the fact. It's not a good way to do business."

Harrington wasn't a big fan of Walker, either, but he was still annoyed by the accusation. "What do you care what happens to him, as long as you get paid?"

"I *don't* care what happens to him. But I *do* care about not getting paid. And his stupidity is either going to get him killed or in jail before that happens and then I *won't* get paid. *That* bothers me."

"If he gets killed, he gets killed. What do you suggest?" Harrington asked, his curiosity now peaked.

"It's simple. If Walker wants to act reckless, let him. We let him do all the dirty work and put his life on the line and then, when he ends up getting himself killed, we step in and reap the rewards."

Harrington's sense of loyalty wanted him to

defend Walker, but he was now invested in the notion. "How would we do that?" he asked, instead.

"Walker wants the J.B. Bar," Spurlock said slyly. "So, we help him get it."

"But that isn't his whole plan," Harrington noted. "He also wants to open a freight line in town, and he's also looking at a saloon."

"I don't care about either of those," Spurlock dismissed. "I've never been one to work inside somewhere. For all I care, you can have the freight office and the saloon and I'll take the ranch. A ranch, I can work. That's all I want."

"Y'know, if Walker heard you even thinking about double-crossing him, he'd kill you on sight," Harrington warned.

Spurlock scoffed out loud. "I'm not afraid of Walker."

Harrington suddenly had a question that he wanted the answer to. "What if Walker tells *me* to kill you?"

Spurlock took another casual sip and gave Harrington an unconcerned glance. "That's not a problem. I'm not afraid of you, either."

Blaine Walker paused outside the hotel door to bask in the morning sun as a smile formed on his face. He had only been in Salt Creek for a relatively short period of time and, yet, he was already making a name for himself. Considering what he had already accomplished, he was very pleased with how things were moving along.

His presence was everywhere, and he submerged himself in as many areas of the town as he could, making friends along the way and building strong relationships with other businesses in the process. His integrity, and his intentions, were only being questioned by one man and he watched that man, Sheriff Vince Redding, as he was slowly losing his grip on the town. The thought brought a smile to Walker's face every time he thought about it.

Walker was already in the process of taking over the Sidewinder Saloon and was in negotiations with the town council to build a new freight office that would tie in with the new railroad carrying goods to and from Salt Creek while further securing his financial stake in the town. After easily unanimously winning over their approval to go ahead with his plans, Walker set out to put his plans into motion. Owning a successful saloon would seal his position with the townspeople and instantly have substantial revenue coming in. Opening a freight office would boost sales and the town's confidence in him while promoting growth for the town and its businesses. Everything was working out according to his plan. That only left one thing that remained out of Walker's reach: the J.B. Bar Ranch.

Try as he may, he could not stop thinking about Abigail's ranch. It was the largest spread in the entire territory, amassing more land than he thought possible by just one person. But her father, Roland Bartlett, had done just that and upon his death, the ownership of the entire empire had reverted to his only living kin, his daughter Abigail. She was the only thing standing between him and owning the most successful ranch around. He had to find a way to get his hands on that land.

After completing his meeting with a liquor supplier, Walker decided to pay Abigail another visit. Walker had worked hard to keep himself in front of her as much as possible, drawing off of her time and making sure he was in her life anytime she wasn't working.

He stopped by the restaurant on his way out of town and had them put together a picnic lunch for him to bring along. He had taken great care to nurture their relationship consistently since his arrival, not wanting to have to compete with another suitor for her affection. The time was ripe to get his hands on the J.B. Bar and Walker wasn't taking any chances that someone else would beat him to it.

He knew Abigail Bartlett was a successful, intelligent woman who would not be easily fooled. But she was also a woman who was lonely. All of her time was being spent running the J.B. Bar, which left her with no time to go looking for companionship and no possibility of it coming looking for her. That was where he came in. He would step in and tell her what she wanted to hear in order to gain her trust. Once he had a firm grip on the ranch, Abigail Bartlett would be nothing more than an added bonus.

He pulled his buggy up to the Bartlett home and climbed down, scanning around him for signs of her until he was satisfied that she was likely inside. His knock on the door was greeted by the maid, Roschell. "Yes?" she asked innocently.

"Is Miss Bartlett in?"

"Yes, sir," Roschell answered with a warm smile. "She's in the library…"

Walker cut her off before she could finish her sentence, pulling off his hat and tossing his riding gloves into it before abruptly handing it to Roschell without commenting and walked down the hallway towards the library while a stunned Roschell remained in the doorway quietly, still holding his hat and gloves and not knowing how to react. Walker found Abigail sitting at her father's desk, going through invoices. She smiled when she looked up and saw who it was.

"Blaine," she fussed as she slid back her chair and greeted him with a warm hug and a quick kiss. "I wasn't expecting you. What brings you out here?"

"No particular reason," he replied with a flashy smile. "I just wanted to see you, that's all."

"Well, I'm glad you came. I could use a little social interaction for a change. Seems like all I ever talk about is ranching and cattle and grass. I could stand to talk about something else for once."

"Good, because I have a picnic waiting for you to take your mind off of things, at least for the time being."

"Oh, Blaine! How wonderful!" she said happily as she threw her arms around his neck and hugged him tightly. "Thank you for thinking of me. It's exactly what I need right about now."

"Then let's go," he said as he motioned for her to head outside. They took a short buggy ride to a shaded spot next to the stream. After opening out a blanket, Blaine began setting out the foods as they settled into their lunch. Their conversation remained light until Abigail caught notice of Blaine's worried look that he was trying to hide.

"Blaine? What's wrong?" she asked with notable concern. "You act like there's something bothering you."

"It's nothing," he answered dismissively with a half-smile.

"Please, tell me."

Walker gathered his thoughts. "I don't think your friend, Sheriff Redding, likes me."

"Why do you say that?"

"He tenses up whenever I'm around. And I know that look he gives me. It's a look of jealousy."

"There's never been anything between us, I promise you. Maybe he just doesn't know you well enough to be comfortable around you."

"I don't see it getting any better."

"Well, it's going to have to. He's going to have to get used to you being around. You aren't going to let him come between us, are you?"

"No, of course not," Walker assured her. "I would never let that happen."

"Good," Abigail replied with a smile, which quickly faded when she caught his concern. "There's something else, isn't there?"

Blaine shook his head dismissively. "It's just something business-related. You needn't worry about it."

"What is it? Maybe I can help."

Walker turned to face Abigail, looking into her large brown eyes to make sure he had her full atten-tion. "It's nothing, really. I shouldn't even be both-ering you with my personal affairs. It's not appropriate for this point in our relationship."

She touched him lightly on his arm in a reassuring way, just as he had hoped. "I'm comfortable enough talking about it if you are."

Walker tossed her a somewhat defeated glance. "I have some investors back in Chicago who had expressed an interest in investing in my new ventures out here. Now that I've gotten possession of the saloon and have plans for the new freight office, they have changed their minds and decided to back out of the deal. I can cover most of the expenses, but after having laid out a substantial amount of money as the payment for the saloon, I was counting on these gentlemen to help fund my expansion into the freight office until I could get it off the ground. But their timing could not be more horrific. I'm afraid they've now put me in a rather difficult position. I've extended myself out to other stations for goods to be brought into town and expansions created, but now I stand to possibly lose everything because a few men have broken their word and suddenly gotten cold feet. I guess you can't rely on a person's word anymore."

"Is it really that bad, Blaine? Are you at risk of losing out on opening a freight office? Because we really need one, especially now that the train comes through here."

"I know," Walker agreed. "That's why I was so anxious to get it opened so we could capitalize on the new rail line."

"Having a freight office here is a necessity," Abigail pointed out. "It'll help Salt Creek to grow even more than it already has. We have to make sure that happens."

Walker glared over at Abigail, a well-rehearsed, surprised look covering his face. "*We?*"

"I can't just stand by and let you lose out on this, Blaine. It'll benefit us all, not just the businesses in town. We have to make sure that freight office opens, and soon. The sooner, the better."

"Abigail, I can't ask you to get financially involved in this," Walker tried to reason. "It's still a gamble, no matter how much it's needed. I couldn't ask you to do that for me."

"Then don't look at it as me doing it for you, Blaine," she reasoned. "Think of me doing it for everyone in Salt Creek. It's a good investment."

"Are you sure you want to do this, Abigail?"

"I'm sure," she answered adamantly. "Have the papers drawn up and I'll sign them."

"Okay, but only if you agree to be my partner, fifty-fifty."

"Agreed."

"Well, now that that's over with, I had something else I wanted to talk to you about."

CHAPTER 14

IT WAS NEARING THE END OF THE DAY WHEN A LIGHT knock at the door brought Blaine Walker's attention away from what he was thinking about as he stared out the window of his hotel room, something he had grown accustomed to doing quite a bit of lately. He abandoned his spot at the window, drew his revolver as he passed his gun belt and cocked it, hiding it behind him while he approached the door. "Yes?"

"It's Will," came a dull voice from the hallway. Walker uncocked the revolver and opened the door, glancing out into the hallway for anyone who could hear them and locking the door as he closed it behind them. Will Spurlock's expression was not one that Blaine Walker was particularly interested in seeing at the moment. "We've got a problem," Spurlock uttered, leading the direction of the conversation.

Walker's demeanor suddenly soured from the statement. "What is it now?"

"Redding's been sniffing around. That's 'what's now'," Spurlock said mockingly.

Walker was agitated by the vague comment. "What are you talking about?"

"I mean, he's going around asking questions about you and where you got your money. He suspects you aren't as well off as you claim to be. He's putting the thought into everybody's head."

"Then put a lid on it before it gets out of hand."

"I've got news for you, Walker," Spurlock retorted solemnly. "It's already out of hand."

"Then get control over it," Walker demanded. "That's what I'm paying you for."

"I'm confused. I thought that was what you were paying Harrington for."

"Harrington has the lead on this. You're here to back him up, if need be."

"I'm not used to being given second place."

"Well, you are this time, so stay out of Redding's sight. Speaking of which, he hasn't seen you, has he?"

"He caught a glimpse of me as he was leaving the bank today, but I lost him down an alley."

"You fool. You can't let him know that you're here or why you're here. If he finds out who you are, he could link you back to me, and I can't have that."

"Relax. Most of the people who can identify me don't live long enough to tell anyone."

"I can't take that kind of chance. I need you to lay low until you're needed."

"Why don't you just let me kill him and be done with it? Why do we keep wasting our time trying to keep him at bay when I could just get rid of him once and for all?"

"Because he's a lawman, and when you kill lawmen, you bring the entire wrath of the law down on you. That's something I'm not willing to do right now. The people in this town love him, so you don't make a move against him unless I authorize it, got it?"

Spurlock scoffed loudly, clearly annoyed by the order. "Well, Walker, you've put me in a difficult spot. You see, I'm not used to working like this. People hire me to eliminate threats, not to coddle 'em like they're a baby. I don't have time for this nonsense," he stated as he turned for the door.

"You'll have time for whatever I'm paying you for," Walker snapped. "If Redding is causing so many problems, then get to him."

"What d'ya mean?"

"What I mean, is that every man has their weak point," Walker pointed out. "You put enough pressure on that point and he'll get the message and back off. You just need to find out what that weak point is. Redding's married. Start there."

Spurlock's interest peaked at learning this bit of information. "Redding's married?"

"Yeah."

"Good. That'll make my job a lot easier."

"No, send Harrington. I need you to be fresh and available when I call on you."

"Are you sure he's up to it? I don't know if he has the stomach for something like that."

"What makes you think you'd be any better for the job? You said you had a problem getting rid of lawmen. Do you also have a problem with hurting a woman?"

"I didn't say I had a problem getting rid of lawmen. I said it would cost you extra."

Walker looked irritated. "Does this mean that dealing with women costs extra, too?"

"No. I'll do that for free."

"I don't care what you or Harrington end up doing. Just let Harrington handle this. I just need you to get busy doing something. I didn't bring you here to sit back and relax. I need to start seeing some results for my money."

"Listen up, Walker," Spurlock snapped. "I came here because you needed me, so don't stand there and try to tell me how to do my job. I don't like anyone trying to pull that on me. Not at all."

"Then start taking some initiative and start earning your pay," Walker fought back. "I don't like to invest money and not see a return, and so far, I'm not impressed with your performance, so show me what I've invested in. Remember, I'm being overly gracious with your pay and I can make things very unpleasant for you if I want to, y'know."

Spurlock turned slowly back to Walker, unhappy with the comment, which was nothing short of an insult. "What are you implying?"

"I'm not implying anything. I'm stating pure fact. You put so much emphasis on your precious reputation as a gunman. Well, I have to maintain a similar reputation as a businessman. I can't have that reputation tarnished. How would you feel if *your* reputation became tarnished? What do you think that would do for your business? There is an honor among outlaws, you know. I can put the word out that Will Spurlock is not a man of his word and that he doesn't live up to his reputation as a man who can get things done. How do you think that would affect your ability to find work? You wouldn't be able to get a job hiring your gun out to start a horse race. When I'm done with you, you'd be lucky if you ended up mucking out stalls in some two-bit town somewhere."

Spurlock did not take kindly to the threat as he launched himself across the floor to where he was face-to-face with Walker, his finger shaking in his face. "Now you listen here," he spouted angrily, "nobody threatens me and lives to talk about it!"

Walker did not back down and stood toe-to-toe with Spurlock. "No, *you* listen! I didn't painstakingly put all of this together and meticulously plan everything out just to have some washed up gun-for-hire ruin it all! *I* run this operation, *not* you! If you don't like it, then take the pay you've earned and get out!"

Spurlock could feel his hand slowly sliding down towards his gun and was staring into Walker's eyes when Walker broke his concentration.

"You'd better be faster than that," Walker said as he cocked his revolver. The distinctive sound suddenly drew Spurlock's attention to the barrel of Walker's revolver that was already pointing at his midsection. Spurlock glanced down at the gun and removed his hand from his holster as he slowly relaxed and a faint, comfortable grin came across his face.

"I see you planned ahead."

Walker smirked. "I *always* plan ahead."

"Alright, Walker," he said reluctantly, slightly pulling back from the gun. "We'll do it *your* way, for now. But this isn't over. And when it is, and it's just you and me, we'll see how you do when you don't have the drop on me."

As the roan stomped up to the hitching rail in front of his house, the exhausted sheriff climbed down from the saddle, feeling lost and defeated. Redding had not experienced such loss of control in the entire time he had been sheriff, and the ramifications of what was happening all around him were beginning to get to him.

After dusting off the remnants of the road from the front of his clothing with his hat, he entered his modest house to find his wife, Grace, toiling away at supper.

"Is that you?" she called from over her shoulder without turning.

"Yeah... it's me," Redding admitted in a crushed tone as he collapsed into the chair on the edge of the kitchen with an exhausted sigh.

Grace finished up with what she was tending to and wiped her hands off on her apron as she walked over to him and hugged him from behind. "Is everything alright, Vince?"

"It could have been better."

"I'm sorry," she whispered in his ear as she kissed him softly on the side of his neck and then returned to her task. "Do you want to talk about it?"

"Nah. It doesn't matter. It's the same old thing."

"I'm sorry you had a bad day."

"Bad day. Bad week. Bad month," Vince Redding muttered under his breath. The murmur was low and quiet, but still just enough to catch Grace's attention.

"Did you say something?"

"No," he replied as he stared off into the low-burning fire she had already made as he returned the conversation. "How was your day?"

"Oh, about the same. Mrs. Watterson down at the mercantile store asked me if I would be interested in working there some, y'know, just a few hours here and there. I'm thinking about saying yes since I have some time on my hands. And we could certainly use the extra money."

It may not be extra, Redding thought to himself. *Not if he didn't get a handle on this Blaine Walker thing or else he might be out of a job.*

"I know you've had a rough time lately," Grace said, jarring him out of his thoughts, as she wiped her hands on her apron and walked from the kitchen over to the table, garnishing a coy smile, "so I bought something for you today, to remind you that I appreciate how hard you work."

Redding took the small bag she handed him and dumped its contents into his palm to see a folding walnut-handle Russell Barlow knife. Engraved on the handle were the initials *V.R.* He longingly stared at it as if it were a nugget of gold.

"That's really nice, Grace. Thank you." He turned as she knelt over and they kissed.

"I know you lost your old knife a few months ago, and you never replaced it. They just got them in at the mercantile store while I was talking to Mrs. Watterson and I thought of you. You never buy anything for yourself and I thought you needed a new one. A sheriff has to have a good knife."

Redding sat the knife next to his plate so he could admire it more as he ate, but his celebration was cut short as his mind focused more on what was transpiring in Dell Reynolds's murder investigation, or rather what *wasn't* transpiring. It was an investigation that had all but stalled.

"Supper is almost ready," she informed him, cutting into his line of thought again. "Why don't you wash up?"

Redding took the hint and stepped over to the basin. After cleaning up the best that he could, he sat down at the table as Grace began transferring food from the stove to the table and then sat down herself. As she opened her napkin over her lap, she noticed his distant demeanor as he stared down at his new knife. "What's wrong, Vince? You don't like the knife?"

"No," he uttered with a smile, feeling ashamed

that he had come across as being unappreciative. "No, I love it. Really. Thank you, again. My mind is just on something else."

"Tell me. Maybe I can't help, but maybe I can."

Vince Redding slowly shook his head as he dished out mashed potatoes for Grace and then for himself. "It's a lot of things and they're all coming down on top of me at once."

"Like what?"

"The first thing that's bothering me is that I'm still no closer to solving Dell Reynolds' death."

"I know you've been working hard on it, but you'll get it figured out. Do you still think he was killed on purpose?"

"I know he was. He was killed to create an opportunity."

"What kind of opportunity, and for who?" she asked as she commenced eating.

"An opportunity for someone to take over his saloon, the Sidewinder."

"Who would be willing to kill him to do that?"

"Blaine Walker."

Grace stopped eating as she stared at him in disbelief. "*Abigail's* Blaine?"

Redding nodded.

"I find that hard to believe, Vince. Why, he doesn't seem like the kind of man who could do such a thing."

"He isn't. He never would be. That's why I know he hired someone else to do his dirty work for him. He would never risk putting himself in that kind of position. He's too smart for that."

"That's not possible, Vince," she replied. "He's not that type of person."

"He *is* that type of person," Vince argued. "That's *exactly* the problem. No one sees him for the type of person he really is but me."

"Do you have any proof that he hired a killer?"

"No," he reluctantly admitted in a lowered voice. "I don't. That's the *other* problem."

"Well, you can't go around accusing someone of something so hideous if you don't have any proof."

"I know the law, Grace," he snipped. "I don't need you to tell me how to do my job." As soon as he uttered the words, he saw the sting in her expression of how his words had hurt her as his temper decreased. "I'm sorry. I didn't mean that. I know you were only trying to help."

"It's alright. Have you talked to Abigail about this?"

"I've tried telling her, but she won't hear any of it. She thinks I'm being too overprotective."

"Are you?"

The comment caused him to look over at her. "What's that supposed to mean?"

"Well, it's an honest question. You do have a history with Abigail."

"I don't have any history with her."

"Vince, she chased you relentlessly. One time, right in front of me in your own office. Remember?"

Vine recalled the incident that she was referring to when Abigail had visited him in his office as she tried to lure him away from Grace and had stolen a kiss from him just as Grace had entered through the door. He cringed uncomfortably at the recollection. "That was different. That was before we were married."

"But we were still together," she pointed out. "And she knew it, but she did it anyway."

"But that was back then," he insisted, trying to find a way out of the subject. "That was just the one time. It was harmless flirting. She isn't interested in me now."

"No, but the whole town knows how biased you are toward her, of how biased you've always been toward her. Biased and maybe even a little overprotective."

"That's because I felt responsible for her being alone. I didn't stop Slade McMahon in time before he killed her father and I ended up having to kill Slade. That left her with no one. That was my fault."

"It wasn't your fault, Vince. You didn't know that

Slade was going to kill Roland Bartlett and you had no choice but to kill Slade. I was there, remember?"

"Yeah," Redding confessed through the difficult memory. "I remember. But none of that matters now. She's so infatuated with Walker that she can't see him for who he really is, even though I keep trying to tell her."

"But that's just it, Vince. You can't tell her. She's in love. You're going to have to show her hard, verifiable proof or you're just wasting your time and she isn't ever going to believe you."

Redding was mulling over what Grace had said when his attention was suddenly drawn to part of her last statement. "Wait...*what* did you just say? What do you mean, she's in love?"

Grace was surprised at his reaction. "You...you mean you didn't know? The word is all over town. Blaine proposed to Abigail. They're to be married next month."

CHAPTER 15

THE RIFLE BARREL WAS POISED ON TOP OF THE ROCKS, overlooking the road below as the man waited. Watching.

Even though there was a cool bite of the mid-morning autumn weather, the air was still, allowing the sun to beat down relentlessly on the man so much so that he had to periodically wipe his eyes with his sleeve as he continued to wait, his patience growing increasingly thinner as he scanned the road for movement. He was not in the habit of ambushing men. It was the coward's way out of fixing things, he had always believed. But this time was different. He felt he had no choice but to take out the one man that was causing so many problems.

He had been waiting for some time now, something that he was not accustomed to. Whenever he had an adversary, he had always initiated the fight, preferring to meet them face-to-face. Lying in wait, like this, and not facing his opponent was not who he was.

Above him, a buzzard quietly floated over his position in circles, patiently waiting, no doubt inviting others to join it, mistaking the unmoving man lying across the rocks for an easy meal. His presence annoyed the man who was wishing it would go away and not chance giving away his position. If he could, he would blast it from the sky and be done with it, but he dared not risk giving away his position, not now. Not after this long. So, annoyed and growing more impatient, he waited.

He hated waiting. He had grown tired of waiting.

But, in the end, it would be worth it to rid himself of this problem, he kept telling himself.

He repositioned himself on the rocks, the escalating heat reflecting off of the slate and stabbing him in the face despite the chilled air around him, making his position even more uncomfortable and frustrating him even more. He was not a patient man to begin with. This was only confirming that even more.

He was acting alone now. He did not have permission to do this. It had been a decision he had made on his own and one that he would certainly catch the devil for doing. There would be repercussions from his actions. He understood that, but that did not dissuade his intentions. He would worry about the fallout from this when it came due. Until then, he was tired of taking orders from someone who knew nothing about what they were doing, even if they were his employer. It was evident that he would have to take matters into his own hands if he ever wanted this to be over.

He had stood patiently and waited for the order to do something, but that order had been put on hold for too long. It was obvious his employer didn't intend to step up and take care of things, and he wasn't willing to wait any longer for the man to grow a backbone. Now, frustrated and out of patience, he was taking matters into his own hands.

When he caught a glimpse of sunlight bouncing off of his rifle barrel, he reached down and scooped up a small handful of sand and brushed it over his rifle barrel to dull the finish and prevent the metal from possibly being spotted up in the rocks. After dusting off the remnants of sand from his hand onto his pants leg, he resumed his watch.

The sun was relentless, beating down on him even more. *How much longer must he lay in wait?*

It was then that he saw him.

Off in the distance, coming in the direction of Salt Creek, was a rider. He squinted to make sure what he was seeing was real. At first, he couldn't be sure. He waited, his patience finally paying off as the rider came closer and then he was sure. It was him. The man he had been waiting all this time for.

He waited as the rider drew nearer. His first instinct was to shoot the man out of the saddle, to kill him and be done with this, but his position could not have been more uncomfortable and he could not afford to miss. He would only have one chance at this. Despite his impulsive behavior, he had to be patient and to wait some more.

He hated waiting.

The rider had not spotted him. The rider's easy demeanor assured him that the rider had not discovered him.

The rider's advancement had caused the shooter to rethink his position and second-guess himself enough to where he would have to move over slightly, finally settling the rifle barrel into a small notch while taking careful aim. This was the last time he would see the rider before he passed between him and a small bluff for a short period of time. After that, the rider would not emerge again until he was right up on him. By then, it would be too easy for the rider to spot him and fire back, and he wasn't sure how good the rider was with a gun. If he was to have a chance to get off a clean shot, it had to be before the rider reached the bluff.

Small beads of sweat continued to annoy the

shooter as they ran down his temples. He tried to focus his eyes on the rider, squinting away the stinging sensation the sweat was causing him. He was within range. He closed his left eye, focusing his attention on lining up the man in his sights. He took in a deep breath and released a small bit before holding the rest as his finger lightly touched the trigger. Just as he squeezed it, a trickle of sweat slipped down and dampened his eye, causing him to flinch and sending the shot off its target.

The bullet danced off the road, startling the rider as well as his horse, sending him reeling and almost tossing its rider out of the saddle. The rider fought to stay atop, pulling back tightly on the reins as he tried to steady the roan's movements with calming words while frantically glancing about into the surrounding rocks for the shooter as he kicked the horse into a run for the nearest cover just as a second shot trailed the roan's hooves.

The shooter cursed and frantically wiped away at his brow as he took a look to see if his second shot had found its mark and cursed again when he realized it had not. His scanning of the surrounding rocks revealed nothing. He had failed. It would be impossible to root the man out of his hiding now.

The rider had jumped from the roan and paused behind a boulder, his revolver already drawn before his feet had touched earth, worried that any movement would invite a bullet. Just as he was about to move, he heard the sounds of a horse retreating off in the distance and he knew that it was far enough away that they would be long gone before he could crawl his way up and around the rocks or ride all the way around the massive outcropping. The pounding of hooves on the rocks was faint, but distinctive, as they faded away.

Whoever had tried to shoot him was gone.

Blaine Walker was causally sitting at his small table sorting through paperwork, engrossed in thought, when he heard the sound of boots briskly coming down the hallway of the Imperial Hotel. At first, he thought nothing of it, but as they grew nearer, he feared they may be destined for him. It was only when he reached for his gun that he realized it was still hanging on the coat rack by the door. But before he could stand and reach for it, the door to his room was violently kicked in and he found himself staring into the face of Sheriff Vince Redding. Redding said nothing as he continued advancing across the room as Walker stood, his face flush with a stunned expression.

"Redding!" he shouted defiantly. "What do you think…"

Redding said nothing as he caught Walker with

an unexpected quick right that sent Walker staggering backwards onto the table. Walker raised his hands to fight back, but Redding delivered another staggering right jab that rocked Walker and sent his head back down onto the table with a thud. His face flush with anger, he gathered a handful of Walker's shirt in his fist before Walker could recover and focused his attention towards him as he leaned closer to him.

"You trying to have me killed now, Walker, is that it?!" Redding spewed through gritted teeth. "What's the matter? Am I getting too close to your plans?!"

"What are you talking about?!" Walker yelled. "I didn't hire anyone to kill you!"

"Oh, yeah?! Then why was I just shot at while coming into town?!" Redding barked viciously, his anger almost consuming him. "You think that was a coincidence?! Because I sure as hell don't!"

Walker tried to struggle free from Redding's grasp, but Redding held onto him and would not relent, forcing him to have to defend himself with his back still pressed against the table while Redding continued to bear down on him. "I don't know what you're talking about!" Walker shouted.

"Just now, I was coming into town and someone took a couple of shots at me from the rocks! You can deny it all you want, but I know you're behind it!"

"It wasn't me! I swear!"

Redding pushed himself away from Walker and took a few steps back, allowing Walker just enough room to pull himself up and roughly straighten his shirt while he cast a careful eye at his attacker. Still breathing heavily from his outburst of anger, he stared him down as he shook his head vehemently. "I don't believe you, Walker. You're lying. It was you. I know it."

"Maybe whoever shot at you mistook you for someone else," Walker reasoned, still trying to gather himself and get over his attack. "Maybe they planned on shooting and then robbing you."

Redding continued shaking his head, his face flushed and his eyes darkened with anger. "No. I was alone, and I was shot at coming into town. Someone was waiting out in the rocks, waiting for *me*. It wasn't a robbery or anything like that. I never even saw them. If they wanted to rob me, I would have seen them. No. They weren't interested in robbing me. They were waiting to kill me and you know it!"

"Well," Walker spouted, after somewhat gathering himself, "despite what you might believe, I didn't order anyone to do that."

"You're a liar, Walker," Redding snapped at him while trying to calm himself down. "You're a liar and a coward. If you wanted me dead, you should be man enough to face me instead of sending someone else to do your dirty work for you. I know you're behind it. You know it and I know it."

"Just like you thought I was behind Dell Reynold's murder?" Walker replied with a smug expression. "And I guess you can prove that, too. Right, sheriff?"

Redding stood his ground, his anger building with every passing second as he clenched his fist even tighter. He wanted to lunge at the man and beat him senseless, but it wouldn't do any good without proof. It always came down to proof. He stared at the confident arrogance in Walker's eyes, the satisfaction that he was, once again, one step ahead of Redding. The realization infuriated him to the point that he thought he might not be able to contain himself. He had to get out of there before he did something that he wouldn't be able to take back. "I'm warning you. Tell your boys to stay away from me, Walker," Redding warned with a pointed finger. "If you've got a quarrel with me, then let's you and me settle this once and for all. Don't be a coward and hide behind the truth and send your boys to do your dirty work for you. Be man enough to handle this yourself."

"Believe me, sheriff," he smirked defiantly, "if I wanted to, I could handle you."

Redding did not back down. "I look forward to it. Anytime. Anywhere." Redding paused just long enough for the words to sink in before he turned and brushed past the hotel clerk who was standing in the open doorway who had obviously heard the commotion coming from upstairs and came over to investigate. His shocked expression rendered him speechless as he watched the sheriff stomp down the stairs towards the lobby before he then turned his attention back to Walker. "Is everything alright, Mr. Walker?"

"Yes, Carl," Walker assured him while he straightened his shirt again. "Everything is fine. The sheriff and I were just having a somewhat heated discussion. I apologize for the disturbance of your hotel."

"Must have been pretty heated," Carl, the clerk, replied as he pointed to Walker's face. "Your mouth's bleeding."

Walker touched his fingers to the side of his mouth and pulled them back to reveal fresh blood from a cut. The sight of his own blood angered him, but he was not going to allow the hotel clerk, or anyone else for that matter, to see how much it bothered him. "Oh, that's nothing. Just a scratch."

"The sheriff done that to you, did he?"

"Like I said, Carl," Walker admitted nonchalantly. "It was nothing more than a heated discussion."

Carl shook his head in disbelief. "Wonder what would cause Sheriff Redding to do that to you?

Never known him to lose his temper like that before."

Walker reached into his pocket as he walked over to Carl and slipped him a folded bill as he smiled coyly. "I don't know, but since no real harm was done let's just keep this between us for the time being, shall we?"

When Carl glanced down at the money being offered, his face suddenly shifted into an innocent smile. "Sure thing, Mr. Walker," he replied as he looked back at Walker. "Whatever you say."

CHAPTER 16

WILL SPURLOCK HEARD THE MAN APPROACHING LONG before he saw him. Such instincts of his had been honed over the years, perfected by his trade, along with his determination to stay alive. He took no unnecessary chances, and that philosophy had proven to be essential in keeping him alive.

The rider was coming from the direction of town and judging from the amount of noise they were creating, whoever it was had not tried to hide their presence. Still, Spurlock waited in anticipation, poised and ready. He had not made it this far by dropping his guard.

He had slipped back in the shadows, waiting just out of sight of his fire, his back to the flames so as not to throw off his ability to see out into the night. A moment later, the horse carrying Blaine Walker eased up to the edge of the camp as Walker searched for the man he had come to see. Walker had made the ride out to his camp because he had not felt comfortable being seen in town with Spurlock.

"That's a good way to get your head blown off," Spurlock announced out of the darkness, revealing himself as he walked slowly into the light of the fire where Walker could see him. Walker wasted no time informing Spurlock what had brought him out there.

"Are you crazy taking a shot at Redding!" Walker shouted, without taking the time to dismount.

The comment caused Spurlock to chuckle under his breath. "I take it that Redding came to pay you a visit," he replied nonchalantly as he poured himself a cup of coffee and nodded in Walker's direction as he glanced over at Walker's face. "Looks like he got the better of you, too."

"Yeah, he did! He broke into my room and assaulted me! Blames me for trying to have him killed! But I didn't authorize that, now did I?!"

"You don't have to authorize everything, Walker. I can think for myself."

"You lunatic! You weren't thinking at all! You can't kill him now. He's the sheriff! It'll draw too much attention to me! We've already discussed this, or have you forgotten?!"

"Lighten up, Walker," Spurlock answered causally

as he sat and leaned back against his overturned saddle. "Even though I missed, hopefully he'll get the message and back off. I wasn't necessarily trying to kill him. I was just trying to get his attention, that's all."

"No, you weren't!" Walker disagreed. "You were trying to kill him! You know it and I know it! Now, what the hell were you thinking?!"

"Relax, Walker. It's all under control," Spurlock assured him. "I thought with Redding out of your hair, you could move on with your plans without having to worry about his interference. Look at it this way: with him gone, there's no one else that's willing to oppose you."

"No, you didn't think! You acted on impulse without thinking and you're going to ruin everything with stupid moves like that!"

Spurlock looked up from his coffee, his ego hurt from the insult. "You'd be wise to watch your mouth around me, Walker," Spurlock warned. "You may have paid me to do things for you, but it doesn't mean you don't need to watch what you say and how you say it."

Walker shifted in his saddle, agitated and impatient, unsure just how far he could push Spurlock before it was too much. "What made you think that killing Redding would make things any better? The only thing killing a sheriff will do is to bring the outside law into town to investigate. What are you gonna do then, kill them, too?"

"If I have to," Spurlock replied coolly as he sipped his coffee.

Walker was taken back by the man's arrogance. "You really are crazy, aren't you?"

"Like it or not, Redding's existence is a complication. Now, you might like complications, Walker, but I don't," Spurlock advised him. "I always like to know what I'm up against because then I know how to deal with it. But you keep pushing Redding off to the side and not dealing with him, like he's going to give up and go away, but he isn't. That's what you're not understanding. As long as he's allowed to stay alive, he's going to complicate things for me and I don't like that. When you complicate things and you don't deal with them, they tend to cause you even more problems. You'd be a lot better off if you would just accept that."

"This has to be handled delicately, or this is going to blow up in our faces," Walker argued. "Right now, I agree that Redding needs to be dealt with, but he isn't causing so many problems that he has to be eliminated completely and right now."

"You let me decide that."

Walker shook his head gently. "I'm beginning to think hiring you was a mistake."

Spurlock immediately tensed up from the

comment. He stood and tossed the remnants of his cup off to the side and dropped the cup onto the ground as he slowly walked towards Walker, locking eyes with him the entire time. "Are you trying to get out of our arrangement, Walker?" he asked, stopping a few feet away from Walker's horse. The question in his eyes was overshadowed by his chilly demeanor. "Because trying to cheat me out of my pay would not be a wise move for you to make."

Walker felt trapped. If he didn't carefully answer Spurlock, he feared the man would kill him now, without hesitation. He needed to choose his words wisely. "I'm not saying I'm cutting you out of anything," Walker admitted as calmly as he could remain. "I'm simply saying you need to be more careful. I need to maintain a low profile. Killing Redding isn't going to accomplish that. In fact, it'll create just the opposite. I don't need that kind of attention when I'm so close to making all of this work out."

"Redding isn't going to be able to live," Spurlock implied. "The sooner you realize that, the better off you'll be. He needs to go, and it needs to be done soon."

"You don't need to make a move unless you clear it through me first. That's the only way we're going to stay on the same page. If you go off shooting up things, you're going to ruin it for all of us."

"Just remember something, Walker. *You* need *me*. *I* don't need you."

"From now on, just keep your gun in its holster. When the time is right, you can kill Redding. But until then, you only use it when I say so. Understand?"

"We'll do it your way unless I see that things are going south. But if I feel like things are getting out of hand, I'll handle them myself, my way, whether you like it or not."

Blaine Walker left Spurlock's camp, equally annoyed as much as concerned. He had the hotel clerk handle getting his horse back over to the livery stable while he ascended the stairs to his room. When he keyed the door and opened it, Ike Harrington was sitting at the table in the dark, nursing a shot glass full of whiskey and a half-empty bottle. The sight of him startled Walker so much that he was speechless.

"You sure are jumpy, Walker," Harrington chuckled as he took a sip. "You look like you could use a drink yourself to steady your nerves. Where you been this late?"

"I just came from meeting with Spurlock," Walker said in a low tone so as not to be heard by others who might be listening outside the room as he quietly shut the door.

"And how is your gunman?"

"He's losing control," Walker warned. "He tried to kill Redding by taking a shot at him outside of town, but luckily he missed. Redding came and paid me a visit and gave me this," he snorted as he pointed to the bruises on his face.

"You think Spurlock will try again?"

"I think he's going to keep doing reckless things until it gets pinned on me. In the end, my plans are going to suffer because he can't contain himself."

"So, what do we do?"

"Spurlock has gotten out of control. I can't have someone working for me being out of control." He looked at Harrington, as if silently implying something. "He's a wild card, and he's messing things up for me."

Harrington moved to the edge of his chair with interest. "You want me to get rid of him?"

"Maybe. Spurlock has outlived his usefulness. I should have never hired him in the first place. He's done nothing but cause me irritation and risk jeopardizing everything I've worked for."

"I told you when all of this started that you didn't need him, remember? I never liked him from the beginning."

"And you were right. I should never have involved him in this. He hasn't been worth the money I've paid him. That's the second time I've lost good money on a gunman."

Harrington gave him a puzzled look. "You talking about me?"

"No," Walker answered. "I'm talking about another gunman I hired before you were brought into the picture. Gunman by the name of Jack Folson."

"How come I've never heard of or run into him?"

"Because he's dead."

"Dead? What happened?"

"I sent him into town before I arrived to get rid of the sheriff. I had heard about Redding before I came here, so in order to have things run more smoothly, I needed to get rid of him before I hit town so it couldn't be connected back to me. I hired him to pick a fight with Redding in a public place so there would be plenty of witnesses, but apparently Folson wasn't good enough and he got himself killed."

"Did Redding ever find out that you hired Folson?"

"No. He would have said something if he knew. Now here I am with another problem."

"How do you want this handled? Y'know, Spurlock isn't the type to go away quietly."

"I don't care how quietly he goes away. I just want to make sure that he goes away permanently."

Harrington sat down his glass and stood, walking slowly over to Walker. "Are you saying what I think you're saying? Because if you are, I need to hear you say it, so I make sure there's no confusion."

"I don't see any other way out of this," Walker reasoned.

"Say it, Walker," Harrington insisted. "Let me hear you say it."

"Fine. I need you to kill Spurlock."

Harrington grabbed his hat as he walked towards the door. "It's about damn time."

CHAPTER 17

SHERIFF VINCE REDDING stared out his window, lost in thought and unsure of what to do next. It annoyed him to have to admit it, but he had let Blaine Walker get to him. He had never let anyone get to him like this before, but then again, he had never been up against someone like Blaine Walker. Walker had brought out the savage in him, forcing him to do things he would not normally consider doing. Things that jeopardized his position as town sheriff. Things that jeopardized his freedom. He could now easily be charged with assault on Walker and possibly lose his job and his freedom. Walker had gotten to him and he hated it.

Whether or not he wanted to admit it, the news of Abigail and Blaine getting married had hit Vince Redding hard. She was headed down a bad road, a road that would only end up with Abigail coming out on the losing end of things. She deserved better. Anyone would be better for her than Walker. He could see that. Why couldn't she?

He was worried that Walker had worked his way so far into Abigail's life that she would never see him for what he really was until it was too late to do anything about it. Walker was nothing more than a conman bent on ruining her and taking over control of Salt Creek and the J.B. Bar Ranch. It was a frustrating situation to be in and a hard reality to have to face alone. No one believed him and he had no proof to back up his suspicions. He felt as if not even his own wife, Grace, believed him.

He was all alone in this.

He sat at his desk, staring out his window, savoring a lukewarm cup of coffee, unable to remember the last time he had taken a sip as he pondered what his next move would be. The infamous wedding was just over three weeks away. How was he going to uncover the truth and then bring all of this to light in such a short amount of time, all by himself? It almost seemed hopeless. He needed something to get his mind off of the dilemma, if only for a brief while. He needed to do rounds.

Sheriff Redding grabbed his hat and pulled on his coat before stepping out into the icy embrace of the autumn morning. It was only late September, but the recent cooler weather told him that winter was coming soon, and with a vengeance. He had heard of very few fall weddings, with couples generally wanting the fresh crispness and the colors of spring or summer to exchange their vows, but he knew that Blaine Walker's plans couldn't wait that long. Walker was working off of a timeline and he was in a hurry to seize control of the J.B. Bar. The sooner he had that in his grasp, the sooner he could work on turning the town into his own property. When that happened, Redding knew that Walker's first order of business would be to get rid of him as sheriff. That is, if he didn't have him killed before then.

He worked his way through the north edge of town, through the businesses, casting his glances and waves at the various townspeople as he went as if everything were fine. He needed the townspeople to think that, even if he didn't. Some gave him responses that appeared to be a little colder than usual, but he brushed it off as being nothing.

He liked this town, liked the people. He had worked his way into the heart of Salt Creek and he was happy here. He couldn't stand the thought of it being turned over to the likes of Blaine Walker.

He decided to go over to the railroad station when he heard the incoming whistle announcing its arrival. He had made it a point to be there as often as he could when the train hit town, just as a precaution. If it had brought Walker into their lives, it could bring others just like him– or possibly even worse.

Redding paused on the end of the landing platform and waited as the locomotive slowly crawled into the station, the piercing release of steam almost too much for him to withstand. After the final clank of the engine coming to a noisy halt was made and a final hissing of white, cloudy steam was released, the passengers began to disperse. Redding watched them with interest as they filed out of the several doors at the end of the passenger cars. It was the usual mixture of businessmen and drifters that he was accustomed to seeing come to town, but no one that overly raised his suspicions. A young man brought up the rear of the group, his smile beaming at the sight of the anxious young woman who had nervously been awaiting his arrival, throwing her arms around his neck tightly as they met and kissed, the smile fixed to her face as if it were permanent before they walked away, clutching each other tightly. Thinking it to be all the passengers, he turned to leave.

And then he saw him.

A cowboy with no bags, alone, with no one there to greet him. The man cut his eyes at Redding only briefly before looking away, as if he were searching for something. Or someone. The man looked suspicious, suspicious enough that he deserved to be questioned. The last time a stranger came to town that he didn't question, it had turned out to be the hidden danger of Blaine Walker. Redding wasn't about to let such a thing happen all over again. He decided to confront this man and find out his interest in coming to town.

He walked over to the man, who had paused long enough to pull out the makings for a smoke. When the man saw Redding approaching him, his eyes first fell to the badge on his vest before he locked eyes with Redding again. His disinterest in Redding was too much to measure.

"You waitin' for someone?"

The man cast a disparaging glance at Redding, his frown telling of his annoyance at the question. "Who's asking?"

Redding pulled his coat open enough to make sure the man saw his badge. "I'm the sheriff here, and I wanted to know the nature of your business here in Salt Creek."

The man pulled the tobacco bag's drawstring tight with his teeth and tucked it into his shirt pocket while he precariously held the sprinkled tobacco on cigarette paper in his other hand. "My business here is none of your concern, mister, badge or no badge."

Redding was not in the mood for resistance. He

took a step closer to the man as he stifled his building anger from the stranger's attitude. "I said, what's the nature of your business here?" he asked again, this time more sternly.

The man, who had previously been turned at an angle to Redding, turned to face him as he finished rolling his cigarette, licked the edge and casually propped it between his lips as he fished a match from his shirt pocket. "And I told you, lawman, that it's none of your damn business." When the man started to walk away, Redding placed his hand against his chest to stop him. As soon as Redding's hand pressed against the man's chest, the man swung.

Redding saw the man's arm moving and easily ducked out of the way just as it passed over his head. He took the opportunity to plunge a devastating fist to the man's midsection, catching him off guard and doubling him over with a whoosh of air being forced from his gut, forcing him to drop his cigarette onto the platform. The man tried to recover enough to counter with a right, but Redding had already started his own right, which caught the man on the cheek and violently snapped his head over to the side. Redding quickly followed it up with an uppercut to the chin and then another right that sent the man on his back to the platform.

He reached down and grabbed the stunned man

by the front of his shirt and pulled his head up off of the platform as his head weaved back and forth while he tried to gather his senses. "Mister, I'm going to ask you again," Redding snapped. "You can either tell me willingly or I can beat it out of you. Your choice. Now, what is the nature of your business here?"

The man looked up at Redding, his expression stunned and dull as the willingness to fight had left him. He struggled to form words through his split mouth. "Wife. I'm… I'm meeting…my… my wife."

Before Redding could respond, he heard a woman scream from behind him. He turned to see a woman rushing over to them and kneeling down to her husband, gently stroking his cheek as she cried. But her worry quickly changed to anger as she stood and punched Redding in the chest. "Let go of him, you bully!" she shouted. "Let go of him right now!" she exclaimed as she punched Redding repeatedly until he released the man's shirt, allowing his head to drop back onto the platform. He stood silently in awe as she returned to checking how much her husband had been injured while she sobbed through her anger.

Redding backed away from the couple and looked around him, stunned and embarrassed, not knowing what to say or do. Everyone within sight of them was watching. *They are judging me,* he thought, *and they had every right to. I just assaulted an innocent man for no reason other than my own paranoia.* He looked out over their faces and saw their disappointment and their disapproval. These were the faces of people who no longer had faith in him or his judgment of others. He could see it clearly in their eyes. He stared at them silently, not knowing how to correct this. He had gone too far this time. Way too far. The woman's sobbing brought him back to the moment. He reached down and lightly touched her on the shoulder. "Ma'am, I'm sorry. Let me…"

"No!' she screamed, snatching her shoulder away from his touch as she stared at him with hatred. "You've done enough! You think that badge gives you the right to beat up anyone you want?! Well, it doesn't! And it doesn't scare me! Get your hands off of me and leave us alone! Go on! Get away!"

Redding pulled back again at her urging, not knowing what else he could do to rectify the situation. He desperately wanted to make this right, but there would be no way to do such. He stepped back as she struggled to help her husband to his feet, which took some doing, knowing she would refuse any help from him that he offered as she struggled to throw his arm over her shoulder, all the while angrily cutting her eyes at him.

"I'm sorry," was all he could manage, though he knew it would not help the situation.

"I don't want your sympathy!" she snapped, glancing over her husband's shoulder at him. "I just want you to leave us alone!"

He felt horrible, but there was no fixing this. No amount of explanation was going to make this any better.

He watched the woman assist her husband as they slowly stumbled their way down the platform, having to catch him as his legs tried numerous times to give way until they were out of sight around the corner of the depot. His attention went back to the spectators, who were still watching him. Judging him. Whispering their disapproval at his actions amongst themselves. There was no need to try to explain his position to them. They wouldn't understand. They wouldn't care that he thought he was in the right to confront the man. They knew nothing of Blaine Walker and how dangerous the man was. For all they knew, Walker was as innocent as the man he had just beaten up since he, Walker, had never given them a reason to think otherwise.

Redding turned to walk away from the scene, wishing he could go back and redo it. This was not who he was, but it was who Walker had driven him to be. It had been Walker's plan all along, to make him out to be the bad guy instead, while Walker sat back and watched with delight. He had just been too obsessed with proving Walker's guilt to see it happening right in front of him. Now it was too late to stop it. The damage had already been done.

His failure to check out Walker had been a mistake, a mistake that was now too late to rectify. These people watching him now had no idea that Redding's intentions had been justified, but not his actions. They couldn't realize that he had acted out of necessity of trying to keep them as safe as he could. To keep Salt Creek safe. His town. *Their* town. But he knew that they weren't thinking about that. All they knew was they had just witnessed their town sheriff beat up an innocent man.

And they would not soon forget it.

CHAPTER 18

SHERIFF VINCE REDDING CLIMBED ONTO THE ROAN, still catching subjective glances from the towns-people who had just witnessed him beat up a man without cause. It was uncharacteristic of him and something he never imagined he would ever do, and yet, it had happened.

Redding was tired. Tired and frustrated from trying to protect Abigail from afar and it was all because of Blaine Walker.

It was hard to help someone when they couldn't see for themselves that they needed it. He could see what was slowly happening with Walker trying to take over Abigail's ranch, but no one would believe him, especially her. Now, to make matters worse, they had announced their short engagement. If they married, she would be in too deep to stop him. He had to stop her before she did something foolish, and he had to do it soon.

He was running out of time.

He had let this whole thing between Abigail and Walker get to him, even more than he knew it should. Was he being ridiculous? It made it look as if he had a bigger interest in the outcome than he did. He felt as if Abigail was a grown woman with a good business sense about her, but she was not reacting clearly and, in fact, was acting blindly out of infatuation. He tried to dismiss her ignorance of the situation. *If she were foolish enough to be taken advantage of, she would have no one to blame but herself. He obviously couldn't help her and, therefore, he couldn't be held accountable for her mistakes,* he tried to tell himself, but he was unconvincing.

The sheriff decided to go back to his office and wait for the inevitable visit from Mayor Bradbury, questioning him about the attack on the man at the train depot, an attack that he had no excuse for. It was the first such incident that had ever happened to him since becoming sheriff. It was enough to warrant disciplinary action, but would it be enough to make him lose his job? Hopefully not.

Redding went back to his office and chose to ride out the rest of the day out of everyone's sight. He felt bad for what he had done to the man at the train station. No doubt, by now the gossip wagon had swept through town and his outburst and assault was the hot topic. He felt better being out of everyone's sight, for the time being, until this thing blew over, if it had any chance of doing so. To his dismay, less than an hour-and-a-half later, the door opened, and a displeased Mayor Bradbury stomped inside, slamming the door behind him. The look on his face spoke volumes before he ever opened his mouth. He knew it would be better to let the mayor get in the first word, so it wouldn't look like he was trying to justify his actions.

"What in the devil is wrong with you, Redding?!" Mayor Bradbury snapped, his arms waving almost hysterically. "Assaulting a town citizen like that! Are you crazy, man?! What's gotten into you?!"

"Mayor, I can explain…"

"No, you can't!" Bradbury exploded. "There is no explanation for what you did. Word has already spread all over town! It's all anyone can talk about! You're lucky that man decided not to press charges against you, Redding, or you'd be a resident in your own jail!"

"Look, mayor, I know I had no right to assault him, but it wasn't completely unjustified. I was under the suspicion that he was hiding something."

"Well, he wasn't! I guess you've figured that out by now! And exactly what would he be hiding? I heard he didn't have any luggage with him, not even a rifle. And yet you still attacked him, so you must have been going off of nothing but his looks. Are you telling me you're able to tell how honest or dishonest a man is based just on what he looks like?"

"No, I'm not."

"That's right, you aren't. Now I've got an injured man, an irate wife and a disturbed town council that is questioning your role as peacemaker here in this town, and my role as mayor. I can't afford to have anything like this taking over this town. Do you know how damaging this could be for the morale in this town, not to mention its growth? How do you think the townspeople feel if they can't even trust their own sheriff, a paid civil servant, a man who was sworn to protect them? I can tell you, Redding, that it doesn't sit well with these people. Once the townspeople lose faith in the law and the people who are sworn to uphold it, all chaos ensues. The law is gone and with it, the lawlessness creeps in and the whole town goes to shambles quicker than you can imagine. I've heard of it happening several times. We can't have that here in Salt Creek."

"I understand, mayor, but..."

"No 'buts', sheriff. Now, I've always liked you. I think you're a good man and you've always done a good job as sheriff. Maybe you've had a bad day and things got out of hand. I don't know this man that you injured personally, but maybe he said something to you that rubbed you the wrong way. Whatever the case, I'm here to tell you that it can't happen again. Understand? I've somehow got to convince them that nothing like this will ever happen again. Can I truthfully tell them that?"

"Yes, mayor," Redding responded while thinking about his attack on Walker that the mayor obviously had not yet heard about. "I promise nothing like this will ever happen again."

"See that it doesn't, Redding," Bradbury huffed while trying to calm himself down. He took in a deep breath as he pulled a handkerchief from his coat and wiped away at the beads of sweat that his outburst had produced. "I went to war for you, Redding. Don't make me regret it." He stuffed the handkerchief into his pocket and started for the door as he spoke. "Now, if you'll excuse me, I've got to get over to the land office and sign some papers for the Sidewinder Saloon so we can get the doors open again. It's always good to see recovery after a tragedy."

Redding had already stood to walk the mayor to the door when he stopped suddenly. "Someone's buying the Sidewinder?"

"Yeah. Now that Dell Reynolds is gone, the saloon was up for sale. Didn't take long for it to be sold, either. Knew it wouldn't. Good location."

Redding was afraid to ask, but he needed to know. "You already have a buyer?"

"Yeah. Blaine Walker." Sheriff Redding recoiled from the name. His shocked expression concerned Mayor Bradbury. "Sheriff? Are you alright?"

Redding stared off into nothing without speaking. His worst fear had just come true. Walker had mentioned that he was looking for a saloon to buy. It looked as if he found one, even if it meant killing the owner to get his hands on it.

Once Redding was able to convince Mayor Bradbury that he was fine, he thanked the mayor for coming by and not firing him, and ushered him out the door as quickly as possible, grabbing his own hat and coat to follow him outside. He allowed the mayor to make it far enough across the street that he wouldn't draw his attention as he jumped into the saddle and pulled the reins sharply towards the J.B. Bar.

He was aware that he could expect resistance from Abigail, but at this point, it didn't matter. He had nothing left to lose. If he didn't step in now, he could be killed before he had another chance. Abigail could be harsh with him if she wanted, but one way or another, he was going to tell her and make her understand that she was in danger. Anyone capable of murdering an innocent man like Dell Reynolds in cold blood, or at the very least having him murdered, couldn't be trusted.

This confrontation would not go well, that much he was sure of, because he had no right to interfere. But if that were the case, why did he feel so strongly about protecting her? He tried to push it out of his mind, but it still troubled him, so much so that he had decided, at the last minute, to try to convince her one more time. If she threw him off of her ranch, so be it. At least, he would know he would have a clear conscience over the matter.

He headed towards the J.B. Bar Ranch, wondering the entire ride how he was going to prove that Blaine Walker had something to do with Dell Reynold's death. It was too big of a coincidence that Reynolds had died right after Walker had expressed his interest in a saloon, but proving it was going to be difficult. Walker knew that and knew that Redding would bury himself, and his career, trying to prove it. In fact, he was counting on it.

As he rode up to the ranch house, he hoped Walker wasn't already there. When he pulled the roan to a stop and tied him off, he realized he was not.

A light tapping on the door brought the maid to let him in and take him back to the library, where

Abigail was talking with her ranch foreman, Luther Gilroy.

"Vince! So good to see you," she exclaimed with a broad smile before she saw the solemn look on Redding's face. Her smile quickly faded as she turned to Gilroy. "Would you excuse us, Luther? If I'm not mistaken, it looks like Sheriff Redding is here on official business."

Gilroy nodded his response and then passed a respectful nod at Redding as he left the library and closed the door behind him. Redding made sure the sound of footsteps faded before he turned back to address Abigail, who was visibly worried about the purpose for his arrival. "Vince, are you alright? You look like someone died."

"They did," Redding announced, "Dell Reynolds died."

"I already knew about that, but that isn't what brought you out here, is it? What's on your mind, Vince?"

"Abigail, you've got to back off from seeing Blaine," he uttered as he awaited her disagreement. "At least for now. I have reason to believe that you could be in serious danger."

Abigail's concern quickly shifted from concern to anger. "*What? This* again? Vince, we've already been over this before. I get it, but I'm losing my patience with you. I know you don't like Blaine, but like it or not, he's not going anywhere."

"No, no, no," Redding tried convincing her. "That's not it. Right now, Blaine is trying to buy the Sidewinder Saloon, Dell Reynold's establishment."

"Yeah, I know. He told me about it. So what? He's also trying to open up a freight office to link with the railroad. Are you going to interfere with that, too?"

"No, Abigail, I just…"

"Are you trying to tell me that he's not allowed to buy a business when it becomes available now?"

"That's not the point, Abigail," Redding tried reasoning. "He's dangerous. I think he had Dell Reynolds killed so he could take over his saloon."

"What are you saying?!" Abigail exploded, slamming her hands down on the desk from rage. "I don't believe you! Who are you? I don't even recognize you anymore, Vince. You already tried to get me to break up with him before, but this is going too far! Now, you're accusing him of murder? You have a real problem, you know that?"

"I'm not saying he did it himself, but he at least had someone else do it for him."

"It's the same thing, Vince! You're saying even if he didn't pull the trigger, he was still the one who had Dell killed, is that right?!"

"Yes," Redding answered, trying to keep his cool.

"I can't believe you're accusing him of that!" she yelled as she paced back and forth behind the desk. "Why don't you just come right out and say it, Vince? You know this all comes down to the fact that you don't like him! Just admit it!"

"Alright!" Redding yelled back. "I don't like him! I've never liked him! Are you happy?! From the moment I first laid eyes on him, I knew there was something wrong about him. I'm a good judge of character and I'm trying to tell you that this man is no good for you! Why else would I be doing this? I don't have any other interest in this, other than to try to keep you safe."

"That's just your opinion, Vince! Nothing more! You don't have any evidence. You don't have any witnesses that saw him do anything. You have nothing. Nothing! And yet, you keep coming to me over and over again trying to talk me out of being with him! Why? Why do you keep trying to do this to me, Vince? Why?!" She paused only for a second before her anger forced her impatience. "Answer me!"

"Because I care about you!" Redding finally shouted. "Alright? You happy now? I care about you! Call me crazy for caring!"

"Oh, my goodness," Abigail suddenly softened as her composure and anger began to subside. "Are you in *love* with me? That's it, isn't it? You don't want

him to be with me because you want me all for yourself. Does Grace know about this?"

"What? No! I'm not saying I'm in love with you.
I'm saying I care about you as a friend and I care
about what happens to you, that's all! Strictly as a
friend!"

"Then, as a friend, why don't you want me to be
happy?"

Redding stepped towards her. "I *do* want you to
be happy, Abigail, but I also want you to be safe and I
don't think you will be if you stay with Blaine."

"Well, I'm staying with Blaine, whether you like it
or not. In fact, I'm marrying Blaine, Vince. You need
to get used to the idea because it isn't going to
change."

"I know. I heard."

"Well, then accept it or don't. I really don't care
anymore. I don't care about what you think, or what
you feel, or what you believe. I don't care about any
of it anymore, Vince. I'm tired of trying to convince
you that Blaine is a good man. I'm not doing it
anymore. And I shouldn't have to. If you were truly
my friend, you would be happy for me. But you
aren't. It obviously doesn't matter what I say, you've
already made your mind up. And we both know how
stubborn you are, even when you're blatantly
wrong."

"Abigail…"

"No, Vince!" she shouted. "Just shut up! I don't want to hear it from you anymore! I'm tired of you running him into the ground for no reason! He's never done anything to you. In fact, he's only been nice to you and yet, you only see him as someone evil. Well, I don't care what you think of him. I love him and we're going to be married, whether you like it or not! Now, I want you to leave!"

"Abigail, please…"

"I said 'get out'!"

"Please, just listen to me…"

"Get… out!" Abigail yelled again, causing the door to the library to suddenly open as Luther Gilroy stepped inside to see what all the commotion was about. He saw how upset Abigail had become and gave Redding a disapproving look with his hand cradling his revolver, waiting to see if Redding would comply with Abigail's demands to leave or if he would be forced to step in.

"You've overstayed your welcome. I think you need to go, sheriff," Gilroy stated firmly with a stern warning. "Now."

Redding cast a glance at Abigail, watching her breathing heavily as she fought to keep from putting her hands on him, disturbed by seeing the hate that he had created within her. He hated what had become of their friendship, but there was nothing he could do about it now. He had only done what he thought was best. He turned and walked to the door, waiting for Luther Gilroy to step to the side to allow him to leave. As he was about to step through the doorway, he turned back to her one last time. "Abigail, I only did it because I care what happens to you."

"Get out," she repeated in a normal tone, ignoring his comment. "And don't bother coming to the wedding," she said as she calmly sat down behind the desk and gave him a disapproving glare. "You aren't invited."

CHAPTER 19

WILL SPURLOCK WAS CASUALLY SIPPING HIS COFFEE, having just finished eating, when the bullet passed right by his head, mere inches from hitting him. He instinctively dove over his saddle, rolling across the ground and leaping to his feet in one fluid motion to make it behind a nearby tree, while he drew his revolver in the process, as a second and then third shot rang out, kicking the dirt up just behind his feet. Then he waited and listened. There was no sound and no movement, both of which were not comforting. It meant that whoever was shooting at him was waiting him out to see if he made a move where they could pinpoint his location and finish him off. At least whoever was after him did not appear to be a very good shot, he thought to himself.

He would have never missed such an ambush. At least he had that going for him.

Spurlock listened intently to the sounds of the night, waiting for anything out of the ordinary that would stand out and give away his attacker's position, but there was nothing. All he knew was that the shots had come from off to his right. He faded back into the trees and headed to his left, approaching his camp from the opposite side and swinging a wide enough girth that he could hopefully come up behind his attacker, assuming they were still in position, which he believed them to be since there had been no movement of a horse, as far as he could tell.

He eased his way down through the foliage, skirting the trees and winding his way towards the shooter. When he reached the far side of his camp, he stalled his movements and waited. If the shooter had remained in his position, they would still be in front of him, hidden in the lush landscape, waiting for another chance at him. But Spurlock wasn't keen on giving him one, and he had no intentions of spending the rest of the night out in the brush, either. One way or another, this had to end.

He expanded his circle, scoping out the trees behind where he believed the shooter to still be hidden, looking for the man's horse. If he couldn't flush him out, he would at least set him on foot.

Spurlock angled his path around the nearest

cluster of trees and stopped. This would be the general area where his shooter should have left his horse, but he still saw nothing. Sufficiently frustrated, he started through the trees, making his way directly towards his camp. He would likely run into the man at some point before he saw his camp, since the size of the area that the man could hide in was quickly dwindling. Spurlock had taken a few more careful steps when he heard the shot at the same time as he felt the bullet graze the side of his head. He collapsed forward, barely catching himself against a tree while trying to maintain his faculties. The burning sensation was like a hot branding iron being pressed against his skin and caused him to curse out loud in anger and disappointment in himself. For a few brief seconds, Spurlock was stunned by the shot and he was having difficulty shaking the cobwebs from his head that had stalled his thinking. He turned, pressing his back against the tree in an effort to clear his thoughts and bring him back to the shooter, but he was struggling just to stay alert. His first instinct was to favor his head and close his eyes to shutter out the brightness of the sun and to offer what relief it could, but he could not afford to lower his defenses this early, not even for a second, for fear that someone would come upon him when he was not able to defend himself. If his attacker happened to come upon him now, in his present condition, he would be helpless to stop him. He had to remain quiet and hope that his shooter would give up his search and leave.

The seconds dragged by like hours as he remained hidden within a small grove of trees. It had turned into a waiting game as both sides were waiting for the other to make a move and divulge their hiding spot, but Spurlock was determined not to be the first to crack under the pressure. It wasn't until he heard the faint sound of a horse galloping off, heading in the direction of town, that he finally relaxed and holstered his revolver. As soon as he realized he was no longer in danger, he collapsed.

Ike Harrington barged into Blaine Walker's room without knocking, startling Walker, who was holding a revolver pointed in Harrington's direction, a habit that he had grown accustomed to doing since Vince Redding had burst into his room and beat him. The look on Walker's face once he recognized that it was Harrington was less than amused. Before Walker could inquire as to why Harrington had broken into his room so suddenly, Harrington spilled his news.

"I just shot Spurlock," he exclaimed as he rushed past Walker and over to the window so he could look out onto the street. He was unsure if Spurlock was following him and wanted to know when he came into town if he in fact did follow him there.

"You shot Spurlock?" Walker asked. "Is he dead?"

"Would I be watching the streets if he was dead?" Harrington snapped viciously. "No, he's not dead, but I'm pretty sure I wounded him. I never saw him again after I shot at him. He could be laying out there dying."

"Then you'd better finish him off before he finds out it was you or you won't get another chance."

"I'm aware of that!" Harrington retorted sharply, cutting Walker a nervous stare.

"Does he know it was you?"

"I don't think so," Harrington stated. "He never saw me. Or at least I don't think he did. You've got to help me. You've got to give me an alibi so he doesn't find out it was me."

"Why should I do that? You should be able to handle Spurlock on your own. You said you could."

"But I didn't plan on missing. If he *is* alive, he'll come looking for me."

"Fine," Walker agreed. "I'll say you were running an errand for me out to Abigail's ranch. He'll never question that and he won't ride out there to check it out, either."

Harrington stayed put by the window, his attention fixated on the streets. It wasn't long before he saw Spurlock riding into town and heading straight for Doc Hastings' office. As Spurlock dismounted, Harrington got a clear view of the blood on his shirt from the wound on the side of his head as he glanced all around him for potential threats before he disappeared inside the doctor's office. Harrington felt a mixture of relief that he knew of Spurlock's whereabouts, along with a sense of distress that Spurlock was still alive. He had tried to take out Spurlock and had failed miserably. Now that Spurlock was aware that someone was after him, Harrington doubted he would get such a clear opportunity again to kill him.

"Do you see him?" Walker asked as he, too, stepped over to the window for a look. "Yeah, he just went into the doc's office. Looks like I grazed the side of his head."

"He's going to be extra careful from now on, which makes your job of killing him that much harder."

"I know," Harrington replied in an annoyed tone.

"Are you sure you're up to it?"

Harrington turned to look at him, still annoyed at the line of questioning being thrown at him. "What's *that* supposed to mean? Are you saying you're gonna bring in another gun to clean up my mistakes?"

"I don't want to, but if I have to, I will," Walker replied. "So don't give me a reason to."

"You wanted Spurlock dead, and that's exactly

what I aim to do. I may have messed up this time, but I won't the next time. So, just keep your other gunmen to yourself. I don't need the help."

Walker stared him down. "You forget that if Spurlock finds out I told you to kill him, he'll come after both of us, so I need to know if you can handle this. I don't know about you, but I personally don't want to spend the rest of my life looking over my shoulder. So, I'll ask you again: are you up to the task? Because if you have even the slightest hesitation or doubt, I need to know so I can plan accordingly."

"I'm fine. I'll handle it," Harrington uttered as he felt the quiet insulting of his abilities. Clearly, Walker had no faith in him that he could take Spurlock, and his failure right now had reinforced that doubt. So, he would have to come up with a new plan. He would take down Spurlock first and then Walker, and then he wouldn't have anything to worry about. He smiled at Walker, knowing that he and Walker were thinking about two very different outcomes.

CHAPTER 20

VINCE REDDING LEFT THE J.B. BAR RANCH A
defeated man. It was a feeling he had grown accustomed to as of late from his assault of the innocent
man at the train station to now with his isolation
from Abigail Bartlett. Even though he felt that all of
his actions had been justified, it still did not change
things. He had tried to do the right thing and
uncover the deception that was clouding Salt Creek,
but it seemed that everything he did simply blew up
in his face and made him out to be the bad guy. As a
result, he was slowly and systematically isolating
himself from virtually everyone in town, and the
worst part was that he had no idea how to stop it.
Thankfully, he still had Grace on his side. He knew
he could count on her if no one else.

Redding made his way back to the sheriff's office

and chose to remain out of sight for much of the remainder of the day, sending Deputy Clint McNeil to do rounds in his place as he pondered his next move. That would give him the much-needed time to try to think of a way out of this mess before it was too late and things could not be rectified.

Redding felt trapped. His investigation into Dell Reynolds' murder had stalled, with the townspeople continuously asking questions about it that he could not answer. His inability to put them at ease was catching up to him. The residents of Salt Creek had always felt protected and safe here under his watch, but that comforting notion was quickly falling away. They wanted answers that he simply could not give them, and that was unacceptable for a lawman. It eroded away at their trust in their sheriff and once that was gone, he might as well turn in his badge and walk away. The problem was, he had answers. They just weren't the answers that anyone in town wanted to hear.

When he walked the streets these days, he received a different response from the townspeople compared to times past. Now, people looked at him with fear, fear that a prominent businessman in town had been murdered and no one had been apprehended. Many even wondered if they were next, but he could not guarantee that they wouldn't be. No one could. Least of all, him.

The impending wedding between Abigail Bartlett and Blaine Walker also weighed heavily on his mind and was fast approaching, another disturbing thought that he preferred not to dwell on. He had tried everything he could to warn Abigail of Walker's true intentions, but that had blown up in his face every time. He often wondered why he was so adamant to convince Abigail since she had been so resistant, but deep down, he knew why. Putting all personal feelings aside, he had a problem with it because he was sworn to uphold the law and here it was being mocked right in front of him and not just to anybody but to a person that he cared about. But caring alone wouldn't save her. She would end up hurt, broke, broken, and alone. Or even possibly dead. Now, here he was. And what did he have to show for caring? No friends, no allies, and no proof. It felt as if the entire town was against him, and it was all because of Blaine Walker. His life had been perfect until the man had entered Salt Creek. Now it was in shambles. He felt helpless, and he did not like it. Not one bit.

Sheriff Redding decided to call it a day and headed home to one of the last people he could count on to back him. When he walked through the front door, he immediately picked up on the tension in the room. His suspicions were confirmed when he tried to hug Grace from behind and not only did she not reciprocate, but it seemed as if she had partially pulled away.

"What's wrong?" he wanted to know, asking the obvious question.

Grace turned to face him. Her lips tightened from the tension she was experiencing. "Vince, we need to talk."

"That's never a good way to start a conversation," Redding replied, confirming his instincts as he leaned his back against the kitchen counter to see her better. "What did I do now?" he added with a soft chuckle to try to lighten the mood.

"This isn't funny, Vince," Grace spoke, her words coming out forcibly as if she were having to restrain herself from what she was about to say. "Has anyone talked to you?"

"Who are you talking about?"

"The mayor. The town council. Anyone. Has anyone talked to you?"

"No. Why?"

Grace stumbled to speak. "Vince, I think your job is in jeopardy."

Redding's soft smile quickly faded as he took in her words. "What? What are you talking about?"

"There's talk around town about whether or not you're still qualified to be sheriff. You attacked that man at the train station and now your obsession with trying to ruin Blaine Walker is consuming you. It's all you ever think or talk about. Some people are questioning if you should keep your job or be fired. Some are even pushing to have you removed now without waiting any longer."

Redding fought back the urge to ask about specific people, though he had no idea who they might be. "Where is this coming from? I've always been there for these people. Why all of a sudden is my loyalty being questioned?"

"It's not your loyalty that's being questioned," Grace corrected him, followed by a short, uncomfortable pause. "It's your discretion."

"My *discretion?*" Redding responded with surprise. "Since when is my discretion not good enough?"

Grace stopped preparing food and turned to face Redding. She sighed heavily before she began. "Vince, you haven't handled this matter with Blaine Walker very well. He has a lot of backers in this town. People like him. They respect him. They trust him. And they're taking offense that you're going after him like you are for no reason."

Redding scoffed out loud at the insinuation. "That's their problem."

"See? *That's* what I'm talking about," she chimed in. "You can't have that kind of attitude towards someone who has done nothing but good for this town. That kind of blatant disregard for the towns-people is what's going to be your downfall."

Redding became adamant about the claim. "He killed Dell Reynolds, Grace, or he at least had him killed."

"You don't know that," Grace insisted, her emotions quickly taking over.

"I *do* know it!" Redding exploded. "I just can't prove it!"

"Knowing isn't enough, Vince, and you know it. You've always told me that when it comes to the law, if it can't be proven, then it isn't real."

"Yeah, I know."

"Well, that applies here, too, Vince. You've done nothing but try to run Blaine into the ground and a lot of people don't like that. They admire him for what he's done for this town and what he's planning on doing in the future. They see him as an asset. Right now, they think of *you* as a liability."

"I really don't care what they think."

"Well, you should care about this: there's also talk around town that a gunman has been hired to either run you out of town or kill you."

"Probably hired by Blaine Walker, too," Redding insisted. "How much of a rumor is it? Or is it just wishful thinking?"

"I don't know if it's true or not. It could just be rumors. Y'know, you've made a lot of people mad."

"You keep saying 'a lot of people'. Who exactly are you talking about?"

"I'm not going to stand here and list names so you can go and confront them because I know you and that's exactly what you'll do. It wouldn't do you any good, anyway, and it would only make matters worse."

"But this is not my fault. They don't see Blaine for what he really is. He's not the kind, generous businessman that everyone thinks he is. He's conniving and shady and he's responsible for Dell Reynold's death. Whether he was the one who pulled the trigger or not, he was just as responsible for it. I'm telling you, Grace, he can't be trusted."

"You do realize that this kind of talk is going to finish off your career, a career that is just barely hanging on by a thread, as it is."

Redding scoffed again. "You make it sound like it's already finished."

"It isn't, but it will be if you don't put a stop to what you're doing," Grace insisted, grabbing him by the arm. "You're sabotaging yourself and you can't even see it because of your hatred for Blaine Walker. It might look bad now, but you can still turn this around, Vince. It's not too late. But you have to stop trying to pin everything on Blaine. The townspeople aren't going to allow it to continue. And unless you have something substantial to charge him with, then you'd be better off just letting it go."

Redding started to speak when a thought hit him. "Someone asked you to talk to me about this, didn't they?"

The question startled Grace, who stood quietly at the accusation for a few seconds before answering. "Yes. Some of the townspeople have approached me and asked if I would talk to you about your behavior."

"My *behavior?* What am I, a child being scolded? First, it was my discretion and now it's my behavior. Next, you're going to try to tell me how to do my job."

"No one is trying to do that, Vince, at least not yet, but they are concerned and they're putting a lot of trust in Blaine and what he's doing. They're not going to back down."

"So they're putting their trust in Blaine and their distrust in me, a man who has done nothing but good for this town. I can't believe this is happening," Redding admitted, frustrated. "I can't believe I'm the only one who sees what's going on here and now, on top of everything else, he's managed to turn the town against me. He knows that I know all about him and he's using his position and his influence to make me out to be the bad guy out of the two of us when it's clearly him."

"Do you hear yourself?" Grace uttered. "This is what everyone is talking about. Your personal vendetta against Blaine. It's consumed you. You're not the sheriff you used to be."

"Is that them talking or you?"

Grace cut her expression at him as if carefully stifling her words so as not to say anything hurtful. "I'm trying to help you here, Vince, but you're not making it any easier for me. You should be thanking me for warning you instead of trying to pick a fight with me. You trying to defend your actions is going to end up ruining you."

Redding suddenly realized her position on the matter. "I don't believe it. They got to you and now you agree with them, don't you? That's why they came to you. Because they knew they could get you over to their side to try to convince me to back off."

"I'm not on their side, Vince," Grace claimed. "I'm trying to be on your side, but you're making that harder and harder to do."

"Well, it sure doesn't look like you're on my side."

"I don't know what you have against Blaine. He makes Abigail happy. You've seen the change in her, and that's something we haven't seen in quite some time. If she's found someone who makes her happy, then why can't you just leave him alone and let her be happy?"

"She's only happy because she doesn't see him for who he really is."

"Will you stop saying that, Vince?" Grace said in an outburst. "You're all alone on this and you can't even see it. I'm trying to help you here and you're ignoring everything I'm telling you."

"Just like you're ignoring everything I'm telling you."

"Alright, then why should *I* be rude towards him? Tell me that. Why, Vince? Just because you say so? He hasn't done anything to me, or to you, for that matter, but I'm still supposed to hate him just because you do?"

"He killed Dell Reynolds," Redding stated firmly.

"Will you stop saying that?! You don't know that! And even if you did, you can't prove it!"

Redding tried to pull back his emotions before he said something he would regret. "They really got to you, didn't they? They've turned my own wife against me and convinced you that I'm making all of this up."

"I'm not against you, Vince, I would never be against you, but I also won't be a part of this personal lynching party you have for Blaine Walker. I just won't do it."

Redding suddenly had a thought as he reached into his pants pocket. When he removed his hand, he was holding the walnut-handle Russell Barlow knife she had given him. "Is that what *this* was for?" he asked, looking at her. "Was this supposed to help shut me up and bring me over to your side?"

Grace looked confused. "There is no 'my' side, Vince. I gave that to you because I thought you might like it, that's all."

Redding sat the knife down on the kitchen table. "Well, now I don't feel right carrying it around, knowing how you feel about me. I'll pick it up when all of this is over."

"Vince, you aren't being reasonable," Grace argued. "You needn't get mad just because no one wants to side with you."

"So, that's it then? You're telling me I'm on my own?"

"This is ridiculous, Vince. All you have to do is leave the man alone. If he is what you say he is, then it'll come out in time. At least that way you won't be held responsible for spreading vicious rumors about him."

"Trust me, they're not just rumors, Grace. They're the truth," he stated through tightened lips, "and everyone will see it. I promise you. I may not have the evidence to prove it right now, but I will." He donned his hat and reached for the door. "I just hope no one else dies before I can get it."

CHAPTER 21

I<small>T WAS AN UNUSUALLY CRISP MORNING AS</small> V<small>INCE</small>
Redding slowly sat up from the bunk in the back of
his office, recalling the incident with Grace that had
brought him there the previous night. He had settled
here to clear his head and try to sort things out
when he felt he couldn't reason with Grace. It wasn't
his first choice for sleep, but it was still far better
than getting into another argument with her. He
should have seen this coming, and now it was too
late to stop it from happening. They had finally
gotten to her. Even his deputy, Clint McNeil, was
shying away from discussing Blaine Walker and his
guilt, as if he had somehow been persuaded by the
townspeople, too. That was everyone. Now, Redding
knew that he was literally on his own in the matter.

He scratched his head and got dressed, putting

on the makings for a fresh pot of coffee in the process. It was a little more than three weeks until Blaine and Abigail's wedding and there was a lot to do. His first order of business was to find a way to tie Walker to Dell Reynolds' murder. That had not been easy before now and it would not be any easier to get it done before the day of the wedding came.

As the pot of water brewed and stuffed the office with its building aroma, he filed through the wanted posters for a likeness of Walker. It was a long shot, but he wanted to make sure all of his possibilities were covered. But, in the end, the effort produced nothing.

Annoyed at the results, Redding decided to abandon his theory and walked over to the bank to see the bank president, Mr. Wainwright. He knew Wainwright was probably one of the ones Grace had admitted was siding with Walker, but it was still a long shot that he could find out something, anything, that could help him prove his case. As he caught Wainwright's glance through the window, he could tell the man was not anxious to see him and saw the man take in a deep sigh as he forced a fake smile and waved him into his office.

"Sheriff, good to see you," Wainwright announced as a lie as he extended his hand.

"Sorry to bother you, but I had a few questions about an account."

Wainwright suddenly shifted uneasily in his chair. "Well now, sheriff, you know I can't divulge any personal information about a customer. It would be unethical, not to mention it being against bank policy."

"I'm not asking for personal information, Mr. Wainwright," Redding insisted. "I just need to ask a few questions about someone who has an account here."

Wainwright hesitated, as if pondering the ramifications of doing so. "Well, I guess I could possibly answer some questions, nothing too personal, mind you, and as long as they weren't too specific or could be considered an intrusion on someone's personal business. Who are you inquiring about?"

"Blaine Walker."

The mention of the man's name caused Wainwright to shift in his chair again. "I'm sorry, sheriff, but that information is confidential."

"I haven't even told you what I needed," Redding professed, "and you're already shooting me down."

"I'm sorry, sheriff, but I can't delve into Mr. Walker's personal finances. It wouldn't be prudent."

"Again, I'm not asking you for specifics. I'm asking you for some general information. It's linked to the investigation into Dell Reynolds' murder. Now, you wouldn't want word to get around to the townspeople that you were willing to interfere with an official murder investigation, would you, Mr. Wainwright?"

Wainwright took in Redding's claim. "Are you suggesting that Mr. Walker has something to do with Mr. Reynolds' death?"

"No, I'm not. I just need to see if there are any links between Walker and Reynolds since Walker bought out his saloon. So, can you help me?"

Wainwright paused to take in Redding's comment. "I have no desire to be a hindrance to an investigation, sheriff. Tell me what questions you're inquiring about and I'll see if I can answer them for you without getting us both into trouble."

Redding gathered as much information as he could before a nervous Mr. Wainwright politely stopped him. As helpful as Mr. Wainwright was, the limited answers Redding got didn't make much of a difference or answer any of his questions. After thanking the man, Redding left the office and headed back to his own office. When he opened the door, he was shocked to see three members of the town council waiting in his office, but the impatience of the men didn't really surprise him.

"Hello. Can I help you gentlemen?" he asked while he hung his hat on the coat rack and walked around them to sit at his desk. It was apparent that one of the men, a local businessman by the name of Percy Brewer, had been designated as the spokesperson for the group.

"Sheriff, we've got a problem," Brewer started.

"What is it?"

"It's you, sheriff," Lucius Childers chimed in rudely, unable to contain himself any longer. Redding was not surprised by the man's tenacity. Over the years, he had been the only town council member that had never really bonded with Redding. Redding had never considered it a great loss.

Redding diverted his attention over to Childers. "What about me, Lucius?"

"You've come unhinged," Percy Brewer spoke up as he took back the conversation. "The town council is concerned with your recent behavior."

The use of the word stabbed at Redding's anger. "The town council is, or just you?"

"See, Percy," Childers ranted as he snapped at Brewer. "This type of behavior is exactly what I was talking about."

"What is it you don't like about my behavior?" Redding asked, glancing over to Childers.

"It's as if you're losing control over your emotions, sheriff," Percy Brewer lowered his tone to try to maintain control of the tone of the group. "Just like when you attacked that poor man at the train station. He was innocent. He'd never done anything to you and yet you beat him to a pulp for no reason, no reason whatsoever."

"That was a simple mistake, Percy. I thought he was someone else. He looked suspicious to me."

"That's still no reason to beat the man up, sheriff," Brewer responded. "If you have any concern about someone, then you detain them and if you have to, you arrest them, but you don't assault them."

"I know what the law is, gentlemen."

"You're lucky he didn't press charges against you."

"I know. I tried to apologize, but his wife pushed me away."

"Of course, she did," Lucius Childers added abruptly. "She had just witnessed you attacking her husband. It wasn't like you could deny it since it happened in front of all those witnesses."

"It was my fault. I admit it. But what does that have to do with me now?"

Percy Bowers joined back in. "If it were an isolated incident, we could probably look past it, but it isn't the only time this has happened recently, is it, sheriff?"

Redding braced himself for what was about to be said. "What are you talking about, Percy?"

"What he's talking about is that we heard about you assaulting Blaine Walker," Lucius Childers answered calmly.

Percy Brewer cut in before Redding could answer. "You *do* admit to hitting him, don't you, sheriff?"

"Yeah. I hit him a couple of times," Redding admitted reluctantly.

"You see? He openly admits it," Lucius Childers ranted, shaking his finger at Redding. "Did *he* look suspicious, too, sheriff?"

"Calm down, Lucius," Brewer suggested as he waved his hand at Childers before turning back to Redding. "What he means is we can't have that kind of behavior in Salt Creek, especially from no less than the town sheriff. It doesn't look good to the townspeople. They've lost faith in you, sheriff," Brewer added. "It's not a good position to be in. Not for you or the town."

"This isn't really about me or my job, is it, gentlemen? It's all about Blaine Walker."

Brewer and Childers exchanged quiet glances before Childers spoke again. "Yes, it involves Mr. Walker."

"You gentlemen don't know what type of person he really is," Redding warned. "But I do. I've seen it many times before. It's part of the job to pick up on people that aren't what they claim to be."

"But this time you were wrong, sheriff," Childers said. "Blaine Walker has done nothing to warrant your hostility."

"Nothing that you're aware of."

"You've taken matters into your own hands and now your hatred for the man has spilled over to your interaction with other people, which is why you assaulted that man at the train station."

"That was different."

"No, it isn't, sheriff," Childers insisted. "It all comes down to the fact that you've become so fixated on Walker that you have let your personal opinion of him cloud your judgement concerning the performance of your job."

"I'm not fixated on him, Lucius. I have reason to believe he's up to something. I just don't know what that is, just yet."

"I believe there's more to it than that. It's my opinion that your judgment is skewed because of your feelings for Abigail Bartlett," Lucius Childers added.

"Now, hold on there," Redding said defensively, his demeanor suddenly hardening. "I don't have any feelings for Abigail. She's just a friend."

"That's not the word around town, sheriff," Percy Bowers spoke. "People see how she acts around you. She's clearly smitten with you, has been for some time, and I think you're jealous of Walker for having something that you can't."

Lucius Childers took advantage of the opening to berate Redding even further. "If it were anyone else, you wouldn't be so obsessed with removing Walker, but since it's Abigail Bartlett, you've lost all reasoning. You aren't thinking clearly. I wouldn't be surprised if there was something going on there, even if Abigail disapproved."

Redding stood his ground, his jaw clenching from the building anger. "I have never been unfaithful to my wife and I'm insulted that you would even imply that."

"I don't mean to be insensitive, sheriff," Lucius responded sternly with a lie, "but facts are facts. You mean to tell me that you have never been attracted to her?"

"She's a beautiful woman, but no, I have never been attracted to her."

Percy Brewer took over. "Be that as it may, sheriff, Mr. Walker only wants to see this town grow. That's all. We all do, and we'll do whatever it takes to make that happen. There's nothing else to it. You're just intent on making more out of this than there is."

"Just let me keep an eye on him and I promise I'll prove it to all of you."

"I wish it were that simple, sheriff, but it isn't. Word around town is that you're a different person. They don't trust your judgement anymore."

"I can bring them around. Just give me some time."

"I'm afraid we don't have that kind of time. Salt

Creek is experiencing substantial growth. Now that the railroad comes through here, businesses want to come here, too. Salt Creek is becoming a metropolis. Why, we could be on our way to becoming another Chicago. People like Blaine Walker can make that come true."

"People like Walker prey on towns like this," Redding stated coldly, speaking a little too openly. "They're professionals. They're more experienced and they know how to operate just outside of the reach of the law. They know how to work their way into your lives and take over before you realize it. By the time you do, it's too late to do anything about it. I can prove it. I know I can."

Lucius Childers sighed heavily, his agitation building. "Why can't you just accept that Mr. Walker is nothing more than a businessman that you've grossly misjudged?"

"There's more to it than that, Lucius. I'm telling you. You'll see."

"I told you this was a waste of time, Percy," Childers erupted. "The man is beyond trying to reason with."

Redding waited for their approval, though he doubted he would be convincing enough to get it at this point. He looked over the troubled faces of the three men and knew that there was something they weren't telling him. "I appreciate you coming over to talk to me about your concerns, but I don't think you gentlemen came over here just to tell me that, did you? There's more to it than that, am I right?"

Childers and Brewer exchanged looks with the third man, Cal Holder, head of the town council, who had not yet spoken. "No, sheriff," Holder finally spoke up. "We didn't."

"Well then, Percy, why don't you gentlemen respect me enough to just come right out and tell me why you're here."

Cal Holder stiffened before he spoke. "Alright, we will. I'm sorry to have to tell you this, sheriff, but I'm afraid we're going to have to take your badge."

Redding sat back in his chair, though not surprised at their intentions. "Is this because of the attack at the train depot? Or is it because Walker has won all of you over with his charm?"

"It's a compilation of many things, sheriff," Holder replied. "It's the assault on the man at the train depot and the assault on Walker. It's also your fixation on a man who clearly has done nothing wrong in the eyes of the law and in the eyes of everyone in town. Your fascination with Blaine Walker can't be overlooked anymore. The man deserves to be left alone and free of harassment. You've shown us that you aren't capable of complying with such a request."

Redding scoffed softly. "So, that's it? Nobody

bothers to look at the good I've done? I make a couple of mistakes and suddenly I'm no longer fit to hold the job? Everybody makes mistakes, but I guess in the grand scheme of things none of that matters now, does it? You've all made up your minds. The problem is, you're all wrong. You just can't see it yet."

The men stood silent, not knowing what to say to him. Redding removed the badge from his vest and tossed it onto the desk as he stood and grabbed his hat and coat and headed for the door.

"It's nothing personal, sheriff," Percy Bowers added in an attempt to soften the blow.

The comment caused Redding to stop at the door and glance back at him. "I don't think you can call me that anymore, Percy."

CHAPTER 22

VINCE REDDING CRADLED A SMALL GLASS OF WHISKEY as he stared off into nothing, slowly tilting the glass slightly to splash the last swallow of liquid from side to side before he downed it in one single gulp. He slammed the empty glass down on the table harder than he anticipated, unknowingly drawing the attention of the Palladium Saloon's owner and bartender, Stan Granger, who had been keeping a watchful eye on the man since his entering the place. The burly man finished wiping the glass he had most recently been working on and flung the cloth over his shoulder as he rounded the end of the bar and walked over to his friend's table.

"You okay, sheriff?" Granger's booming voice echoed despite his attempts to keep it quiet.

"I'm not the sheriff anymore, Stan," Redding

confessed softly as he poured himself another shot full. "I'm just another regular customer coming in here to drink, just like everybody else."

"What are you talking about?" Granger asked.

Redding pulled back the lapel of his coat back to show Granger that he was not wearing a badge. "They took it from me."

"Who's 'they'?" Granger questioned, still brandishing a confused look. "Why would they do that?"

Redding shook his head as he tossed back the whiskey without hesitation. "It doesn't matter, Stan," he spoke, pulling the taste deep into his gut. "They got what they wanted. They wanted me out of here, out of the way, where I couldn't cause any trouble. They wanted me quiet. Well, they got it."

"Sheriff… I mean, why? I don't understand."

"I rubbed them the wrong way," Redding professed. "I had it in for Blaine Walker and they let me go over it. Well, that's fine. They can have him. Let him take over Abigail Bartlett. Let him take over the J.B. Bar. Hell, let him take over this whole stinking town, for all I care. I tried to warn them, but they just wouldn't listen."

"Who, sheriff?" Granger asked while pulling out a chair next to Redding and sat. "Who wouldn't listen?"

"The town council, for one. The mayor," Redding

scoffed. "Even my own wife is against me on this one."

"Grace isn't against you, sheriff. Grace loves you."

"She let 'em get to her, Stan. I tried to tell her, and them, and even Abigail Bartlett, that Walker is no good, but nobody will listen to me. But they'll see that I'm right. You wait. It'll be too late, but in the end, they'll see."

"Why don't you go home, sheriff, and spend some time with Grace?" Granger suggested. "All of this will blow over. You'll see."

"I can't go home," Redding admitted under his breath. "We had an argument. I needed to get out of there to cool off before I said something I'd regret."

"Well, that's the smart thing to do. Stay as long as you like, sheri…" Granger caught himself before he could finish. "I can't get used to not calling you that."

Redding slid his chair back and stood, fishing a couple of coins from his pocket and handing them to Granger. "Well, you'd better get used to it." He patted the big man on the shoulder as he passed him. "Thanks for lending me your ear."

Vince Redding stepped out onto the boardwalk, the brisk, steady wind immediately forcing him to cinch his coat up closer to his neck as he shrugged his shoulders to contain what little body heat he still had. He had to gather his things from his old office and then he could head home, despite what he had just told Granger. Knowing Grace like he did, she would have calmed down, too, and they could start to put all of this behind them.

He entered the sheriff's office. It was the first time he had done so since being fired. It suddenly felt strange to be there, an odd feeling considering he had spent so much time there. But he was no longer welcome there. He was in the process of stuffing his clothes into his saddlebags when he heard the front door open. His suspicions were confirmed when his stirring brought Deputy Clint McNeil to the doorway to check on him.

"Hey… there," McNeil fumbled his words with an uneasy pause.

"I know. You don't know what to call me," Redding chuckled softly. "That seems to be the problem with everyone."

"It just doesn't seem right not to call you 'sheriff.'"

"I know," Redding replied. "It's all I've known for what seems like a long time. It'll take some getting used to."

"So, what do you do now?" McNeil asked.

"I'm not sure. I guess I could try my hand at ranching. I do own some land, y'know, and I'm not without experience. I just never thought I'd have to go back to it as my primary occupation, especially this soon."

"If there's anything I can do, just let me know," McNeil offered.

"Thanks," Redding responded before he turned and smiled at the young man. "So, have they found my replacement yet?"

A look of despair came over McNeil's face as he slowly pulled back his coat to reveal the sheriff's badge pinned on his vest. "They said it's just temporary, for now," McNeil said, trying to dismiss the appointment as much as possible, "Until they can find a replacement for you. Said I was too young to take over permanently, which is fine with me. I didn't want it, believe me, not even temporarily, but they didn't really give me a choice. They told me if I wanted to keep working here, I had to agree to it until they could come up with someone else."

Redding could see how uncomfortable talking about it was to the young man, so he tried to put him at ease. "Yeah, they like to do that. It's okay, Clint. I'm not mad, if that's what you're concerned about. I don't doubt that you can handle it. You know the job and you're definitely qualified. The question is: are you up to it?"

"Yes, sir. I just don't like seeing you without this badge. It rightfully belongs to you."

"Well, the town council didn't see it that way," Redding stated. "They think they're doing what's best for the town, but they're gonna see that they were wrong." Redding picked up his saddlebags and tossed them over his shoulder. "Well, it's not my problem anymore, Clint," he said as he walked past McNeil, patting him on the shoulder with a slight smile. "Now, it's yours."

The sun had just set, majestically retreating below the mountaintops and ushering in the night. The weather had turned cold recently; the evenings forcing those wandering about into heavier coats as an inkling of the first possible snow threatened to make an appearance sometime in the near future.

Grace pulled the shades after taking a final glance out onto the land while it was still dipped in the remnants of light that had not already spilled over the mountaintops. Vince might have been agitated when he left the night before, but he still had made sure to leave her plenty of firewood before he had gone to spend the night in the sheriff's office. She had expected no less from the man.

The discussion had marked a milestone for the young couple. It had been their first argument since being together. She knew that eventually the time would come when they would disagree on a matter, even the elder women in town had warned her of its coming, no matter how solid the relationship was, but she had hoped they were wrong or that that time

would be considerably farther down the road. This
was an uncomfortable feeling, one that she did not
care for. She could not imagine being at odds with
her husband. He might have been obstinate, but he
was still a good man. A kind man. And he loved her
more than she could ever imagine, and she loved
him. But here they were. Him sleeping at the sheriff's office and her tidying up the house in anticipation of him returning once he had cooled off
enough. Since she had no frame of reference, she
had no idea when that might be.

She had made herself a winter stew with some of
the venison they had stored away from his last
hunting expedition, the smell of the game perme-
ating the entire dwelling and causing her stomach to
growl as it anticipated its taking. She had not eaten
alone very often, only when Vince's job had required
it of him and had taken him away from her. But this
time was different. He had left on his own and not
from a call of duty, and she had no idea when he
would return. She assumed it would be soon, hoped
it would be, but she was unsure since they had never
been faced with this type of situation before. *He
would be home soon*, she kept telling herself. *He just
needed to cool off. Then he would come back to her.*

She could hear that the wind was picking up
outside, the stirrings of the cooler air filtering
through the gap under the front door and chilling

her feet. She had asked Vince several times to fix such a gap, but he had yet to do so. It would be the first thing she asked of him when he returned, after she gave him a big apologetic hug.

She had dished out a generous portion of the stew, taking in its wafting aroma as she walked it over from the stove to the chair across from the fireplace where she could sit quietly as a steady blaze warmed her on the outside while the stew did likewise to her insides. She sampled a spoonful after cooling it slightly, enjoying its generous and robust taste. *This was Vince's favorite. He'll be sorry he missed such a treat.*

She was bringing another spoonful to her mouth, blowing on it to cool it as she did so when she thought she heard the faint whinny of a horse. *He was home. Just in time to eat with her.*

She sat her bowl down on the end table and wiped her mouth with her apron as she walked to the door, a sense of relief overtaking her. "I was hoping you'd come home soon," she spoke with a smile as she opened the door to see Ike Harrington sitting on his horse just beyond the hitching rail.

Grace froze.

CHAPTER 23

Ike Harrington sat atop his horse; a sinister smile spread over his face as he took in her features. "Well, well, looky here," he uttered casually. "Looks like the sheriff did pretty well for himself."

Grace tried to remain as calm as possible, suppressing her panic as best as she could. She knew men like this. They fed off of the fear of others, even reveled in doing so. But she would do her best not to give him the satisfaction. The more frightened he believed her to be, the worse the situation would become and the greater the danger she would be placing herself in. "Can I help you?" she finally asked, with subdued anxiety, after taking in a full, deep breath.

Harrington slowly climbed down, not willing or wanting to take his eyes off the woman. She was attractive, that much was for sure. She could feel his glare covering her. The thought of it almost made her nauseous. "I don't suppose your husband is home," he stated calmly, "or else you wouldn't be the one answering the door."

Grace tried to remain cool, firming up her stance to ward off her fears. "He's not here right now, but I'm expecting him any minute."

"Now, Mrs. Redding, we both know that's a lie," Harrington said calmly, all the while he continued slowly walking towards the front door. Grace partially pulled it to as a precaution but had not closed it. "It's almost dark. Now, why would your husband not be home this late in the day, especially since he no longer has a job to keep him away?"

Grace had opened her mouth to respond but was caught off-guard by the comment. Harrington caught the surprised look on her face. "You look surprised," he added before it occurred to him that this was something she was not aware of. "Oh, you mean, you don't know? Redding is no longer the sheriff, honey. They fired him."

Grace took in a deep breath as she stood defiantly. "I… I don't believe you."

"You don't have to take my word for it," Harrington proclaimed with a building arrogance while taking a few more cautious steps. "Ask him yourself. I'm sure he wouldn't lie to a pretty little thing like you."

"I will, when he comes home," she replied, becoming increasingly nervous as his approach continued. "That's far enough," she finally warned.

Harrington stopped his movements. "Do I make you nervous, Mrs. Redding? What are you gonna do if I don't stop? Throw a frying pan at me because you don't have a gun on you? Unless you have one tucked away somewhere under that pretty little dress of yours. Y'know what? Maybe I should just pat you down, for my own safety, just to make sure. What do you think?"

"Don't you dare even think about putting your hands on me," she threatened, as she secretly fought for courage.

"Too late," he answered as he lunged for her. She tried to slip back inside the doorway and slam the door shut, but she had allowed him to come too close and Harrington slid his foot in the opening and prevented it from closing, wedging it between the door and the frame. She struggled to push it closed, but his foot was preventing it until he could brace himself enough to forcibly push it open with his shoulder, throwing her back onto the floor in the process. She whipped her head around to see him stepping inside and slowly closing the door behind him, still watching her carefully. He quickly accessed the room, glancing around it for weapons and continued walking towards her as she slid across the floor with her hands behind her, afraid to take her eyes off of him.

"That wasn't very lady-like, Mrs. Redding," Harrington joked with a weak smile as he toyed with her.

"You stay away from me," Grace warned him, her fear turning to anger as she continued slowly sliding backward. "You touch me and my husband will kill you."

By now, Harrington had closed the gap between them considerably and was right in front of her. "I'd like to see him try it," he boasted. "It'd give me a reason to kill him, not that I need one."

"You've got it all wrong. He'll kill you, and I look forward to watching him do it," she replied, her anger swelling and giving her more resistance. The insult tore away at his pride. It implied that Redding was faster than him. That was when Harrington hit her.

He swung the back of his hand without warning, catching her on the mouth and splitting her lips in several places. She tasted the coppery taste of her own blood and slid back once more, but Harrington was right on top of her as he brutally slapped her across the face again, this time with his right hand. The popping sound was almost as painful to hear as the blow was as her head was flung backwards. She grunted from the impact, trying to regain her senses before he was on her again. As he reached for her, she faked being incoherent and waited for him to get close enough to allow her to kick him in the groin as hard as her position on the floor would allow her.

Harrington groaned loudly, his legs having partially collapsed, his body somewhat buckling. When she tried to make a run for the door, Harrington was in the way and reached out for her, grabbing her by the arm and pulling her closer to him. His rage erupted as he swung the back of his left hand solidly against her face, snapping her head backwards so harshly that she feared it might break her neck. The blow knocked her back onto the floor. Still grimacing from the pain of being kicked in his groin, Harrington took the opportunity and jumped on top of her, pinning her arms to the floor next to her head as she fought back with everything she had left in her. His teeth were gritted, his eyes wide with rage as he looked down at her bloodied face.

"I was just to going to rough you up a bit, but you left me with no choice trying to hurt me like that!" He swung a hard right, catching the side of her cheek and splitting it, his anger feeding off of her helplessness. The punch rattled her senses and made her brain foggy. She was helpless to stop him. She feared he would kill her before he realized how much he was hurting her.

He struck her again with a left and then followed it up with a stinging right. He wanted to do more to her, but began to worry that she might have been right about Redding returning soon. The last thing he needed was to have to confront and kill Redding in his own home. That would mean he would have to kill his wife, too, and that would bring unnecessary heat down on Blaine Walker, something that Walker would not put up with. It would be better for him to wait and kill Redding somewhere else, so it would be less likely to be linked directly to Walker. Besides, he was sure he had made his point by beating her.

With Grace lying limp on the floor, having succumbed to her beating, Harrington slowly stood while gingerly nursing his groin. He stepped from over her and had looked down at her battered face covered in blood when the anger of what she had done to him took over his discomfort and got the better of him and he kicked her violently in the side. Grace grunted loudly over the sound of breaking ribs, her breathing instantly challenged as she fought for air. She was partially rolling on the floor as she favored her side and began to cry through the intense pain, her face already beginning to swell.

Harrington looked around the home and located

a dish towel, which he used to wipe the sweat from his face that his abuse had generated before tossing it onto the floor. He was turning to grab his hat from off of the floor when he spotted Redding's new Barlow knife that Grace had given him, sitting on the table. He admired it briefly, smiling at the initials, knowing that taking it would agitate Redding, and slipped it into his pocket as a memento before retrieving his hat.

"You're lucky, Mrs. Redding," he advised her as he smoothed back his hair with one hand while he donned his hat with the other. "I had planned on spending more time with you, but I don't need your husband catching me here right now, since killing both of you would mess things up for my employer. But tell him now that he's no longer sheriff, he has no need to keep after Blaine Walker." He turned to leave, but stopped short and turned back to face her. "Oh, and tell him if he tries to pin any of this on Mr. Walker, neither of you will ever live long enough to see it go anywhere."

Harrington walked through the still open door and climbed into the saddle. Grace could not sit up enough to make sure Harrington had left, but the creaking of the leather saddle and the soft whinnying of the horse told her that her attacker had ridden away, leaving Grace lying on the floor, crying and writhing in pain. She tried to get up, but the stabbing pain in her side was unbearable and she quickly collapsed onto her back before she could even place an arm under her.

At some point, she lost consciousness.

Vince Redding was puzzled.

As he neared his home, he noticed that he could see the inside light too clearly and saw the front door standing open, as a sick feeling suddenly came over him. He instantly kicked the roan into action, galloping the remainder of the way to his home and sliding out of the saddle before the roan even had a chance to come to a stop. He rushed inside to find Grace severely beaten and lying on the floor, unresponsive, her breathing shallow and weak.

"Grace!" he shouted as he collapsed onto the floor and scooped her up in his arms. The sudden stabbing of pain from being moved abruptly startled her awake as she screamed from the agony of her broken ribs.

"Oh, my God, Grace!" he screamed again, gingerly holding her in his arms and relaxing his hold on her. She began crying profusely as he lightly moved the stray strands of hair from her face that were attached to it with dried blood from her facial wounds and exposed the extent of her wounds. "Stay with me, Grace. Please, stay with me." He felt helpless as he looked down at her swollen, bleeding face and began to cry.

"Who did this to you?" he asked through sobbing tears, but Grace was in too much pain to answer with more than painful moans as she floated dangerously close to death. He scooped her up into his arms and carefully walked over to the roan, grabbing the horse's reins and leading it into the barn. After gently laying Grace down on a busted bale of hay he quickly hitched the wagon to the roan and padded the seat with all of the extra saddles blankets he could find before carefully laying Grace across the seat and then climbing onto it himself, lifting her head to rest it in his lap as he urged the roan into movement.

As he pulled away into the chilly night, his thoughts were focused solely on Grace. It pained him to see her so feeble. So fragile. So close to dying. *Who would do such a thing to a woman?* Whoever it was, they would have to be twisted, twisted and dark, unlike anyone he had ever encountered. He had seen some rough men in his time, ruthless and uncaring men who could easily kill a man without any remorse, but this was something entirely different. The individual responsible for this was cold and obviously had no respect for human life of any kind. To beat up a woman was unforgivable, but to do so to such an extent with their bare hands was something unimaginable, no matter who it was.

Redding wiped away the tears creeping down his face and took in a deep breath to compose himself. He did not want her to see him so broken apart, should she wake. He stole a glance at her to check to make sure she was still breathing as he continued towards town, worried the entire trip that she might not make it that far. But she had to make it.

She just had to.

CHAPTER 24

THE SOUND OF THE WAGON CAREENING DOWN THE street and Redding calling out commands to urge the animal on broke the silence of Salt Creek. The few townspeople who were still out and about in the evening stopped to catch a glimpse of the wagon as it rounded the last corner before reaching the office of Doctor Hastings. Redding pulled back sharply on the reins while stomping the brake, sliding the wagon to a stop and jumping down in one swift motion. He hurried around and scooped Grace up to carry her to the office door, where he began furiously kicking it until he saw a light coming from the back room into the front parlor. A second later, Doc Hastings opened it as Redding pushed past him and entered, with Hastings following right behind him before the doctor could ask what had happened.

"Bring her in here," he said, ushering Redding into the examination room and motioning for him to lay her down on the table. Hastings gently nudged Redding out of the way and began working on Grace, while Redding tried to slip past him and look over his shoulder, though his crowding was interfering with Hasting's work. "Vince, I need you to go wait in the parlor," Hastings finally confessed, prompting Redding to reluctantly leave his wife in the doctor's hands and sit alone to find out her fate.

The time dragged by as he waited anxiously for some report on Grace's condition, trying to keep his courage up while preparing himself to fear the worst. A thousand responses concerning her condition came to mind, none of them appealing. He fought back the disparaging thoughts as he tried to maintain his composure. It took everything he had in him not to rush back and be by her side in the event that she somehow miraculously woke up. He had to be sure to be there if she opened her eyes again, and he would need to see her again if she didn't. It was over an hour later before Doc Hastings appeared in the doorway, wiping away the labored and worrisome sweat that had beaded his forehead from his efforts. Redding jumped to his feet in anticipation of his report.

"She was beaten pretty severely, but I think I finally got her stable, at least for now," Doc Hastings informed him in a somber tone. "She's still in a lot of pain, so I gave her some laudanum to help her rest. I have to be honest with you, Vince. I don't know for sure, either way. The next twenty-four hours are going to be crucial as to how extensive the damage is, or," Doc Hastings hesitated, "if she will even make it."

The horrid words beat down on Redding, who felt as if he would vomit. *This couldn't be happening. This was all his fault. She had been beaten because of him. No, she had been beaten because of Blaine Walker.*

His rage swelled up inside of him, almost choking him. It was one thing to take a shot at him on the road, but to go into his home and viciously assault his wife, someone who had nothing to do with any of this, was wrong. It was so wrong.

"Can I see her?" Redding asked timidly, his spirit and his bravery being put to the test.

"Yes, but only for a few minutes. Her body has been through a lot and, more than anything, she needs to rest now. Don't try to talk to her. She's delirious and it'll only confuse and upset her. That's what she doesn't need right now. I doubt her swollen jaw and mouth would allow her to form any recognizable words, anyway. Alright?" Doc Hastings waited until Redding nodded simply, his face etched with worry and fear before he led him into the back room. The scene horrified him.

Grace was laying under a thin blanket, her face cleaned up enough for him to see the extensive bruising and swelling she had suffered. She looked so much worse just from the time he had brought her in to see the doctor. Redding was stunned and taken back by her appearance, the swelling making her look like a corpse or, at the very least, someone he didn't recognize. Her left eye was swollen shut and her lips were swollen from bruising and bleeding. He couldn't believe he was looking at her in this condition.

"It doesn't even look like her," he spoke softly, not able to take his eyes off of her.

"She took a lot of abuse, that's for sure. Someone was really out to hurt her. It's a miracle they didn't kill her."

"Looks like they were trying to."

"Any idea who it was?"

Redding shook his head gently, still unable to take his eyes off of Grace. "No. They were already gone when I found her."

"I heard what they did to you," Doc Hastings said, surprising Redding by changing the subject. "Taking your badge from you the way they did. That wasn't right."

"They don't see it that way."

"They've made a big mistake."

Redding motioned at Grace. "Now they've made two."

"Why would anyone do this? It's so senseless."

"They think I'm out to get Blaine Walker."

"Are you?"

"I was out to prove that he isn't who he seems. I guess it came back to bite me. Of course, I also gave them plenty to use against me."

"I heard about the assault at the train station. Can't say I blame you. I probably would have done the same thing that you did."

"Then you're the only one. I also assaulted Walker."

"I heard about that, too. Knowing you like I do, I'm sure you had a good reason for doing it."

"Apparently not good enough to warrant beating the man."

"Everybody makes mistakes. You've done a lot for this town, Vince," Hastings said poignantly. "Too bad they can't look past a few indiscretions and see that. If they could, maybe you could be sheriff again."

"I can't worry about me getting my old job back right now. I need to find out who did this to Grace." Redding walked into the parlor, followed by Doc Hastings.

"Don't worry about moving her. It wouldn't be wise, anyway. She can stay here for a few days," Hastings offered, keeping his voice low in case

Grace was coherent enough to listen in. "I need to keep a close eye on her anyway, to make sure she doesn't suffer any setbacks. She needs constant care."

"Doc, I don't know how to repay you for all this. Thank you."

"You can thank me by not getting yourself killed. Grace is going to need you for her recovery once she's out of the woods."

Redding feared asking what he was about to ask. "Level with me, doc. What are her chances?"

"Fair to possibly good, if I had to bet on it. She's young and in good health, so she has that going for her. I won't know if there's any damage to her brain until she wakes up. That's my main concern at this point. I know this is an odd thing to say, but she's really lucky, Vince. Whoever beat her stopped at the right time. She couldn't have endured much more. A few more blows like the ones she sustained and she would have never made it and if she had, she would never be the same again."

"Thanks again, doc," Redding replied, offering his hand. "I'll come by and check on her tomorrow morning."

"Go get some rest. I promise I'll take good care of her."

Redding passed the man a faint, concerned smile and walked outside, gathering his coat to face the chilly evening. Nudging the roan gently towards home, he worried about having to leave her behind, but at least she was in the best hands anywhere around. He trusted Doc Hastings. In fact, Hastings was probably the only one he could trust.

He would go home tonight, though he doubted he would get much sleep. He was too worried about Grace and if she would recover.

He couldn't rest, anyway.

He had men to kill.

Vince Redding awoke the following morning and skipped eating to get to Doc Hastings' office as early as possible. When Hastings motioned him into the back room, Redding stopped short at the sight of his wife.

Grace was laying asleep, her face so distorted from bruising and swelling that he didn't recognize her. He had to fight back the instinct to break down, not wanting to do so for fear that he would not be able to regather himself. He reached down, softly holding her hand as he fought back the tears.

"I know it looks bad, but I think she's past the worst of it," Doc Hastings said as he tried comforting him. "I know I said give it twenty-four hours, but she seems to have stabilized sooner than I expected, which is a good sign that the possibility of permanent damage is lowered."

"It doesn't surprise me. She's a strong woman," Redding added, without taking his eyes off of her.

"Yeah, she is," Hastings agreed with a nod. "Thank goodness."

"Can I stay in here with her for a while?"

"Sure," Doc Hastings answered. "Take as much time as you need."

Redding gently nodded his appreciation and stood over Grace, holding her hand and wishing she would wake and prove to be alright as he continued watching over her. He would gladly have taken her place if he had been given the chance. She had endured so much punishment for him. It wasn't fair. It wasn't right. And he would make sure that it did not happen again, and that whoever did this to her would pay.

After some time, it was clear that Grace was not going to awaken anytime soon. As Doc Hastings had warned him, she needed her rest. He was relieved to have heard the good news about her recovery, which was as good as could be expected, given her circumstances. He waited a little longer and conceded to the notion that she would remain unconscious for quite some time. After thanking Doc Hastings for his help, Redding left the doctor's office and stepped out onto the boardwalk, embracing the chilled morning air. He wasn't concerned with eating, but he knew he needed to keep up his strength in case something happened.

He walked over to the restaurant and ate a late lunch, chatting with the owner, Millie Williamson, about Grace's condition. By now, the entire town was engulfed in gossip about what had happened to her. Good. He wanted to make sure Blaine Walker wasn't hiding behind the secret. Everyone needed to know what had happened and that this time, Redding wasn't making it up.

Upon leaving the restaurant, Redding couldn't help but go back to check on Grace. Doc Hastings had to leave to go out to a ranch to check on another patient, leaving Redding alone with Grace. He remained there until Hastings returned a few hours later.

At the urging of Hastings, Redding was finally persuaded to go and get away for a while, to try to give himself a break from the stress of waiting for Grace to awaken. He reluctantly agreed, but only with the understanding that he would be back later, which Doc Hastings agreed to.

Redding left the doctor's office, not sure where to go from there, although he had a good idea where he needed to go next. He needed answers. Answers about Grace. After what had happened to her, he deserved them. She deserved them. A flood of thoughts was going through his mind and all of them involved Blaine Walker. He knew it was a bad idea and one that would surely bring him trouble, but he couldn't put it off any longer. He needed to go pay a visit to Walker.

And he was going to make sure that it wasn't going to be a pleasant one.

CHAPTER 25

Will Spurlock tossed in his bed, unable to sleep, something that was uncharacteristic of him.

He had been having trouble sleeping since being ambushed, forcing him to break down his camp outside of town and move into the Imperial Hotel, down the hall from Walker. He had told Walker that he wanted to have better security versus being a target out in the open, but the truth was he wanted to be nearer to Walker to keep an eye on him until all this was over. He kept running it through his mind. *Keep your friends close and your enemies closer.* He couldn't prove it, but deep down, he knew Walker had something to do with his attack.

The shooting had changed him. He worried that he was no longer as confident as he was before. He was not meant to be on the receiving end of a bullet.

Of course, he had been shot at before. That was nothing new. But this was different. This time not only had he not been the aggressor, but he had unwillingly lowered his guard enough that it almost got him killed. That was not like him. Why had he been so careless? That was out of character for him, and it was a good way for a hired gun to get himself killed. Going after someone and gunning them down for profit was who he was and how he had chosen to live. Until now, it had not affected him. This, hiding away like this, was not him, and he hated being forced to live like it.

He sat up in his bed, the incessant throbbing of the fresh wound on the side of his head immediately drawing his attention and his annoyance. The shot had been close, a little too close for his liking, in fact, closer than anytime he had ever been shot at. Although he despised the idea of being forced to live out of a hotel room, he had no choice. Until he pieced together who was trying to kill him, or prove who he suspected it to be, he needed to have as much protection as possible and, unfortunately, being in a hotel was the best way to ensure that.

He found himself on edge, something that he was not accustomed to. Although he couldn't prove it, deep down, he knew that Harrington was responsible for the ambush. Walker had done this to him. Walker had Harrington bring him out into the open, like an exposed nerve, where he was not comfortable being and where he was suddenly, and uncharacteristically vulnerable. He was not meant to be a target, and frankly, he hated it.

Harrington had obviously been given the task of killing him, ordered to do so at the direction of Walker. Spurlock was a good dozen years older than Harrington and, though he was more seasoned with a gun than Harrington, he was also showing his age and feared he could also be losing his edge. Slowing down was a hired gun's worst nightmare and one that they knew would, sooner or later, inevitably catch up to every one of them. The problem was that most hired guns only found out when that time was when they were gunned down by someone younger and faster. The goal was to retire and disappear from the public eye and from the sights of the next group of hired guns coming up and looking to make a name for themselves before that happened. But now, he felt trapped.

Had he waited too long?

Spurlock walked over to the bowl on the basin and doused his face with cool water to shake away the sleep-deprived fatigue that was consuming him. He looked at himself in the mirror, wondering. So far, he had been given very little to do for Blaine Walker. It was unlike any job he had ever been hired for. Was that on purpose or were his skills being held in reserve until something bigger was needed of him?

Spurlock was getting antsy. The longer he stayed there in the hotel, the less his patience was holding out. He wasn't accustomed to being inside like this and it was already starting to wear on him. He needed to get out of the room and clear his head, so he decided to go downstairs to get a breather.

As he stepped out onto the boardwalk, he felt an immediate sense of relief. It was as if the walls of his room had been closing in on him and now, he was being released. He took in a deep breath of the cool morning air and savored its sweetness as he glanced over the townspeople moving about on the streets. His mind was thinking about Blaine Walker and how he was going to confront him when he locked eyes with Vince Redding. Redding was across the street and several buildings down from him but had noticed seeing the man that had eluded him several days earlier by darting down between the buildings with his horse. Without hesitation, Vince Redding started towards him.

Spurlock saw Redding's movements and turned to go back inside the hotel, hoping to lose Redding by going out the back of the building and down the rear stairs to the stables for the bay. He slipped past the clerk's desk and up the stairs, paying careful attention that neither Walker nor

Harrington would emerge from Walker's room as he passed it. He made his way down the long hallway and out the back door, scaling the stairs in little time down to the alley behind. As he turned to head towards the livery stables, the sound of a gun being cocked behind him stopped him in his tracks.

"I know you're fast," Redding spoke, "but you aren't faster than a trigger being pulled. Now, grab the butt of your gun with your left hand and drop it onto the ground, slowly."

Spurlock did as he was instructed and then raised his hands as he slowly turned to face his adversary. It was the first time the two had actually met face-to- face.

"I know you. You're Redding. You used to be the town sheriff."

"I'm afraid I don't know you," Redding admitted calmly, "but I do know of you. You're Will Spurlock."

"In the flesh," Spurlock acknowledged with a slight, respectful nod as his hands began to drop slightly.

"I also know your reputation, Spurlock, so don't make me kill you before I get the answers I'm looking for."

"Fair enough," Spurlock conceded as he raised his hands back to their original positions. "What can I do for you, Redding?"

"You can start by telling me what you know about the attack on my wife."

"Well, then, this is going to be a short conversation because I don't know anything about that."

"I'm not saying you did it, but I know you know who was responsible. I just want their name and you can be on your way."

"Now, why would you be willing to let me go? Aren't you at least mildly curious about why I came to town?"

"If I had to guess, I'd say Blaine Walker brought you here to get rid of me."

"What if I told you that you were right? Would you gun me down right here and now?"

"I'm not a cold-blooded killer like you, Spurlock. If I draw on you, it'll be a fair fight. Right now, I just want answers."

"What makes you think I know anything?" Spurlock asked suspiciously, unsure of what Redding knew.

"Because you work for Walker, and *he* does. I know he's calling all the shots."

"Then you should be talking to him, not me."

"We don't get along. That's why I'm talking to you."

"I can't help you, Redding," Spurlock said solidly.

"Can't, or won't?" Redding noted. "I see you moved into the Imperial. Now, I was thinking: why would a hired gun do that? Seems like a man of your reputation would want to put as much distance between you and the law as possible, and yet here you are living in a room right around the corner from his office. Could it have anything to do with you being ambushed and almost killed the other day? And don't try to deny it didn't happen because I know better," Redding added as he motioned to the gash on the side of Spurlock's head.

Spurlock's body tensed from the comment. He had worried that word of his encounter with the hired assassin would get out, and it had. Now, he had to try to deal with the fallout that it had created, a fallout that could easily jeopardize his movements. "What do you know about that?"

"It's all over town, Spurlock," Redding insisted. "Everyone's talking about it. You're a hot topic for the townspeople, and one that concerns them. Till now, they only had to worry about the risk of your kind arriving to help take over the town. Now, they know that time has come and they're wondering how they're going to deal with it."

"Redding, your problem is that you give the townspeople too much credit."

"And your problem is that you don't give Walker enough," Redding pointed out. "I know you worked for him, but I don't think you understand just how distrustful he is. When are you going to realize that you can't trust him? After he's gotten you killed?"

"That's a mighty big accusation, Redding," Spurlock stated boldly. "I hope you can back that up with facts."

"I think you already know the facts, Spurlock. But for some reason I just don't think you're ready to admit them to yourself."

Spurlock scoffed out loud. "Admit what, exactly? That my employer is trying to have me killed? That's absurd."

"Is it? You get shot at and then you move into the Imperial. Are you telling me that was a coincidence? You can't trust Walker and you know it. I'm telling you, if you aren't responsible for attacking my wife, then I give you my word that I'm not after you. I just want a name and I'll handle it from there."

"What makes you think I can give you a name?"

"I'm not here to play games, Spurlock. I just want a name and we can both move on."

Spurlock stood silent, quietly studying Redding. He believed what Redding was telling him, and he knew he was right. Walker clearly could not be trusted; that much was for certain. But could he divulge what he suspected and still maintain his loyalty to Walker, however fractured that loyalty might be? He knew that Harrington was likely the one who had tried to kill him and that it was likely at

the bidding of Blaine Walker. Did he really owe
either of the men any loyalty?

"Ike Harrington," Spurlock spilled after a brief
hesitation. "You need to look at him. And you never
heard it from me."

"Much obliged," Redding replied as he nodded
simply and began slowly backing away, while still
being careful to cover Spurlock with his gun.

"That's the only time I'm going to help you,
Redding," Spurlock announced calmly. "The next
time you point a gun at me, you can be sure that I'll
be pointing one back."

CHAPTER 26

DEPUTY CLINT MCNEIL MOSEYED INTO THE SHERIFF'S office just ahead of his new boss, Augustus Copeland. Both men retired their coats to the rack while Deputy McNeil started a new pot of coffee for them.

"Thanks for showing me the ropes, Clint," Copeland stated as he sat down at his new desk. "I feel better having done a set of rounds with you. I didn't know being a sheriff was so involved. I always thought it was just being a badge to keep order."

"No, there's a lot more to it than people think," McNeil reiterated as he went about filing up the coffeepot with water. "Like Sheriff Redding always said: 'being a sheriff isn't about carrying a gun; it's about building relationships.'"

"Wise man," Copeland added, noting the young man's reaction. "You miss him, don't you?"

McNeil stopped what he was doing and looked his way. "Yes, sir. I sure do. He was a good man. I don't care what they say about him. He done a lot of good for this town."

"I didn't know him personally, but I never heard bad things about him, that is, until he got into trouble. It's not fair to forget about all the good he did before that. Well, I'll try to live up to his reputation," Copeland stated.

Deputy McNeil dismissed the statement and was placing the pot on top of the stove when the office door opened and Doc Hastings emerged in the doorway. "Doc, anything wrong?" Copeland asked the man as Hastings stepped in and closed the door behind him. He shook off the chill in the air as he stepped over to the desk, facing Copeland.

"Augustus, you've got a problem."

"What's wrong?"

"It's Vince Redding," Doc Hastings noted. "His wife was severely beaten last night. She's over at my office right now. She was in pretty bad shape. In fact, she almost died."

Sheriff Copeland's attention deepened. "What about Redding?"

"I'm afraid he's gonna do something crazy and go

after Blaine Walker. He blames him for his wife getting beat."

"Does he know for a fact that Walker was behind it?"

"No, but he suspects. In Redding's eyes, that might be good enough to act upon."

Sheriff Copeland rose and donned his coat and hat. "Where's Redding now?"

"I saw him go eat at Millie's Restaurant, and then I don't know where he went from there. I assume he's going to end up at Walker's before it's over."

"I need to go warn Walker," Copeland announced. "Clint, stay here in case Redding comes by. If he does, stall him until I can make it back, or at least find out where he's headed next so I can talk to him."

"Yes sir, sheriff."

"Thanks, doc," Copeland said to Hastings as he followed the man outside. "I'm sure Redding will come back to check on his wife. When he does, let me know as soon as you can. I need to try to talk some sense into him before he goes and does something stupid."

"I will," Hastings assured him as he headed back to his office while Sheriff Copeland headed out in the direction of the Imperial Hotel.

. . .

A light tapping at the door broke Blaine Walker from his thoughts and startled him at the same time. There were only two people it could possibly be. It was either Ike Harrington coming to tell him that he had taken care of Spurlock, or it was a very angry Spurlock seeking revenge for Walker putting a contract on his head. He pulled the revolver from his waistband and stood poised behind the door.

"Yeah?"

"It's me," Harrington announced quietly through the door. Walker tucked the gun back into his waistband as he unlocked and opened the door, allowing Harrington inside before closing it back and locking it behind him.

"Harrington, what are you doing here? Is Spurlock taken care of?" he asked, hoping for the best.

"No," Harrington answered, a noticeable hint of disappointment in his voice. "I can't find him."

"What do you mean, you can't find him?" Walker asked with concern. "There's only so many places he can be."

"I know that, but that doesn't make it any easier finding him."

"Did you check the saloons?"

Harrington was annoyed by the simplicity of the question. "Yeah, I checked the saloons. Nothing. I even rode out to his camp, but he's moved it."

"That doesn't make any sense. Why would he move his camp?"

"To be careful, I guess. Once someone that's looking to hurt you knows where you're camping, you leave yourself open for an attack. Makes perfect sense to move it. That's what I would have done."

Walker was not amused by the news. "Now what do we do? I need to find him."

"He'll turn up," Harrington assured him. "It's just a matter…"

The sound of approaching footsteps jostled the two men from talking, each one straining to hear who could be outside in the hallway. Harrington motioned for Walker to go to the back of the room as he drew his revolver and hurried over to the door just as the footsteps stopped somewhere down from the door. *They heard us stop talking,* Harrington thought to himself. *That's why they stopped. They know we're listening.*

Harrington lightly grasped the doorknob and turned it slowly until the latch released and the door eased open slightly. He stepped back from the light slipping in the opening of the door into the darkness of the room and waited against the wall, but there was no movement out in the hall. His patience was wearing thin as he waited, but no one moved out in the hall. Then a man spoke up.

"Freeze, Redding," they heard him say. "Drop the gun."

Harrington and Walker heard the sound of a revolver hitting the hallway floor and then the man's voice again. "Alright, Mr. Walker. You can come on out."

Harrington nodded to Walker, who slowly walked over to the door and opened it to see Sheriff Copeland standing behind Redding, covering him with his gun. Redding had his hands up as he waited for Harrington and Walker to emerge from the room.

"Well, look who was trying to ambush me," Walker announced. "Good work, sheriff."

"You shouldn't have gone after my wife, Walker," Redding warned, his voice stiff with anger. "You have a problem with me? You take it up with me and only me. But you crossed the line this time, going after a defenseless woman, you coward."

"I didn't touch your wife, I swear it," Walker insisted.

"I think you did. I think you couldn't kill me, so you went after the one thing in this world that I care about."

"You can't prove that, Redding, and you know it. I've been in town all this time. Ask the desk clerk. Ask Wainwright over at the bank. They've both seen me here for the past two days."

"Then you sent someone to do it for you because you didn't want to get implicated in it. Either way, it all comes back to you. You might as well have beaten her yourself."

"That's a pretty big accusation, Redding," Sheriff Copeland spoke up. "I assume you have some type of proof of that."

"Mr. Redding doesn't believe in proof, sheriff," Walker said tauntingly, cutting Redding off before he could answer. "He goes off of blind faith and unfounded accusations."

"I'll have proof as soon as my wife wakes up," Redding stated boldly.

"Then come back when you do," Walker replied as he shot a look at Harrington while Harrington eyed Redding with renewed interest.

"So, you're the famous Vince Redding, the ex-sheriff," Harrington said in a mocking tone, unwilling to miss the opportunity to take a jab at Redding. He looked Redding up and down slowly. "You sure don't look like much."

"Do I know you?" an irritated Redding asked, sidestepping the insult.

"Not yet," Harrington answered confidently, "but if you keep harassing Mr. Walker, you will."

"You must be the latest hired gunman for Walker to hide behind."

The insult stung Harrington, his cocky mood

suddenly turning dark. "He isn't hiding. And neither am I."

"Well, he certainly doesn't face his enemies head-on. Tell me, in addition to your babysitting duties, do you pick up after him and do his laundry, too?"

Harrington lunged at Redding, but Walker was close enough that he managed to grab him and hold him back before he could advance towards him. Harrington's hatred was evident in his eyes and his facial expression. It was clear that he wanted Redding dead. Redding never so much as flinched, taking great pleasure in having ruffled Harrington. "You'll pay for that, Redding," Harrington warned through gritted teeth. "I promise you that. You'll pay for that kind of talk."

"Anytime you're ready," Redding replied through a stone-cold stare.

"Alright, fellas, that's enough," Sheriff Copeland said, breaking up the challenge. "Redding, you need to get out of here and stay out of here. Pick up your gun and let's go, before things get any more out of hand."

"They're already out of hand," Redding noted under his breath as he retrieved his revolver and holstered it, while Sheriff Copeland maintained his gun covering him. "But that's about to change."

"I look forward to it," Harrington added as he was pulled back into the room by Walker as the door shut. Redding turned and was escorted out of the hotel by Sheriff Copeland. Copeland stopped when they made it to the boardwalk just outside the main hotel door.

"Redding, I don't know you personally, but Deputy McNeil does, so let me give you a piece of advice. Stay away from Walker unless you have proof that he's done something wrong. You're only going to make things worse for you, not him."

"He attacked my wife, or at least he hired someone to do it for him."

Sheriff Copeland was clearly shocked by the news. "I heard your wife was attacked and I'm sorry to hear that. When did this happen?"

"Last night, before I made it home. Almost beat her to death. She's fighting for her life right now over at Doc Hastings."

Sheriff Copeland's demeanor suddenly relaxed. "I'm sorry, Redding. I really am, but you can't go off chasing and threatening Mr. Walker without proof that he did something wrong. You used to be sheriff. You know that."

Redding turned to walk away, but Copeland grabbed his arm to prevent it. "Redding, watch yourself. Blaine Walker is not the type of man you want to cross. I know he hasn't been here that long, but he's already made friends, friends in powerful positions that could make your life a living hell if they wanted to. Or possibly even end it. These men will do anything to protect what they've built."

"I appreciate your concern, sheriff, but I have to do what I can to bring Walker down before anyone else gets hurt."

"He's a dangerous man, Redding, and I can't protect you from the likes of him, and especially not from his hired guns. If you try to go after him without sufficient proof, I'll have no other choice but to bring you in."

Redding turned to face Sheriff Copeland. "You seem like a decent man, Copeland, but Blaine Walker is not only dirty, he's dangerous, just like you said. I could overlook everything else that he's done to me, but not that he tried to have my wife killed. I'm not going to let that go unpunished. Before this is over, people are going to get hurt, but that doesn't mean that it must include you."

"As much as I agree with you, as the former lawman in this town, you, of all people, know I can't just stand by and allow that to happen. I wouldn't be doing my job if I did."

"Then go ahead and do your job, sheriff," Redding advised him. "But when you do, just make sure you stay out of my way."

CHAPTER 27

BLAINE WALKER LEFT SHERIFF COPELAND AND
Vince Redding in the hallway as he slammed the
door to his room shut and whipped around to
face Harrington, enraged and looking for
answers. "What in the hell is Redding talking
about? What was that about his wife being
beaten?"

"I worked his wife over for 'ya pretty good,"
Harrington bragged. "I gotta tell 'ya, I kinda enjoyed
it."

"You idiot!" Walker shouted, trying to suppress
his rage so no one outside of the room could hear.
"Are you *trying* to get me arrested?"

"Relax," Harrington replied dismissively. "I made
sure you aren't involved in this."

"I hired you, you idiot! Of course, I'm involved!

They'll see that I paid you to work on my behalf! What you do comes back directly to me!"

"No one saw me," Harrington argued. "They can't prove I was there."

"You fool, when Redding's wife wakes up, she'll be able to identify you! And then what?! They'll come straight to me asking questions!"

"Then we make sure she doesn't wake up."

Walker had turned to pace the floor, but immediately turned back at hearing the comment. "Are you out of your mind? You're talking about going into the doctor's office and killing his patient right there in front of him!"

"You got a better answer?"

Walker wanted to say something, but he was at a loss for words. Nothing seemed to be the answer to this problem. Walker tried to calm himself down as best he could. "I can't have Redding's wife pointing you out as her attacker. It'll ruin me for sure."

"So, what are you gonna do? Have Spurlock kill me like you wanted me to kill him? Y'know, Spurlock and I should both be concerned. You seem to only be loyal to the person who can help you out at the time, whoever that turns out to be."

Walker was taken back by the comment. "What are you saying? You saying you can't trust me?"

"All I'm saying is that when you didn't like what Spurlock was doing, you wanted to have him killed,"

Harrington stated boldly. "Now, you don't like what I did and you're implying the same thing should happen to me."

"I never said I wanted to have you killed."

Harrington shook his head as he answered. "You didn't say that you didn't."

Walker began pacing the floor again, his mind racing to come up with a solution that would benefit them both. Finally, he stopped and faced Harrington. "There's a way out of this for both of us."

"Go ahead. I'm all ears."

"We pin the assault of Redding's wife on Spurlock," Walker announced proudly.

Harrington's confusion showed. "How's that going to work? Redding's wife will finger me, not Spurlock."

"*He* doesn't know that. We let him believe that Redding's wife is accusing him of being her attacker. He'll kill her to shut her up and then he's on the hook for murder. He'll profess his innocence right up to when they hang him."

"How can you be sure Spurlock will be willing to kill Redding's wife just to shut her up when he knows it's not true?"

"Because he told me as much," Walker confessed. "He told me himself that he had no problem killing a woman. And he's very protective of his reputation. If word got out that he beat up a woman, even if it weren't true, it would ruin his business. Believe me, he isn't about to let anything, or anyone, do that to him. Even if it means having to kill a woman."

After leaving from his failed confrontation with Blaine Walker, Vince Redding went straight back to Doc Hastings' office to check on Grace. The doctor motioned him back to see her still sleeping.

"How's she doing?" he asked, unsure if he wanted to hear the answer.

"She's not out of the woods yet, but she's holding her own," Hastings advised him. "She still needs plenty of rest and care."

"When can I take her home?"

"She's starting to come to some, and she's been half drifting in and out of consciousness over the last hour or so. I expect her to be waking soon. If she does and she appears to check out okay, then it means the worst is over and you can take her home, provided you let me know as soon as anything changes with her."

"You've got my word, doc," Redding agreed wholeheartedly. "I'll watch over her like a hawk until she's better. Don't have much else to do these days."

"Just have a seat out there and let me keep an eye on her to see if she wakes up."

An exhausted Redding nodded his understanding

and took a seat out in the waiting room and waited as instructed. He was nudged awake some time later by Doc Hastings. "She's awake", Hastings informed him, prompting Redding to jump up from his chair.

"How long have I been asleep?" he asked, while rubbing the drowsiness away from his eyes.

"Couple of hours," Hastings replied. "You obviously needed it," he added as they entered the exam room, where he saw Grace look his way when she saw his movement. Though her left eye was still swollen shut, both of her eyes immediately filled with tears as she lost her composure at seeing him. He leaned over and hugged her, being careful not to push too hard on her injured side.

"How are you feeling?" he asked quietly as he tried to ignore the injuries to her face.

"Sore," was all she could reply as she fought to control her tears.

"Are you ready to go home?" She nodded yes, breaking out into more crying as she hugged him again. "Grace, who did this to you?" he asked when they had separated again.

"I… didn't know him," she answered. "He didn't say his name or why he was doing what he did. He just said he was looking to kill you."

"I'll find out who it is, Grace. I promise."

She reached down and grabbed his forearm, holding onto it tightly. "No, Vince. That's exactly what they want. They're using me to get to you. They're counting on you to make a mistake that they can use to their advantage. They want to get you angry enough to give them a reason to kill you. Don't give them the satisfaction."

"They already had enough reason to try to kill me, Grace, but I'm not letting them get away with this."

"And where does it end, Vince? With you dead? Why don't we just sell the house and the land and move away from here. We'll go somewhere they can't find us. We'll change our names if we have to."

"I'm not uprooting our lives just because of them. Everything we own is here. Our lives are here. I'm not running, Grace. It's not fair, and it's not right."

"No, it's not, but at least we'll be alive and together."

"I'm sorry, grace, but I can't let them get away with this. I have to put an end to it right now so we won't have to run." He then turned to Doc Hastings. "Is she okay to go home, doc?"

"Besides the obvious facial contusions, she has a concussion and some broken ribs, but I think she's good enough for a wagon ride home, as long as you agree to take it slow getting her there. But that's it, understand? She's to go straight to bed, and she's not to exert herself at all. I'll drop by tomorrow and check on her progress."

"Thank you," she softly uttered through swollen lips and a painful, partial smile.

"Yeah, thanks, doc," Redding said as they shook hands before he helped Grace up from the table and outside to the waiting wagon.

"I'm scared for you, Vince," Grace admitted as she gingerly climbed into the wagon. "I'm afraid you'll do something without worrying about the risks you're taking."

"I know you worry about me, Grace, and I'm sorry that you do, but I have to do this."

Grace did not like the answer but knew there was no talking her husband out of it. He was determined to put a stop to things, even if it meant jeopardizing his safety in the process. She had feared for his safety the entire time when he was a lawman, but this was the first time she actually feared for his life. There was also the fact that the man who had attacked her was still out there. Was he waiting for another chance to try to kill her? She was afraid to be alone for fear that he would return. But how did she relay her fears to Redding when he was determined to bring Blaine Walker down? He was so consumed by Walker that he was putting his life, and now hers, on the line. Where did it all end? When they were both dead?

Vince Redding was overly careful as he helped Grace into the chair before retrieving the breakfast he had made for her. It was the second day after she had come home, and things were slowly coming together. The swelling of her face had somewhat subsided, and she was beginning to act like her old self again, which was a relief for Redding but not enough to satisfy his thirst for revenge. He would help her recover as much as possible, but, at the same time, he also would not forget what he had to do.

Redding was moving Grace back to their bed so she could get some rest when he heard a horse approaching. He quickly and carefully slid Grace back down into her chair, instead, and reached for his revolver hanging next to the door as he peered out the window. He watched, relieved, as Abigail Bartlett rode up to the front of the house in a buggy. Redding holstered his gun and met her outside.

"Hello, Abigail," he addressed her as she stiffened up from his appearance. He could tell by her disposition that she was feeling awkward having to talk to him after the way they had left things the last time they had talked. She hesitated, almost unsure of what to say to him.

"Hello, Vince," she responded coolly as she climbed down from the buggy and reached into the back to retrieve a basket. "I wasn't sure if you would be here. I brought some food for Grace so she wouldn't have to worry about trying to cook."

"We appreciate it, but she wouldn't have to cook. I'm here. I don't know if you had heard or not, but I'm no longer the sheriff."

"Yes," she replied in a stiff, stern tone. "I heard. I'm sorry you lost your job, Vince. I hope you don't think I had anything to do with it because I didn't. I know we've had our share of disagreements, but I would never wish someone to lose their livelihood because of something I did or said."

"No, I never thought that," Redding replied. "By the way, how's the planning of the wedding going?"

Abigail turned defensive. "I don't want to fight with you, Vince..."

"I know," he stopped her. "I was only asking. I'm not trying to pick a fight with you. I was genuinely asking just because I wanted to know, that's all."

"Oh, well, yes," she answered awkwardly and cautiously. "It's going well. Only two more weeks."

"Good," he added with an understanding nod. "I'm glad to hear it."

Abigail stopped as if she had something that needed to be said. "Vince, I hope you know that although I didn't appreciate your accusations about Blaine, and I don't have anything against you, but I still think it would be best for everyone involved if you weren't at the wedding. I hope you understand."

"Oh, yeah, I understand," Redding responded,

feeling awkward himself at the subject. "I wouldn't want anything to take away from your ceremony."

"Thank you for understanding," she said, somewhat relaxing her demeanor. "I hate that things turned out this way between us."

Redding nodded, his expression softened and solemn. "Yeah. I am, too."

There was a slight pause before Abigail broke the uneasy silence. "How's Grace?"

"She's doing good, considering what she's been through. She's awake if you want to come inside."

"I will for a few minutes. I don't want to tire her out. I know she needs her rest. I just wanted to bring this food by that Consquella made for you."

"Well, tell her 'thank you' for us."

Redding stood off to the side, allowing Abigail to go inside. He remained outside, admiring her black stallion so the two women could speak in private. It was only a few minutes later that Abigail reappeared.

"It's hard to see her like that," Abigail commented as she climbed into the buggy with Redding's assistance. "I didn't ask her because I didn't want to stir up any bad memories of what happened to her, but do you have any leads on who attacked her?"

"No, nothing yet," Redding hated to admit.

Abigail looked at him with compassion. "I hate that this happened to you two, Vince, but I hope you don't think that Blaine had anything to do with it.

You might not like him, but he isn't capable of doing something so horrendous."

"I've put my feelings about him aside, Abigail. I'm not implying that Blaine was in any way involved. If being with him makes you happy, then I just want you two to be happy. And thanks again for the food."

Abigail smiled and leaned over to give him a hug. "Thank you, Vince," she responded with a noticeable sense of relief in her expression. "That means a lot to me."

She tugged on the reins and sent the stallion into motion, pulling away from Redding with a renewed smile. He watched her ride away and turned to walk back into his home to check on Grace. He had told Abigail that he was not implying Blaine had something to do with Grace's assault. That was true.

He wasn't implying that Blaine had something to do with it.

He *knew* he did.

CHAPTER 28

ABIGAIL BARTLETT DROVE HER BUGGY BACK TO THE
J.B. Bar Ranch, all the while wondering what she had
just witnessed. She couldn't believe that Vince had
finally given up his mission of trying to ruin Blaine.
It was as if something had come over him. But what
could have caused such a drastic change in his
demeanor towards Blaine? Could it have been his
fear of losing Grace? Perhaps. But the explanation
seemed to be deeper than that. Or was he just telling
her what he thought she wanted to hear? That was
more of a plausible explanation. But again, if that
were the case, he was certainly putting on quite a
show for her and was being very convincing. She
wanted to think that Vince had dropped his infatuation with bringing down Blaine, but she knew Vince
too well to ever suspect that things had smoothed

over that easily. There was something more going on here, and she was determined to find out what it was before she married.

The rest of the ride back to the ranch was consumed with Abigail not being able to get the thought of Vince's odd behavior out of her mind. Something about it still bothered her. She just couldn't put her finger on what it was. She decided to question Blaine about what he knew of Grace's attack when he came over later that day. Maybe he had heard something in town that Vince might not have. It was certainly worth a try.

She spent the remainder of the morning and the first part of the afternoon mulling around the house, awaiting Blaine's visit. The more she thought about it, the more she questioned Vince's motives. She didn't like how mistrusting she had become of Vince. Hopefully, Blaine would have some news that would help put her mind at ease.

Blaine arrived mid-afternoon and kissed her as soon as he could get out of his wagon, as was customary. But this time, the change in her reception was cool enough that he could tell something was bothering her.

"What's wrong, my dear?" he asked her as he took in the obvious distance in her expression.

"I went out to see how Grace Redding was this morning," she answered.

"And how was she? Doing better, I'm hoping, considering the circumstances."

"Yes, she's doing well, considering," Abigail replied. She paused briefly before she began again. "Blaine, have you heard anything about her attack? I mean, the new sheriff has very little to go on, if anything. Has there been any talk around town about who might have done this?"

"No," Blaine said with a convincing shaking of his head. "Are you worried, my dear? You aren't concerned that the same thing could happen to you, are you? Because I would never let anything happen to you. I hope you know that."

"I know. And in answer to your question, no, I'm not concerned that it could happen to me. But that's just it. Why did it happen to *her*? She's lived out there for some time now and she was alone every day while Vince was sheriff. If anything, he would have been subjected to his enemies more while he was still sheriff."

"But, my dear, it was likely some drifter. Drifters come and go through here all the time. You know that."

"Of course. They come here all the time looking for work."

"There, you see? There's nothing strange about a drifter coming through. That's probably what happened to her."

"But that's too much of a coincidence," she reasoned. "What are the chances that a drifter would just happen to come through there on the only night that her husband wasn't home?"

"Maybe he was watching the place," Blaine argued. "Maybe he had been watching it for some time and waiting for his opportunity for her to be alone to attack her."

"But a drifter wouldn't invest that kind of time in watching a small, one shack ranch. No offense to Vince or Grace, but there's nothing significant about that ranch, nothing that was of such value that a drifter would feel they just had to have."

Walker pulled back slightly from her. "Where is this coming from, Abigail? What is your sudden interest in the Reddings?"

"When I saw Vince today, I got to wondering about it.

It was apparent to her that the news of her seeing Redding did not sit well with Walker. "And why were you over at the Reddings?"

"I went over to see how Grace was doing and he just happened to be there. Y'know, he's no longer the sheriff."

"And what did he say to you? Obviously, he said something to you or else you wouldn't have such an interest in his wife's attack."

"He didn't have to say anything to me, Blaine.

Grace and Vince are my friends," she said, immediately turning defensive. "I don't need a reason to go talk to them. And I don't need your permission to do so, either."

"Of course not, my dear," Walker said apologetically. "I meant no disrespect of it. I never meant to insinuate that you did. I was merely wondering why the sudden interest in their lives."

The sting of his line of questioning was still too raw for Abigail to let go of. "I went by there to bring them some food and I ran into Vince, who was there taking care of his wife that he had just brought home from the doctor's office, where she almost died."

Walker saw the anger in her swell and that he had said too much. He was now receiving the brunt of her wrath, but he had to put his foot down to try to stop her relationship with Redding.

"I don't want you to see Vince Redding. He's not the type of man that you need to be around. He's nothing but trouble. Just look at all the conflict he's caused recently."

"You're just saying that because you two don't get along."

"I think I have a right to feel the way I do about Redding," Walker professed. "He has done nothing but try to ruin me since I arrived and, yet, I have done nothing to provoke such hatred. Why you would want to associate yourself with such a derelict is beyond me. He's managed to assault several honest citizens, including me, and now he has disgraced his position as town sheriff to the point that the very same townspeople that he swore to protect have fired him. That should tell you volumes about the type of person that he is."

"I know Vince has had his share of problems, but deep down, he's a good man and an honest man."

"If I didn't know any better, I might tend to think that you believe him more than you believe me, your own fiancé. I have to admit, my dear, that such an outlook is quite hurtful to me. I think it would be best for us if you distance yourself from him. I'm afraid I must insist."

"Blaine, I will not be told who I can and cannot associate with," she stated angrily. "And I resent your implication that I care more for him than I do you."

"I'm sorry. I didn't mean to upset you. I know this is a trying time for them and I didn't wish to sound insensitive to what they've gone through. I know you and Redding have some history and I guess I let my petty jealousy get the better of me. I apologize."

"Our history was a long time ago, and it has nothing to do with you and I," she advised him sharply. "I would appreciate it if you wouldn't throw that in my face every time his name is brought up. We happen to live in the same town and we're sure

to run into one another from time to time. I hope
you remember that."

"Again, my apologies, my dear," he said with a
respectful bow.

"I don't like the fact that there hasn't been any
news about who attacked Grace. I think I'll go into
town and talk to the new sheriff. I haven't met him,
and I need to so I can get acquainted with him."

"That's an outstanding idea, my dear. I'll leave
you to your task and see you later on this evening.
We are still on for dinner, aren't we?"

"I suppose," she replied with a hint of agitation in
her voice. "But I don't want to talk about this
anymore."

"Agreed," he answered, trying to smooth things
over with a smile, but she did not reciprocate the
gesture. Walker was sensitive to her mood and
decided it was best to leave the subject alone. It had
been an enlightening discussion and one that proved
there were some loose ends that demanded his
immediate attention. For one, it was only a matter of
time before Grace Redding identified Ike
Harrington as her attacker and when she did, it
wouldn't take long before Harrington was connected
back to him. He simply could not allow that to
happen. Grace Redding had to go. But this had also
proven something else to him. Vince Redding was
no less of a threat than was his wife. Whatever he

needed to do to get rid of both Grace and Vince Redding needed to be done.

Soon.

Ike Harrington had to act fast.

It would not be long before Grace Redding spotted him somewhere around town and pointed him out as her attacker. When that happened, it would be a race to see which happened first: if he were to be arrested or if Will Spurlock were sent to kill him to keep him quiet. Either way, Harrington wasn't amused at being placed in such a position.

Harrington did not fear Spurlock, but he had good reason not to trust him. He did not trust Blaine Walker, either. Not one bit. Walker had confided in Spurlock and would do whatever was necessary to keep himself clean of all that had occurred, and that meant throwing Harrington to the wolves, should his plan fall apart, which was becoming more and more of a possibility with each passing day. Harrington wasn't about to take the fall for everything, but he knew that was exactly what Walker and Spurlock had planned on. And he knew Walker had Spurlock backing him up, just in case he, Harrington, became wise to things. He had followed his orders given to him by Walker and yet he had still somehow managed to put himself in a very precarious position. A position that could get him killed from more than one source.

He had attacked Grace Redding on his own accord, but he had only done that to help Walker advance his cause. Now, that move had backfired on him and he had unknowingly set himself up to take the fall. It was the perfect way for Walker to rid himself of Harrington. Walker would turn Harrington into the authorities for the attack and any information Harrington tried to give up on Walker would be dismissed and construed as someone being desperate enough to lie about Walker to try to save their own neck. Walker had known Harrington would act to protect him out of loyalty and had even counted on it. Now, Walker had backed him into a corner, and the worst part was, he had let him. It was clear that he was now on his own.

CHAPTER 29

IKE HARRINGTON DECIDED TO MAKE A BOLD MOVE, out of nothing short of desperation. It was a move that would either free him of risk or seal his fate. He would alert the sheriff that Will Spurlock had been the one to attack Grace Redding. That would buy him some time to implement the rest of his plan, a plan that would not only ensure his safety, but would also bring Blaine Walker down at the same time, since Walker was the only other one who could implicate him in any wrongdoing. With Will Spurlock behind bars and Walker facing humiliation and then financial ruin, he, Harrington, could take Walker's place, taking over the town as a free man without a care in the world, with Walker having opened the door for him. *That would teach them to try to mess with him.*

The more he thought about it, the more he didn't understand what had brought him to this spot. Walker had hired him to do a job for him and then, without warning and without his approval, he had hired Spurlock as a backup. But why? If Walker had not trusted that Harrington could do the job, then why hire him in the first place? Why not just go straight to Spurlock with the job? The answer puzzled him, and at the same time angered him. It was exactly why he had grown to not trust Walker. It appeared as if Walker had hired Harrington to clean up his mess and then hired Spurlock to get rid of Harrington along with any evidence tying him to anything. At least that was how Harrington perceived it. It was a bold plan. A neat and tidy plan, except for one thing: Harrington wasn't going down that easily.

Harrington headed over to the sheriff's office to put the first part of his plan into motion. As he entered the office, Sheriff Copeland was just coming out of the back room where the cells were located. The sheriff looked up at him as Harrington closed the door behind him.

"Can I help you?" Sheriff Copeland asked.

"It's more like I 'can help you', sheriff," Harrington bragged. "I have information about who attacked Vince Redding's wife."

The news stunned Copeland, bringing him over

to sit down behind his desk. "And might I ask how you happened to come upon this information?"

"I heard a fella bragging about it in the saloon last night. I thought someone should know about it before he gets away."

"Is he planning on leaving town?"

"I don't know," Harrington said, "but I thought you should know, just in case he does decide to leave."

"I appreciate you telling me. Would you be willing to make a statement to the effect?"

Sheriff Copeland asked as he retrieved paper and pencil from his desk drawer.

"Sure thing, sheriff," Harrington gladly agreed. "Anything to help bring this fella in for what he did."

Sheriff Copeland handed the paper and pencil over to Harrington, who scribbled out a statement and then signed the bottom. Copeland took back the paper and glanced it over. "That'll do, Mr. Perkins, is it?"

"Yeah," Harrington replied, "Walter Perkins."

"Well, thank you for coming in, Mr. Perkins. I appreciate you coming forward as a concerned citizen of this town. Not everyone would have done that."

"Glad to help, sheriff," Harrington responded honestly with a coy smile. "I'm happy to do anything that I can do to put this man behind bars."

"Could you give me a description of what this fella looks like so I can be on the lookout for him?"

"He's mid-to-late thirties, a little taller than me, a little over six feet, medium build, sandy-colored hair down to his shoulders, wears a black Stetson. Looks like he can take care of himself. Rides a bay with a white face. I heard the bartender call him by name. Spurlock."

"Thanks. By the way, you wouldn't happen to know where I can find this man right now, do you?"

"No, sorry, sheriff. I haven't seen him today. But he probably isn't in a hurry to leave town since he thinks he got away with it. If I do happen to see him, I'll be sure to let you know right away."

"Thanks, Mr. Perkins," Sheriff Copeland replied.

Harrington gave Sheriff Copeland an affirming nod before leaving his office. He stepped out onto the boardwalk; a satisfying grin spread over his face. Spurlock had messed with the wrong man and now he would pay for it dearly.

As soon as Will Spurlock stepped inside the Imperial Hotel, he could tell something was wrong. From the streets to inside the hotel, everyone was watching him, but not just as they typically did from being a stranger to town, but from something else. It was as if they were suddenly afraid of him.

He walked to the stairs, stealing a glance back
over those who were in the dining room, watching
their eyes following him. It was bizarre behavior.
Why were they looking at him that way? They had
seen him multiple times before without giving him a
second thought. Why was seeing him any different
this time?

He ascended the stairs and headed straight to his
room, passing Blaine Walker's room, hoping he
didn't draw his attention. He slowed his pace,
listening through the door for movement inside, but
heard nothing. There had been little evidence of
Walker around town recently. Walker was likely out
at Abigail Bartlett's ranch, finalizing something to do
with their wedding plans. Since his unexpected
meeting with Vince Redding, he had left the bay tied
up out front just in case he needed to make a quick
getaway. Things were moving way too fast and were
getting more unpredictable with Walker and
Harrington and because of that, he might only get a
moment's notice to leave town. He would need to be
ready, just in case.

Locking the door behind him, he wedged a chair
under the doorknob and sat his gun on the nightstand, loosening it in its holster to make pulling it
out easier before collapsing on his bed.

His mind couldn't shake the reception he had
received in the hotel lobby. It had been the same icy,

standoffish reception everywhere he had gone that day. They had all looked at him differently. But why? No doubt Walker would have an idea of what was going on and could likely even be responsible for it, but he didn't care to involve the man in his business right now. He would find out soon enough, without Walker's interference.

At some point, Spurlock had fallen asleep and was jolted awake by footsteps in the hallway outside his room. He eased his hand over and retrieved his gun as he listened. The footsteps stopped.

He slid out of bed, carefully walking in his socks over to the door and leaning his ear towards it to pick up any sound. Still nothing. He was about to crack open the door when a man spoke from the hallway.

"Spurlock? This is Sheriff Copeland. I need to have a word with you."

Spurlock tucked his gun in the back of his waistband and opened the door to find Sheriff Copeland standing there with Deputy Clint McNeil next to him. Deputy McNeil was brandishing a shotgun while Copeland was clearly edgy with his hand resting on the butt of his revolver as if anticipating trouble.

"You Spurlock?" the sheriff asked with a hint of nervousness.

"You know I am, sheriff. What's this all about?"

"Get your boots on. I'm going to need you to come with me to my office and answer a few questions."

"I can answer them just fine right here," Spurlock stated firmly. Sheriff Copeland was taken back by the resistance but decided it was best not to push a man he knew very little about.

"Alright," Copeland began. "I received word that you were involved in the assault on one of our residents, Grace Redding. Her husband used to be sheriff here."

"That's not a question," Spurlock pointed out dryly.

"Fine, then I'll ask you outright. What do you know about Grace Redding's assault?"

"I don't know anything, sheriff. Never even met the woman."

"That's not what I hear, Mr. Spurlock," Sheriff Copeland replied. "I've got a sworn statement that says they heard you in the saloon bragging about beating up Mrs. Redding."

"I can prove that's a lie," Spurlock reasoned, his agitation quickly escalating.

"And just how do you plan to do that, Mr. Spurlock?" Copeland asked confidently.

"Because I don't drink," he stated firmly. "Haven't for years. Dulls the senses."

Sheriff Copeland was caught off guard by the

admission, unsure just where to go with his questioning. Spurlock continued before he could form a response. "I challenge you to find one bartender or citizen in this town that has seen me in one of your establishments. I don't know where you got your information, sheriff, but it's dead wrong."

Copeland was at a loss for words. He had expected a lot of different replies, but this clearly was not one of them. He was left with no recourse.

"Of course, I'll have to follow up with this matter with the locals, you understand, to collaborate your story," Copeland finally admitted, feeling rather humiliated and embarrassed.

"I understand," Spurlock responded. "Anything else, sheriff?" he asked in an annoyed tone.

"No," Copeland replied humbly. "Sorry to bother you, Mr. Spurlock."

Spurlock started to close the door but opened it back up as a thought occurred to him. "Sheriff, who was it that swore out the statement on me?"

Copeland stumbled with his answer. "I... uh... I..."

"Let me guess: young fella, full of spunk, dark hair, wears a fancy two-gun rig, rides a chestnut with a white mane? I won't bother asking what name he gave you since he would have used an alias."

Copeland suddenly became fidgety and uneasy at the accuracy of the description, trying to shun it off as much as possible, but before he could lie, Spurlock spoke. "That's what I thought," he added as he closed the door in Copeland's face. He stood behind it as he listened to the pair of footsteps until they were gone. *Harrington had done this*, he thought to himself, making his way over to get his boots on. He had wondered why those in the hotel and on the streets had looked at him with such trepidation, and now he knew. They had all heard the rumor that he was responsible for the assault on Grace Redding. *He had known he couldn't trust Walker. Now, he officially couldn't trust Harrington, either.*

CHAPTER 30

THE MORE IKE HARRINGTON THOUGHT ABOUT IT, THE more it bothered him. It was the same problem that had been bothering him for some time.

Grace Redding.

It was a loose end that needed to be addressed and dealt with, and there was only one way to deal with it so it would go away for good.

Grace Redding was at home, recuperating from her attack, an attack that he had decided upon and carried out. He had done it not only to frame Will Spurlock to get him out of the picture, even temporarily but to show Blaine Walker that he could handle things on his own. He could just as easily have gunned down Spurlock, but there was still a small bit of doubt in the back of his mind as to whether he could take Spurlock in a gunfight. He knew Spurlock had to be fast to be in this line of work, but just how fast, he wasn't sure. And uncertainty like that could easily get him killed.

Once he had Walker's trust and Spurlock was safely out of the picture, he, Harrington, would move in, eliminate Walker however he saw fit and take over his whole operation. It would be easy. He would let Walker do all the work and he would reap the rewards.

When he left the sheriff's office, Harrington went straight across the street to the Broken Branch Saloon for a celebratory drink. It felt good to have framed Spurlock, knowing the law would be watching his every move from then on. He realized that his victory would be short-lived– however long it took the law to realize that he had lied to them, but it should still be enough to set his plan into motion.

But right now, his main concern had to be Grace Redding. She could still identify him and ruin everything. She was the link to all of this working out for him, and she was the only one who could link him to any of it. He had mulled over his options, which were getting to be fewer as time went on because of the position he had been placed in.

Then, he decided, it was settled.

As much as he hated to admit it, Grace Redding had to die.

. . .

After being humiliated by Will Spurlock, Sheriff Augustus Copeland wandered back to his office, having given Deputy McNeil the rest of the day off so he would not have to look the young man in the eye, disgraced. It had been his first big act as sheriff and not only had he failed at it miserably, but to make matters worse, he had done so in front of his deputy. He now realized that the only way of rectifying this was to talk to the victim herself, Grace Redding, and get as much accurate information as possible and go from there.

After checking back at his office one final time, Sheriff Copeland left Salt Creek, riding out to the Redding ranch to see if Grace was well enough to answer questions, his hopes renewed that he could finally get some information that would help him solve the question of who was responsible for her attack.

As he left the images of town behind him in a trail of dust, hoping it would not be a wasted trip, Ike Harrington had been watching from the door of the Broken Branch Saloon. Upon leaving the sheriff's office after making his false statement, Harrington knew Copeland would make a beeline for Spurlock's room in the hopes that he could bring Spurlock in for questioning and hopefully identify the person behind Grace Redding's assault. He wanted to see, firsthand, as Spurlock was being led off to the jail.

But when he saw Sheriff Copeland reappear only a few minutes later without Spurlock in custody, his hopes quickly faded to worry. Why wasn't he being locked up? How had Spurlock talked his way out of it? He knew Spurlock was in his room, so there was no reason why he hadn't been arrested. Harrington wasn't sure of the answer, but he did know where that left him: with a witness that needed to be silenced. When he saw Sheriff Copeland mount his horse and ride in the direction of the Redding ranch, his heart sank. Copeland would soon find out the truth.

He walked his empty glass over to the bar and hurried outside and onto his chestnut, pulling the animal west towards the Redding ranch. He wasn't sure what he would do when he got there, but it would involve killing Grace Redding and probably her husband, too.

Harrington rode hard, trying to make up the distance between him and Sheriff Copeland. When Copeland made it back into town, he would have a description of Harrington. From that point on, his time in town would be limited before the authorities came knocking on his door.

He topped a small rise, pushing the chestnut as

hard as he dared. As he rounded a small curve in the road just before the Redding ranch, he saw a rider up ahead, who he recognized as Sheriff Copeland.

Harrington rode straight for the man, who was not yet aware of his presence. While Harrington was still a short distance away, Sheriff Copeland heard a horse behind him and turned to face him, instantly recognizing Harrington and confused by his appearance. Before he could respond to Harrington being there, Harrington panicked, drew, and fired. He watched as Copeland toppled from his horse and onto the road. Harrington pulled his horse back, stopping him as he stared down at the man. He quickly glanced to make sure no one else was around and kicked the chestnut into a trot the short distance over to the fallen man. His panic increased when he climbed down and felt no pulse. Now he had done it. He had killed a lawman, something he had promised himself he would never do. He had talked a big talk to Walker about killing a sheriff, but deep down, he didn't like the notion and had even feared having to do it. Killing drifters, ranchers and other men he was hired to deal with was one thing, but killing a lawman was something that he would never be able to shake from his reputation or his mind. He had intentionally brought severe trouble down on himself. For the first time in his life, he worried about the consequences of his actions.

What was he going to do now?

Despite the chilly afternoon air, Vince Redding had worked up quite a sweat from moving hay into the barn and readying things for the onslaught of the approaching winter. Although he missed being sheriff, it felt good to once again be doing back-breaking hard work for a change. It was the outlook of a new life that he had promised Grace while she was recovering, a life that didn't involve him being shot at.

He decided to take a break, sitting on a short stack of hay bales and wiping the building perspiration from his face with the back of his hand as he caught his breath. He needed to go check in on Grace, anyway, and this seemed as good of a time as any to use that as an excuse to stop work. Grabbing his shirt on his way out of the barn, Redding started to cross the front toward his house when he saw a riderless horse walking up the road towards him.

The scene disturbed him. It didn't matter that he didn't recognize the horse. What concerned him was finding out who the horse belonged to and where they were. After quickly saddling the roan, he grabbed the reins of the mystery horse as he trotted down the road. It was less than three miles down the road when he spotted Sheriff Copeland's dead body lying on the road. He wondered what had happened to the sheriff until he turned him over onto his back and saw the bullet hole still leaking blood that had saturated his shirt and left a dried patch of blood on the road.

Redding carefully studied the scene, putting his experience with shootings to work. It was obvious that Copeland apparently either knew his killer since he hadn't drawn his gun, or he was taken by surprise. A search of Copeland's pockets revealed that he still had his money on him, along with his gun belt and revolver. His horse had been allowed to wander off without being taken, all of which proved that this wasn't a robbery.

The location of Copeland's body proved that he was going out to Redding's ranch, since it was the only one in the direction he was heading. Redding suddenly had an uneasy feeling creep over him. If Copeland had been killed on purpose going to his ranch, then he was coming to see Redding about something that was so important that he couldn't wait for Redding to come back into town. So, the question was: Was Copeland was coming to tell him something, or coming for him, Redding, to verify something that Copeland had heard? The only one he could think of who could possibly answer that question was Deputy Clint McNeil.

Redding strapped Copeland's body across his horse and led it into town, instantly drawing the attention of everyone out on the streets. All traffic came to a halt, and the murmuring began and quickly spread through the crowds as Redding led the dead man and his horse slowly towards the sheriff's office. He tried the door, but Deputy McNeil wasn't there so he walked the two horses and headed over to Doc Hastings' office. A knock at his door brought Doc Hastings outside, where he saw the dead man's body.

"Is that Sheriff Copeland?" Hastings asked while he walked over and lifted Copeland's head to verify.

"Yeah," Redding confirmed. "He's been shot," he added as a crowd had already begun to form around them.

Doc Hastings looked back at Redding. "Who did it?"

"Don't know. His horse wandered up to my place. I found him lying on the road."

"No need to take him down from there," Hastings stated dryly with a slight shaking of his head. "Nothing I can do for him. Might as well go ahead and take him to the undertaker."

"This doesn't make sense," Redding noted. "He hasn't been sheriff long enough to have any enemies. Seemed like a real likable guy. Why would someone shoot him?"

"You tell us, Redding," a man snapped from the crowd, drawing Redding's attention.

"I didn't shoot him," Redding professed, giving the man his attention. "I didn't have any problem with him."

"That's not true. I heard you threaten him," came a voice from the back of the group. The bystanders were parted by a small, mousy-looking man with wire glasses, the clerk at the Imperial Hotel where Blaine Walker was staying. "I heard you threaten Sheriff Copeland yesterday. You said he had better stay out of your way. I heard it, and so did his deputy, Clint."

Doc Hastings cast his glance over to Redding, who was growing increasingly uncomfortable by the uneasiness of the crowd, which had continued to grow as the scene was drawing more and more spectators, all of which were appearing to side with the accusations. The low growling of those surrounding him was starting to concern him.

"He shot the sheriff!" someone called out.

"Now everybody, calm down!" Doc Hastings shouted, trying to quell the growing dissension. "No one knows that for a fact!"

"He needs to hang!" another voice demanded, creating more accompanying shouts and further fueling the anger in the group.

"Everybody, settle down!" Doc Hastings yelled over the growing animosity as he stepped between Redding and the group. "No one's hanging anyone!

We don't know what happened and until we do, this man is not to be harmed!"

"If he killed Sheriff Copeland, he needs to hang!"

"Yeah!"

"String him up!"

"What you're saying doesn't make sense! Think about it: if he killed Sheriff Copeland, why would he put himself in jeopardy by bringing in the body?"

"Hang him!" someone shouted, ignoring Hastings' logic.

"Let's get him!"

"People, please!" Hastings shouted with his hands raised to try to overcome the building tension, but it had already escalated into an angry, uncontrollable crowd. They were getting restless, and the uneasiness was unsettling to Redding. These had been his friends only a few short days ago. Friends that he had known for years. Friends that had elected him into the office of sheriff and had supported him. Friends that had come to his and Grace's wedding and had even helped them settle into their new home. Now, those same people he had once called friends were ready to lynch him, and with Doc Hastings was the only thing preventing them from doing so.

Redding was growing increasingly uncomfortable with their reactions as his hand slowly slid down towards his revolver without taking his eyes off the group. He wanted to voice his innocence, but he had seen this type of crowds before, crowds that were caught up in the moment and being ruled by emotion. They were so wrapped up in the sheriff's murder that he knew they would never listen to him.

He had to get out of there.

CHAPTER 31

VINCE REDDING KEPT A CLOSE WATCH OVER THE growing animosity of the townspeople as he thought of a way out. He didn't like the idea of having to draw on these people, but if they rushed him, he would have no choice. And if he did draw on them, he was taking a chance that they would call his bluff and he would be forced to use his gun and possibly shoot someone. Once guns started being pulled, there were bound to be those who fired back. People would likely be hurt or even killed, and he couldn't have that. His only option was to make a run for it. The problem was, if he did try to get away, it would come off as looking guilty of the very thing he was being accused of. He was being left without a choice. In order to avoid bloodshed, he would have to flee and deal with the consequences later.

The townspeople were growing more restless. Those in the front of the group were slowly inching their way forward as their confidence grew. Redding knew if he started backing up it would be the final straw that would encourage them to rush him. If he was going to get out of this alive, he was going to be forced to make the first move. He was about to grab the roan's reins when a man in the front suddenly leapt forward towards him.

Redding kicked at the man, striking him in the chest and driving him back into the crowd. At the same time, he reached over and grabbed Doc Hastings by the coat, snatching him closer to him as he pulled his revolver. He held Hastings close to him, pointing his gun at Hastings' head, placing the doctor between himself and the crowd. "Everybody stay back!" Redding yelled, stopping those who had moved towards him in their tracks.

"Redding! Are you crazy? What in the world are you doing?!" Doc Hastings shouted, his face full of fear from being caught off-guard while Redding maintained his hold on him as he backed up.

"Stay where you are!" Redding reinforced his command as he reached and grabbed the roan's reins, quickly slipping into his saddle as he relaxed his hold on Hastings. He kicked the roan into moving, running it at full speed down the street while laying over the saddle to minimize himself as a target while the horse's hooves kicked up a spray of dust to help aid his escape. As he fled down the street, several of the townspeople fired shots at him.

"Stop shooting!" Doc Hastings screamed over the shots. "Put your guns away!" he added.

"Let's go after him!" a man called out, sending several of the men running for their horses, but Hastings stepped out into the street in front of them, waving his arms wildly to stop them.

"Stop! Stay where you are!" he shouted again, stopping the men before they could go after Redding. "Let him go!"

"He killed the sheriff!" one of the men argued.

"You don't know that!" Hastings reasoned. "Let him go! We'll get the federal marshal and bring him here! Let him deal with it!"

"He's getting away!"

"He isn't going anywhere!" Hastings argued. "He's one of us! He lives here!"

"Let's go to his house!" someone yelled. "He'll go there because his wife is there!"

Hastings instantly worried about Grace's safety. "I promise you, anyone that goes near that house will have to answer to the federal marshal! I'll make sure of it!"

The threat worked, stalling their pursuit amid a collection of scorns and disgruntled murmurs. The discord it created was passed among the group as they continued to be displeased that he had sided with Redding, but prevented anyone from pursuing Redding, for now.

"Why are you protecting him, doc?" someone asked.

"You can't lynch a man just because you think he's guilty," Hastings pointed out. "Now, go back to your own business and let the marshal handle this. I'll contact him myself. Redding isn't going anywhere," Hastings repeated forcibly. "Now, let it go!"

The final command worked to cause the group to slowly disperse and go about their ways, some still grumbling under their breath at having their plans interrupted. Hastings stood his ground until the last of them had moved on before he headed for the undertaker's office while leading Sheriff Copeland's horse carrying his body.

From his hotel window, Blaine Walker had watched the entire sequence of events involving Redding bringing Sheriff Copeland's body into town until the crowd forced Redding to leave in haste. He smiled as he reveled in his luck. He had wanted to smear Redding's name and reputation to prevent him from being an obstacle, but from what he witnessed, it seemed as if Redding had managed to do that all by himself.

There was, however, one thing that still bothered Walker. Who had killed Sheriff Copeland? He knew it had not been Redding. There was no reasoning behind it. Was it Spurlock or Harrington? That was more than likely the case. But which one was it and why would they have done such a stupid thing this close to him, having executed the rest of his plan? His guess was that Spurlock had killed him after Sheriff Copeland confronted him in his hotel room. He hoped his theory was right since it would give Spurlock the perfect reason for leaving town for good.

Walker paced the room anxiously as a thought suddenly came to him. If Will Spurlock had not killed Sheriff Copeland, that brought up another problem. It meant that Harrington had, which would come back onto him, Walker. But that wasn't the only problem facing Walker. Despite Harrington's best efforts, he had failed to pin Grace Redding's assault on Spurlock and now Spurlock would know that he had been framed by either him or Harrington. Either way, Spurlock would come after him. That was an open problem that needed rectifying. He wasn't sure how it was going to be resolved, but it required immediate attention and, until then, he would have to wait until later to come up with an alternate plan to get rid of Spurlock.

It was less than two weeks until his wedding to Abigail Bartlett, and he was ready to finalize his plans. She had already become a silent partner with him to purchase the Sidewinder Saloon. Next, he would marry her and seal the deal by becoming half owner of the J.B. Bar Ranch. Then, when the timing was right, it would just be the matter of Abigail falling victim to a terrible tragedy and he would have unlimited access to her wealth– wealth that would allow him to buy out anyone in town that he wanted. By then, Will Spurlock would either be run out of town or dead by Harrington's hands, leaving Harrington there to assist him in persuading those who were stubborn enough to oppose him.

He needed to get a message to Harrington on what was needed of him next, but, oddly enough, he had not seen him around town for several hours. In fact, he had not seen Harrington since he had instructed Harrington to pin Grace Redding's assault on Spurlock. It wasn't like Harrington to be out of pocket for that long. He hated the idea of Harrington having free reign to roam around town since the combination of his loose mouth and his arrogance would eventually get him into trouble.

Walker paced more urgently, his patience all but depleted. Spurlock had become too hard to control, which was the reason why he had wanted him killed, but now Harrington's incompetence had made a mess of things and had put his, Walker's, life in jeopardy. One thing was for certain: his hotel room was no longer safe. But that wasn't what worried him the most. He had no idea where Harrington was, and, right now, Harrington was the only thing keeping him safe from Spurlock.

He had to find Harrington before Spurlock came looking for him.

Will Spurlock sat in the lobby of the Imperial Hotel, his back against the wall at the far end of the room where he could keep an eye on both the main hotel entrance as well as the stairs. He was waiting for the appearance of either of two men: Ike Harrington or Blaine Walker, both of which he wanted to confront since both of them wanted him dead.

He sat quietly, nursing the remnants of a beer he had coaxed from the hotel clerk, contemplating what he would do when he spotted these men. It would take all his restraint not to end their lives right then and there, but he couldn't kill them outright, not here in front of all these witnesses. He *would*, however, let them know that he was aware of their intentions. *Let them look over their shoulders.*

That would make them sweat for a while. They deserved it.

Spurlock was growing impatient when he saw Ike Harrington ride up and tie off his horse in front of the Imperial. Harrington entered the hotel, but he did not notice Spurlock situated in the back of the room. Spurlock waited until Harrington walked up the stairs and had enough time to make it to Walker's room before he slipped up the stairs behind him. But when he reached the top of the stairs, Harrington was nowhere to be seen. He inched his way over to Walker's door and pressed his ear against it but heard no voices inside.

"He's not in there," Harrington's voice spoke softly from the stairs behind him as Spurlock instinctively raised his hands, knowing Harrington had already drawn on him.

"Where is he?" Spurlock asked calmly.

"Why?" Harrington asked as Spurlock felt a hand pull his revolver from his holster and threw it onto the floor far behind him. "You gonna kill him?"

"That's the plan. It only seems fair. He tried to have me killed."

"I know. I'm the one who tried to kill you."

"I know," Spurlock said as he moved his hat just enough to expose the gash the bullet had carved into his skull. "You just about did."

"I hoped it would be enough to run you off, but I

should have known better. Men like you aren't chased off that easily."

"Tell me something: why does Walker want me dead so bad?"

"He thinks you've outgrown your usefulness," Harrington replied while maintaining his gun covering Spurlock.

"Is that why you tried to implicate me in the Redding woman's beating?"

"I tried running you out of town and that didn't work, so, yeah, I turned your name over to the sheriff," Harrington admitted freely. "Turns out that didn't work, either."

"Why'd you go after Redding's wife, anyway?"

"Because I was trying to help him," Harrington stated. "Redding wouldn't leave him alone. He kept coming and digging and putting his nose where it didn't belong. I thought I was doing Walker a favor, but it blew up in my face. So, when Walker told me to get rid of you, it seemed like the likely solution to both problems. You'd take the fall for her attack and Redding would leave town with her and leave Walker alone."

"But that didn't work out either, did it?" Spurlock pointed out.

"No," Harrington reluctantly agreed, his voice downcast with frustration. "That's why I had to up the ante."

The comment caught Spurlock's attention more than the rest. He did not like what he was hearing. "*What* did you do, Harrington?"

"Redding just brought Sheriff Copeland's body into town," Harrington began, causing Spurlock to slowly turn to face him. "He was ambushed on his way to Redding's place by you."

Spurlock's hatred began to show in his features. "You'll never make that stick."

"Oh, yeah, I will, because I have the perfect witness to back up my story. Copeland's own deputy."

"How do you figure?" Spurlock asked, his eyes firmly locked onto Harrington's.

"Copeland's deputy was a witness when Copeland came to confront you about attacking Redding's wife. He'll testify that Sheriff Copeland suspected you."

"Suspected, but without proof."

"The fact that he's dead, and you were the last one he talked to will fit together nicely," Harrington bragged. "Besides, you can't account for where you were at the time of his murder, can you? I knew you weren't in town at the time, which made the timing perfect. Now, all I have to do is walk you over to the sheriff's office and turn you over to his deputy."

Spurlock found it almost impossible to contain himself as his rage increased. "You son of a…"

"Easy, Spurlock," Harrington warned confidently. "Now," he added, motioning with his gun, "head over to the sheriff's office so I can…"

Harrington's words were cut short as the door of the room next to them suddenly opened and a man appeared, startled to see the two men standing there as his eyes immediately fixed on Harrington's gun. His sudden appearance drew Harrington's eyes away for only a split second, but it was enough of a distraction for Spurlock to make a move.

Spurlock kicked the gun from Harrington's right hand and lunged just as Harrington went for his second gun. Spurlock managed to grab his hand as he instinctively drew, holding it towards the floor as the two men struggled and sending the bystander back into his room, slamming the door shut behind him.

The two men continued fighting for control of Harrington's revolver until Spurlock abruptly released his grip on Harrington's right arm and swung hard, connecting with Harrington's chin and sending him to the floor while he continued holding his gun. As soon as he hit Harrington, Spurlock turned and ran the few feet to the stairs and started down them just as a bullet tore through the wood at the corner of the wall next to his head. A stunned Harrington rolled onto his feet to pursue Spurlock, but Spurlock had just made it through the door to the outside of the hotel. As he entered the alley, Spurlock saw a small wooden crate sitting with a few discarded items next to the building. He quickly grabbed the crate and wedged it under the doorknob before turning and running between the buildings towards the front of the hotel, where he climbed onto his horse and tore out into the street.

As he hurried out of town, he wondered where Blaine Walker was hiding.

CHAPTER 32

THE ROAN GALLOPED A SHORT DISTANCE FROM TOWN before Vince Redding felt comfortable enough to pull him to a stop and swing around to check his back trail. Luckily, there was no sign of anyone following him, but he knew that could quickly change.

He wondered what his next move would be. He certainly couldn't go home for any amount of time since that would be the first place they'd come looking for him, putting Grace in harm's way. But he also couldn't leave Grace alone, either. Not only would she be helpless to care for herself, but there was also the fact of the person who attacked her having never been caught. He couldn't stand the thought of leaving her so vulnerable to another attack. Once word got out that Redding was on the run, there would be nothing stopping her attacker from coming back and finishing what he started. He would have to forget running for now. He had to make sure she was safe before he worried about his own predicament.

He headed straight for his house as fast as the roan could carry him; the horse sensing his urgency and responding accordingly. In no time, he was coming to a sliding stop in front of his house as he hurried out of the saddle and ran through the front door so quickly that it startled Grace, who was sitting in front of the fireplace. Her face went flush from surprise at seeing Redding in such a panic.

"Vince, what's wrong?"

"I've got to leave, Grace. Everyone in town is after me. They think I killed Sheriff Copeland," Redding hurriedly responded as he quickly ruffled through his drawers and began gathering extra ammunition and a clean shirt.

The news shocked her. "*What?* Sheriff Copeland is *dead?*"

"His horse wandered up here a little while ago. I didn't know whose it was, so I went looking and found him out on the road. He'd been shot."

"He was already dead when you found him?"

"Yeah, but not long."

"Where is he now?"

"I tried to do the right thing and take him into

town, but the townspeople tried to pin his murder on me."

"What do you mean? You didn't kill him. You said yourself that he had been shot when you found him," she reasoned as she stood and walked over to him, but Redding did not slow down his efforts.

"I know that, but it doesn't matter," Redding insisted while hurriedly walking into the kitchen and grabbing a handful of biscuits that Grace had made earlier and stuffing them into the pocket of his coat. "They're looking for someone to blame and they've already made their minds up and they'll be coming here first, looking for me. I need to be gone before they get here."

"Where will you go?" she asked with deep concern in her eyes as she fought back the worry and tears.

"I dunno," he answered, "but it's best if you don't know. The less you know, the safer you'll be."

"Then I'm coming with you." Grace stated as she tried to stand, but Redding stopped her.

"No. You can't go, and you can't stay here, either. I'm dropping you off at the J.B. Bar. Abigail will make sure you're protected until this thing is over."

"But I don't want to go to Abigail's," she insisted, her face full of worry for him. "I want to go with you."

"We don't have a choice, Grace. I can't leave you

here alone, not with your attacker not being caught. I won't be around to protect you, and if they catch me here, they'll put me in jail, and then I really won't be around to protect you."

"I understand, but how will I find you?"

"I'll keep in touch," he insisted as he stopped long enough to look into her distraught eyes. "Don't worry. I'll be fine. I promise."

She hugged him tightly, fighting back the tears more than ever, trying to stay strong. "I'll get my things."

"Hurry. I don't know how far behind me they are."

Grace went into the room for only a minute and returned with a small bag stuffed with her things.

"Ready?" he asked.

She nodded.

With no time to hitch the wagon, he helped her outside and onto the roan before sliding into the saddle behind her and wheeled the horse, heading straight to the J.B. Bar Ranch.

Neither spoke the entire ride, as much out of not knowing what to say as fearing they would speak of how scary and uncertain their future was. As they rode up to the J.B. Bar, one of the two men who were standing out front talking ran inside and a moment later reemerged with Abigail Bartlett and Luther Gilroy. Abigail and Gilroy walked over to

them as Redding climbed down and tied off the
roan.

As he helped Grace down from his horse,
Redding told Abigail the whole story from Sheriff
Copeland's riderless horse coming up to their house
to him being run out of town for fear of his life from
being wrongly accused of murder. Though he
suspected Blaine Walker of being behind it all, he
purposely didn't mention Walker's name to Abigail.
"I hate to involve you in this, Abigail, but I didn't
know where else to go. It doesn't matter what
happens to me, but I need to make sure Grace is safe
until this is over. I know she'll be safe here until I
can figure things out."

"Don't worry, Vince," Abigail replied confidently
as she gently put her arms around Grace, "they'll
have to come through me if anyone wants to get to
her."

Redding looked humbled by the gesture, giving
Abigail a fractured smile of worry and relief.
"Thanks, Abigail."

She returned the awkward gesture as best as she
could. "I know we've grown apart, Vince, and I'm
sorry that's happened, but I want you to know that
regardless of what came between us, I'll take good
care of her. I promise."

"I know," he uttered simply.

Redding nodded softly and then turned to Grace,

whose face was full of fear for him. She didn't want him to go, but she knew it was the only way to put an end to things. "I'll worry about you until you come back to me," she stated through trembling lips.

"I know," he replied as he leaned down and kissed her gingerly and climbed into his saddle as Luther Gilroy walked up carrying a small bundle and offered it to Redding, who looked over at her with confusion.

"I had Luther pack you a few things," she noted. "Thought you could use it. Sounds like you're going to be on the run for a while."

Redding took the bundle from Luther Gilroy, who gave Redding a slight nod of reassurance and understanding. Redding returned the nod and stuffed the bundle into his saddlebag before he gave Grace a final faint smile and turned the roan, kicking it into a run down the road as Abigail and Luther Gilroy helped Grace into the house.

As he rode away from the J.B. Bar, Redding wondered what lay ahead for him. But that was not his main concern at that moment. He was tired of seeing those he cared about being hurt, always having to look over his shoulders, always being on guard, not knowing when or where would be the next time someone tried to kill him. And now, they had gone too far and made the mistake of going after someone he loved.

Enough was enough.

He was fed up with the situation. They had come after him long enough. If they wanted a fight, he would give them one, but not on their terms and not when they were ready, but rather when he was ready and he was able to call the shots. From now on, things would be different. From now on, he would not give them the advantage. From now on, instead of waiting for them to make a move, he would bring the fight to them, and before it was over, he would either kill them all, or die trying.

CHAPTER 33

JUST AFTER NIGHT FELL OVER SALT CREEK, THE ROAN slipped into town with Vince Redding trying to look as inconspicuous as possible. He was still garnishing the usual looks of the townspeople, but with his coat pulled close around his neck and his hat tilted downward, he was unlikely to be identified.

By now, the entire town knew what had happened to Grace, yet they were still out to try to pin Sheriff Copeland's murder on him, even though they had not a shred of evidence to the effect. He thought it ironic that the townspeople had no evidence and, yet, he had been fired for the same thing. He had no worry that anyone would approach him with their sympathies, even if he were spotted. The town had not been loyal to him, which bothered him more than he let on. Even after all he had done for them, they had been easily willing to hang him without sufficient evidence or witnesses to back up their accusations. It had been painful to see their distrust in him. He wouldn't forget it.

Redding slipped down the alley and stopped the roan just short of the back stairs of the Imperial Hotel so as not to attract too much attention. He had no plan, no escape route and very little hope that this would work out, but he had to at least try. He needed answers, and there was only one man he could think of that all of this had been caused by and who could give them to him.

Redding slipped the hammer loop from his revolver and quietly went up the stairs towards Blaine Walker's room. At the top of the stairs, he paused and listened. He would not allow himself to be caught outside Walker's door this time, since the last encounter had ended so badly. When he was confident that no one was around, he slowly made his way over to Walker's door and pressed his ear against it, but he heard nothing coming from the room. Walker was gone.

Redding slipped back downstairs and climbed into his saddle, taking a glance down both directions of the alley, worried he would be spotted. He was about to pull the reins when he caught a glimpse of a horse and rider at the other end of the alley. Whoever it was, they were looking directly at him.

But, oddly enough, they weren't making a move to confront him, which meant they probably weren't one of the townspeople. Who else could it be? Was it Walker's hired gun that Grace had warned him about hired to get rid of him? Maybe. Whoever it was, he was about to find out.

Redding started walking his horse towards the man, who had still not made an effort to move from his position since being spotted. Redding continued walking the roan, becoming leery of how brazen the man was. Was he leading him into a trap? An ambush? Redding did not like the situation and stopped his horse to take it all in before he advanced any farther, leaving the stranger just close enough that he could see him clearly. He could not make out the stranger's face completely, only that he was younger than himself, wearing a two-gun rig and riding a chestnut with a white mane. The move prompted the stranger to finally speak.

"I knew you'd show up, sooner or later. You must be Redding," the young man stated, more as a fact than a question. "I've been looking for you."

Redding's eyes went hard. "Well, now you've found me."

"Good," the man replied calmly. "I don't like loose ends, and you're a loose end."

"A loose end from what?"

"From this whole mess. You should have left

town when you were humiliated and run out of your sheriff job. But you must be a slow learner because you're still here. Either that or you're stupid."

Redding knew the man was trying to coax him into a fight, but he wasn't taking the bait so easily. This man, who Redding assumed had been hired by Blaine Walker, clearly wanted a fight and wanted him to draw so the shooting would be all nice and neat. That's what Walker wanted, for everything to be tidy and resolved so he could resume his plan unopposed. But Redding had to be careful not to be pulled into a bad situation because of his emotions, and because of that, it was going to take a lot more than a few insulting words to lure him into a gunfight. Redding decided to pump the man for information.

"And you are?"

"Ike Harrington," the young man offered proudly and without hesitation. Redding had heard bits and pieces about the name, but the only thing he knew for certain was that the man was no good.

"Walker must be getting awful concerned if he felt the need to bring in a hired gunman."

"Who says I work for Walker?"

"You must work for him," Redding said with keen interest. "You didn't even ask me who 'Walker' was."

Ike Harrington chuckled softly. "Well, you got me there, Redding. But it won't matter in a minute, because you'll be dead and out of Mr. Walker's hair, once and for all."

"Listen, kid, I know Walker paid you to clean up his messes, but this has nothing to do with you. You don't need to do this. Just turn your horse and leave town now and let me deal with Walker in my own way."

Harrington shook his head. "I can't do that. It's like you said, Redding," Harrington noted as his expression turned more serious. "I'm a hired gun, which means I was hired to do a job. Now, what kind of reputation do you think I'd have if I didn't use the gun that someone was paying for?"

"You forget one thing: A reputation won't do you any good if you're dead."

The comment stiffened Harrington's position in his saddle. "Well, now, that sounds like a threat."

"You take it any way you want," Redding uttered. Harrington's glare hardened as his hand went for his gun.

Redding anticipated the move and had reached for his own gun, drawing and firing just as Harrington did the same. Redding felt a violent tug in his right side as he watched Harrington buckle in his saddle, slumping forward as another of his shots discharged innocently into the ground right in front of Redding's horse. Harrington slowly slid out of his saddle and onto the ground in a crumpled pile, his revolver dropping from his hand as he landed. It was only when he was certain that Harrington posed no threat that he noticed the stabbing pain in his side. After holstering his weapon, Redding pulled back his coat and felt the hole in his side just below his armpit where the bullet had passed through, narrowly missing his lung. As his adrenaline began to subside, the severity of his wound became all too real to him. He pulled the handkerchief from around his neck with his free hand and delicately stuffed it into the hole in the front, cringing from the pain it generated as he did so. He suddenly remembered Harrington and looked down the alley to verify that he had not moved since he had fallen.

Redding knew that the sound of the shots was sure to bring townspeople who would not be willing to listen to his claim of self-defense, even if it were true. He would find no allies here tonight. There would likely be those who would shoot him on sight, especially with him standing over a dead body. All they would see was another dead man by his hand, and he was in no condition to fight them off or even make a run for it, knowing he would collapse out of the saddle before he could get far enough away. He had to act fast.

Redding gently nudged the roan into walking over to Harrington's body and took great care in climbing down. He checked between the buildings before kneeling down next to Harrington's body and began rummaging through his pockets, looking for anything that he could use to tie the dead man to Blaine Walker. He was still searching Harrington's pockets just as he caught a glimpse of someone running across the other end of the alley next to the boardwalk. The man caught sight of Redding and stopped abruptly, immediately calling out in panic for others to come to him as Redding disappeared into the cover of night, heading straight for the J.B. Bar Ranch.

It took all the resolve he could muster to remain in the saddle long enough for the roan to make it to the J.B. Bar. His head was swimming, and he was fighting to remain conscious as his horse stopped at the hitching rail in front of Abigail Bartlett's home. The piercing pain was making it difficult to take in a deep breath. Unable to take in enough air to call out, he tugged on the reins sharply, generating a whinny from the roan that caught the attention of some of the ranch hands that he had managed to slip past and who were milling about just outside of the bunkhouse. A moment later, he felt hands helping him down from his saddle, carrying him into the house, and placing him on a bed. Redding tried to speak, but his delirium was setting in, and he passed out before he could say what had happened.

Redding's eyes opened just as the sun was revealing itself over the mountain range. For a brief second, he forgot about his wound and tried to sit up, but the sharp stab of pain shooting through his side and out his back convinced him that doing so was not in his best interest as his head collapsed back onto the pillow. His grunt of discomfort mixed with defeat alerted the person sitting next to his bed in a rocker.

"Don't try to move," Grace said softly through her own muffled swelling as she dabbed his head with a folded rag. He nodded his understanding while trying to focus his eyes on her. "Who shot you, Vince?"

Redding wet his parched lips with his tongue enough so he could respond. "Said he was Ike Harrington. I didn't know him," he started slowly and carefully. "Ran into him in the alley. He knew me. Drew on me," he added, slowly shaking his head. "I had no choice."

"Did you kill him?" Grace asked hesitantly.

Redding nodded.

"Why would he shoot at you?"

Redding struggled to reach into his pocket and retrieve the Barlow knife Grace had given him, dropping it into her open hand as he spoke. "He was tying up loose ends."

Grace glanced down at the knife, her mouth hanging open in disbelief. She turned it over to verify that Redding's initials were etched into it. "Where did you get this?"

"Off the fella I shot," Redding uttered in a somewhat weakened voice. "He must have taken it as a trophy when he beat you."

Grace was amazed at the turn of events. "What did he look like?"

"Young kid, brown hair, wore two guns."

Grace swallowed hard before she dared to ask. "And his horse?"

"Chestnut... white mane."

"That's the man that attacked me," Grace said through trembling lips as tears began to fill her eyes.

"I know," Redding replied, licking his lips again. "But he can't hurt you anymore."

Just then, there was a light tapping on the door before it slowly opened and Abigail Bartlett entered the room. She glanced at Grace before turning her attention over to Redding. "Is everything okay?" she asked innocently.

"Yeah," Redding responded. "I just gave Grace some news."

Before Abigail could ask, Grace held up the Barlow knife for Abigail to see. "Vince took this off the man he killed last night. Turns out it was the same man who attacked me."

"Oh, my gosh," Abigail's expression turned to one of disbelief. "Are you sure it was the same man?" she asked as both Redding and Grace nodded. "Why would he want the two of you dead?"

Redding hesitated before answering, unsure what type of response he would get in return from Abigail. "He didn't," he hesitated before adding. "He was hired by someone else." His pause caught her attention.

"You think it was Blaine, don't you?"

"I didn't say that, Abigail," Redding tried to cover up his suspicions as he readied for her wrath. "But he did." To his surprise, Abigail did not become upset.

"It's okay, Vince," Abigail reluctantly admitted. "As much as I hate to admit it, I'm afraid you may be right."

CHAPTER 34

TWO DAYS HAD PASSED SINCE REDDING HAD KILLED Ike Harrington and was shot in the process. His strength had returned, and his faculties were as sharp as before. The only residual effect from the shooting was the intense pain shooting through his side every time he moved, thanks to Harrington's bullet. But none of that mattered now. He had disposed of Ike Harrington. Will Spurlock and Blaine Walker were next.

Redding struggled to get dressed by the faint glow of the lantern on the nightstand while trying not to make too much noise that would alert the others in the house of his exploits. It took some time, but he was finally able to pull on the clean shirt Grace had laid out for him when he was ready to get dressed again. She had no idea it would be this soon.

After pulling on his pants, he strapped on his gun belt, grabbed his boots, and started for the door. Despite his best efforts at remaining quiet, the door opened just as he reached for the knob.

"And just where do you think you're going?" Grace asked with irritation.

"I'm going to finish this," Redding stated as he tried to step past her, but she repositioned herself in his path to stop his movements.

"No, you aren't," she declared sternly. "You're going to get back in that bed and rest, Vince Redding. You've been shot."

"Believe me, I know I've been shot, but I'm not going to just lay here and wait for someone to make a move against us. Sooner or later, they're going to realize where we are and come after us. Abigail doesn't deserve to have to defend her own property." He tried to walk around her, but she stepped in his way again, causing him to sigh heavily from frustration.

"Grace, get out of the way," he reasoned, but she would not move.

"No, Vince. I'm not going to let you go out there and get yourself killed. You killed the man who attacked me. That should be good enough."

"Well, it's not," Redding spoke. "I want the man who hired him, too."

"You may think Blaine Walker is behind all of

this, but you still don't have any more proof than you did when it started. Your only witness is dead."

"Forget proof. He needs to be stopped, and I'm going into town to stop him. I'll worry about proof later. Right now, I'm trying to save more people from being hurt or killed."

"You know they'll arrest you as soon as you set foot in town, that is if someone doesn't go wild and shoot you first."

"I'll take that chance."

"You go trying to ride a horse all the way into town and you'll open up those wounds again," she reasoned. "Doc Hastings said you need to stay put for at least a week or more to make sure they heal properly."

"That's not gonna happen. This whole thing will be over by then, and we'll all come out on the losing end."

"But Doc Hastings was very adamant."

"Doc Hastings doesn't know everything."

"He knows about this. And I would consider being nice to him if I were you," she replied. "He's still pretty mad that you used him as a human shield to get yourself out of town. Did you *really* do that?"

"Didn't have much of a choice. It was the only way I could get away without getting shot."

"So, what makes you think you can go back in there now without getting shot?"

"I'm not going to argue with you about this, Grace. Just let me go so I can do what I need to do. I want to make sure Walker can't get away with this."

"He won't get away with it," Abigail said as she entered the room through the open door. "If he *is* the one who's behind all of this, then I need to know for myself. That's why I'm going with you."

Redding was shaking his head. "I don't know what you have planned, Abigail, but the answer is 'no.'"

"You don't get to say what I can and can't do, Vince," she protested adamantly. "I need to know the truth, whatever that turns out to be. If what you've been saying is true, then some of this is my fault for not believing you."

Redding disagreed. "If you go there to face Walker all alone, you're liable to get hurt."

"She won't be alone," Luther Gilroy announced as he walked up to the group, tossing Redding a confident nod. Redding returned the gesture. Redding relaxed his position, turning his full attention over to Abigail. "Alright, Abigail," he answered as he sighed. "What do you have in mind?"

A soft clomping of hooves was the only sound to be heard as the group of Vince Redding, Abigail Bartlett and Luther Gilroy rode quietly into Salt Creek under the cover of darkness as gentle gusts of cold air splashed their faces.

The streets were relatively deserted except for the rowdy crowds spilling out of the four saloons lining the streets, with some customers hanging around the boardwalk chatting loudly among themselves or alone and simply too inebriated to move any farther towards their homes. Redding tilted his hat slightly to shadow his features as they rode past the first saloon with Abigail and Gilroy stopping one building down from the Sidewinder Saloon to give Redding time to execute his part of the plan as Redding continued deeper into town. Their presence there went virtually unnoticed as the liquor worked to dull the senses of anyone who was within sight of the trio.

While Abigail and Gilroy waited just outside the Sidewinder Saloon in the shadows, Redding pulled up in front of the sheriff's office, glancing inside at the lamp still burning. He could make out the outline of someone sitting behind the desk, hoping that his hunch was right and that it was his friend, Deputy Clint McNeil.

His side stabbed him with pain as he carefully climbed down and scanned both directions of the street before walking right into the office to a startled McNeil, who was drinking coffee. The expression on the young deputy's face looked like he had seen a ghost, as he was so surprised that he spilled his coffee.

"Sheriff Redding," McNeil stammered as he jumped to his feet and nervously pulled his gun. "What… are *you* doing here? Y'know, the whole town's looking for you."

Redding already had his hands raised as he stopped a few feet in front of the desk. "I know, Clint. Good to see you. I've come to turn myself in," he added, turning his body slightly in the deputy's direction. "Here. You can take my gun."

Deputy McNeil hesitated at first, unsure if he was being tricked before he slowly stepped around the desk and over to Redding, all the while pointing his gun at him, his hand barely able to control the nervous shaking he was experiencing. He stopped almost too far away from Redding, leaning in and stretching an almost uncomfortable amount to retrieve Redding's gun without getting too close to him. "Don't worry, Clint. I'm not going to resist," Redding reassured him as he tried to ease the young deputy's mind. Only when McNeil had Redding's gun in his hand and had backed far enough away did he take in a deep sigh of relief.

"Why did you turn yourself in, sheriff?" McNeil asked with a puzzled expression. "You know they're looking to hang you for killing Sheriff Copeland."

"I know, but I didn't do it," Redding stated.

"I know that, sheriff," McNeil agreed. "But I have to lock you up, anyway. You understand, don't ya'? As acting sheriff, I don't have a choice."

Redding chuckled softly. "I understand, Clint, which is why I turned myself in. Just show me which cell you want me in."

"Alright," Deputy McNeil responded as he reluctantly started leading Redding down the short hall towards the cells. "I hate to do this, sheriff, but I have…"

"Sorry to have to do this, Clint," Redding whispered to himself. Deputy McNeil never got to finish his sentence as Redding reached behind him to his waistband and pulled his spare revolver, striking McNeil on the back of the head and dropping him to the floor with a painful grunt. He tucked the revolver back in its hiding place and grabbed McNeil under the arms and pulling him into the far back cell. He hurried to the desk and retrieved a set of handcuffs and used them to lock McNeil's hands behind his back to the wall of the cell and gagged him with his handkerchief.

"At least you'll be safe in here," Redding whispered while double-checking his handiwork, as if the young deputy could still hear him. "Sorry, Clint, but I can't risk you walking into the mess that's about to hit town."

. . .

Redding holstered his gun and dimmed the lamp before slipping out of the sheriff's office and gathering the reins of the roan. He used the roan to shield him from those who were out on the boardwalk as he made his way between buildings and up to the rear of the Sidewinder Saloon.

At the same time, out in front of the building next to the Sidewinder, Luther Gilroy checked his pocket watch. "Redding's five minutes are up," Gilroy spoke softly to Abigail before he replaced the watch and removed the hammer loop on his holster. Abigail nodded quietly and led Gilroy down the boardwalk and into the doors of the Sidewinder. For a brief instant, eyes were diverted to her appearance as the congested murmuring dulled, but it was only a few seconds later that the volume resumed, and everyone resumed their activities. Abigail led Gilroy and weaved her way through the dense crowd until they ascended the stairs to the large room at the end of the catwalk, which she took to be Blaine Walker's office because of the large gentleman guarding it. She lifted her chin and walked right up to the man.

"I'd like to see Mr. Walker," she announced sternly, looking the man in the eyes.

"Mr. Walker's not available," the man replied stiffly, his features unchanging and unforgiving.

"I demand to see him immediately," she snapped. "Tell him Abigail Bartlett is here to see him."

"Look, lady," the guard said rigidly, "Why don't you just go back home…"

"Blaine!" Abigail yelled around him. "Blaine, I need to speak to you!" she yelled over him as he forcibly grabbed her arm, his temper flaring.

"Lady! I told you…"

Before he could finish, Luther Gilroy stepped forward and caught the man with a solid right, which caused him to stagger and stunned him long enough for Gilroy to follow it up with a jabbing left and another powerful right that sent the man to the floor. The man shook his head, trying to relieve the delirium that was trying to take over and was attempting to get back to his feet when the door suddenly opened, and Blaine Walker stepped into the opening with a surprised look on his face. "Why, Abigail. What are you doing here, my dear?"

Abigail's expression did not falter. "Blaine, we need to talk."

CHAPTER 35

BLAINE WALKER STEPPED OFF TO THE SIDE, ALLOWING Abigail to enter. "Yes, by all means. Please come in," he offered with an outstretched hand. Abigail walked past him, followed closely by Luther Gilroy. Walker glanced down at his guard, a disappointed look covering his face as he surveyed the bloody cheek and lip Gilroy had just served him. "Go downstairs and clean yourself up," he ordered the man, who said nothing as he nodded his understanding and slowly got to his feet, gently rubbing his cheek to lessen the pain as Walker slammed the door in his face before the man could offer his excuse. Walker walked over and took a seat at his desk, flashing his signature fake smile while one of his henchmen stood next to him. Abigail took the seat across from him while Luther Gilroy stood just behind her.

"Now, what can I do for you, my dear?"

"Do you know a man by the name of Ike Harrington?" she started, wasting no time.

Walker pretended as if he were putting the question to deep thought. "No, I can't say that I do. Why? Should I know him? What did he do?"

"He's the man who tried to kill Grace Redding," Abigail informed him as she fought back her urge to accuse him of lying. Vince Redding had shown her the knife he had taken off Harrington's body after killing him– the same knife that Harrington had stolen from their home the night he had assaulted Grace.

"Where is this man now?" Walker asked with renewed interest.

"He's dead," Abigail informed him, as she watched for his reaction. Her suspicions were confirmed when she saw the noticeable change of relief in his demeanor.

"Well, then that is good news," Walker spilled. "We certainly can't have individuals like that occupying our fine streets."

Abigail could wait no longer. "Blaine, in light of recent events, I've had to reassess my position at the ranch and my holdings in this town. Since I have no next of kin, I need to make sure that the J.B. Bar is protected and that if anything were to happen to me, it would be turned over to the ranch hands who have worked it and stood by my side faithfully for all these years." She paused, waiting for his reaction, and saw his jaw tighten as he desperately tried to fight back his anger.

"But, my dear, I assumed I would be taking over partial control of the ranch when we wed," he said, struggling to maintain his control. "Is that not the standard practice?"

"That's another thing, Blaine," she replied. "With everything going on lately– Grace Redding being assaulted, Sheriff Copeland being murdered, and Vince Redding being accused of it– I think it would be best if we postponed the wedding, just until things settle down some."

The announcement did not sit well with Walker, who leaned forward and interlocked his hands together tightly as his body stiffened. "Wh… why would you think postponing the wedding will make a difference? Those things have already occurred. We cannot change them. We must move on with our lives."

Abigail stood her ground. "I would still feel better postponing it, for a while, until things resume back to normal. That includes my investment in your business and the ranch. It's already been handled."

Walker could not get his mind off her plans for the ranch. "What are you doing with the J.B. Bar?"

"I've rewritten my will. In the event that anything

should happen to me, the ownership of the ranch reverts to the ranch hands to be divided evenly. They can either choose to continue running it and enjoy the profits or if they unanimously choose to sell it, the profits would be dispersed equally among them."

Walker sat quietly, his rage almost too much to contain. He had waited and counted on Abigail turning over control of her ranch and her wealth to him in order to finance his plans. Now, all of that was being jeopardized. He was beside himself with anger.

"Abigail, you can't be serious," he reasoned, his voice changing to show the rising level of frustration as he tried to think of a way out of this predicament that wouldn't make him sound greedy. "You can't possibly be entertaining the notion of turning over your ranch to a bunch of saddle bums?"

Abigail took in the change in Walker's personality as she finally saw what she had not wanted to admit to herself. "They are not saddle bums, Blaine," she corrected him. "They are good and decent hard-working men who have stood by me through the years, and they deserve to be rewarded for their loyalty. They've earned it."

"They've earned nothing!" Walker exploded, slamming his fist down onto the desk. "That ranch is mine! How can you even consider giving it to them?!"

"Did you hear that?" Abigail asked openly to the room.

Suddenly, the side door to the room opened and Redding stepped in, his gun drawn, covering the man next to Walker's desk. "Yeah, I heard it," Redding said as he kept an eye on the man.

"Redding!" Walker snapped. "I should have known you were in the middle of this!"

"Hello, Walker," Redding said smugly. He watched as the man standing next to Walker slowly slid his hand down towards his gun. "You'd better tell your man there not to grab for his gun if he wants to live to see tomorrow."

Walker cut his eyes over to the man. "Don't be a damn fool, Frank. Keep your hands away from your gun." He then returned his look to Redding. "So, I assume you two were in this deception together?" He turned back to Abigail. "I take it there is no new will, is there?"

"No," Abigail answered sternly. "There isn't. I just needed to hear your greed for myself. Vince was right about you all along."

Walker nodded, his face filled with aggravation. "I should have known. You never got over him, did you, my dear?" he asked sarcastically. "You still have a thing for him, don't you? Well, you two deserve one another!" He then turned his attention back to Redding. "I presume you were the one who killed Mr. Harrington?"

Redding nodded slightly. "Yeah."

"Good," a voice from behind Redding spoke, startling everyone in the room. They all turned to see Will Spurlock standing in the doorway, his gun pointing right into Redding's back. "You saved me the trouble of having to do it myself."

"Spurlock, you snake!" Walker quipped. "What rock have you been hiding under?"

"I wasn't hiding, Walker," he announced calmly as he nudged Redding forward with the barrel of his gun and entered the room, stepping closer to the group. "Drop the gun, Redding," he demanded as Redding released his gun to fall to the floor. "Now, step over there with the others." Redding complied and moved over next to Luther Gilroy. He was the first to speak.

"So," Redding asked, "Where were you when all of this was going down?"

"I was just sitting back, waiting for things to start falling apart. Looks like they have. I saw you coming into town and followed you. I figured you would lead me to Walker, and you did."

"I should have had you killed when I had the chance," Walker admitted through clenched teeth.

"You tried to," Spurlock replied calmly. "But

Redding here took Harrington out before he could finish what you sent him to do."

"I won't forget this, Spurlock. You double-crossed me," Walker hissed.

"And you tried to have me killed," Spurlock replied in anger. "Guess that makes us even."

The man standing next to Walker suddenly reached for his gun, only clearing half of his holster as Spurlock spun his direction and fired, striking the man in the chest. As the man fell, he released his grip on his gun, dropping it right in front of Redding as Luther Gilroy went for his own gun. Spurlock spun and shot Gilroy just as Redding dove to the floor and scooped up the henchman's gun and rolled over, firing twice at Spurlock. Both bullets found their mark, digging holes deep into Spurlock's gut as his legs began to fail him. But before Redding could relax, Walker reached into his desk drawer and produced a revolver, pointing it at Redding, but Redding swung his gun around and managed to squeeze off another shot, drilling Walker in the chest. The bullet produced a dull moan from the man as his body jolted and his eyes opened wide with surprise while his face fell forward onto the desk. Redding holstered his gun and rolled onto his back as he cringed from the stabbing pain in his side that his movement had generated.

Abigail immediately jumped from her chair and

knelt down next to Luther Gilroy, who was already applying pressure to the wound in his lower gut through his left hip. Redding staggered to his feet and walked over to see if he could offer her any assistance. He pulled back Gilroy's hand to examine the wound. When they heard footsteps running down the hall towards them, Redding drew his gun and pointed it towards the door as it flew open. The three men who were coming inside abruptly stopped at the sight of Redding's gun pointed directly at them. One of the three was the man Gilroy had beaten outside of Walker's door.

"Get Doc Hastings," Redding ordered them, but all three men were still in disbelief as they took in the scene of the room, unable to move, stuck in their footsteps. Their hesitation in moving angered Redding. "Now!" Redding shouted, prompting the three men to leave and run downstairs as Redding holstered his revolver and went back to tending to Gilroy. He examined the bullet wound in the man's hip again. "You're lucky. I think it missed everything important," he noted before pulling the man's shirt back down and placing Gilroy's hand over it. "Hold down on this," he instructed Gilroy, who nodded and pressed down on his wound. Redding tried to stand but fell backward onto the floor as he pinned his arm against his burning side. Abigail abandoned Gilroy long enough to pull back Redding's vest to see that his wound was bleeding. "Looks like you popped some stitches."

Redding cringed through the pain. "That's the least of my worries. Any second now, townspeople are going to be filing in here wanting to either arrest me or hang me."

She reached over and picked up Gilroy's' revolver and cocked it. "Let 'em try. They'll have to get through me first," she declared.

"Y'know, this is the second time you've come to my aid," Redding pointed out as he favored his side. "It's getting to be a habit with you."

Abigail smiled slightly as she looked over at Walker lying face down in a collected pool of his own blood, her smile quickly diminishing at the sight. "I guess you were right about Blaine after all."

Redding also glanced over at the dead man. "Is it too early to say 'I told you so'?"

CHAPTER 36

THE RELENTLESS WIND TOSSED SWIRLS OF SNOW across the streets of Salt Creek, dusting everything in its path with white powder and slowing movement almost to a standstill. The bite of the early winter was taking its toll on the townspeople, urging them to seek refuge from the bitterly low temperatures as much as possible.

As the wagon came to a stop in front of the mercantile store, Vince Redding set the parking brake and climbed down, helping Grace out afterwards before they scurried inside, bringing in with them a rush of powdered snow as the door slid shut. Redding brushed off the remnants of the flakes as Grace unwound the thick wool muffler she had strategically wrapped around her neck while she shook the dusting off her hat.

It had been almost two months since the incident with Blaine Walker and Will Spurlock had occurred. The town had resumed its normal pace and, most importantly, Vince Redding had been cleared of all charges in the death of Sheriff Copeland and, despite fallback from Lucius Childers, the other members of the town council, Percy Brewer and Cal Holder, reinstated Redding as sheriff. The Reddings headed straight for the owner of the store, Mr. Finley, and picked up the supplies they had ordered. As Vince Redding was busy loading the last of the things onto the wagon, Grace walked outside just as Abigail Bartlett and Luther Gilroy rode up in a buggy.

"Hello, Vince," Abigail spoke as she looked behind him. "Hi, Grace," she added as Grace walked up to the trio.

"Abigail, Luther," Redding replied, tossing each of them a proper tipping of his hat. "How's the hip, Luther?"

"Still a little tender," Luther responded, rubbing the area lightly as he picked up a cane lying next to his leg. "Doc Hastings said I'll probably be using one of these for the rest of my days. How's the side?" he asked, motioning to Redding's wound.

"Still tender. Hurts sometimes when I breathe in deep. Still beats the alternative," he added, generating a nod and a snicker from Gilroy.

"So, how are you two doing?" Grace asked with a mischievous smile.

"We're doing good," Abigail offered as she grabbed onto Luther's arm. "It's funny how we've worked together all these years and I never knew he was feeling for me what I felt for him," she answered as they looked at one another. "I always thought of him as being more than a ranch foreman, more like a close friend, but I just couldn't see just how much he really meant to me. Of course, with my history, we're taking it slow."

Grace smiled at the comment. "Well, I'm glad to hear that you're giving it a chance."

"You off today, sheriff?" Abigail asked.

"Yeah. I had some things I wanted to finish up around the house before the next big storm hits. I left Clint in charge."

Luther cut in. "Did he ever get over you knocking him on the head the night of the shootout with Walker?"

Redding smiled faintly. "He doesn't bring it up much, but I think he's still a little ticked about it. Likes to hold it over my head. Doc Hastings is the same way. Still brings up me using him as a shield when the town thought I'd killed Sheriff Copeland."

"I think that would be a little hard to get over," Luther agreed.

"Well, we need to get a few things and then head

back to the ranch before it gets dark," Abigail said. "Come out and see us sometime," she added with a smile as she nudged Luther. "You ready?"

"Ready," Luther replied as he tipped his hat to Vince and Grace and slowly pulled away in the buggy. The Reddings watched them drive off, and then Vince helped Grace up into the wagon. "Anywhere else we need to go before we leave town?" he asked.

"Yeah. I need to go by the drugstore and pick up some peppermint."

"Still feeling poorly in the mornings?"

"Yeah."

"Hope you ain't gettin' sick. A lot of stuff going around lately."

"No, I'm not getting sick," she said as she gently placed her hand on her stomach. "But there *is* something I need to tell you."

To read all of Lee Everett's books, visit his Amazon author page HERE.

Made in United States
North Haven, CT
14 October 2022

25446936R00221